THE TRAIL

OF THE SNAKE

VOLUME I

Do what needs doing –

Martha McKeeth Ireland

Martha McKeeth Ireland

The Trail of the Snake is a work of fiction. Plot lines and characters were developed by the author and should not be construed as real or confused with any actual incidents or individuals, living or dead.

All locations cited and products named are based on historical records, but are used in a fictional manner and may have been altered to better serve the storyline.

This four-part series, published in two volumes, is set in the 1880s, when people made their own music, often singing as they rode, worked or relaxed. All songs used in the text were sung in this period, during which traveling evangelists held lively camp meetings, and the production and distribution of gospel songs supported prolific songwriters and publishing houses. Scripture quotations are from the King James Version, used most commonly at that time.

The horses described are inspired by horses the author has known, with names and details altered, except in the case of her father's big black gelding, "SoBig."

Scenic photographs are from the Norris A. McKeeth collection.

Cover art incorporates a historical map from 1882, archived in the Idaho State Historical Library in Boise, Idaho.

Volume I includes

Part I - *When Sorrows Like Sea Billows Roll...* and

Part II - *...though trials should come...*

Copyright 2016 by Martha McKeeth Ireland
Published by Ireland Farms
ISBN: 978-1-941840-04-7

THE TRAIL

OF THE SNAKE

PART I

*When sorrows
like sea-billows roll...*

CHAPTER 1

Owyhee County, Idaho Territory, August 1883

The Snake River flowed like a green satin ribbon across the knobby velvet tapestry of the sagebrush plain.

Seated on a sack of oats in the shade of Biladeau's Grand View Mercantile, Jadene Box sketched the familiar rimrock-crowned bluffs across the river while the merchant gathered the few items on Mother's list.

"Thought you might bring your watercolors again," the storekeeper said, returning with the order that easily fit in one hand.

"Mother said not to dawdle," the girl smiled, "and you know I do more than dawdle when I paint your grand view."

"Does tend to grab hold of a body, even when it's sizzling like today," the man said, handing over a couple sewing sundries. "Better take this, too," he added, holding out an envelope.

She wrinkled her nose when she saw the letter was from her middle sister, but she tucked it into the small pack behind the cantle of the saddle on her faded roan pony.

Mr. Biladeau offered her a hand up, which she declined, but she let him hold the leadline of the foal she was ponying, while she got settled atop Soldier.

"Take care not to fall off, settin' all catawampus, like you are," the storekeeper cautioned.

1

"Catawampus is the right word for it," Jady laughed. "But don't you worry, Mr. Biladeau, I keep Soldier to a walk when Mother has me ride lady-style."

Keeping Soldier to a walk was easy. The pony had been packing children around since before Jadene was born and now plodded along on a loose rein, head drooping, in the oven-like heat. The buckskin foal, however, couldn't seem to keep his hooves from dancing.

Jadene dallied the lead rope around the saddlehorn, pulling it up short to keep Dustdevil's nose beside her knee.

"Easy, Dusty," she murmured, caressing the foal that was nearly as tall as Soldier. "It's too hot for a run and I'm not set for it, having to ride sidesaddle like this."

Sitting sidesaddle was not Jadene's choice, but there was no help for it.

"Folks will be scandalized if you ride into town straddling your horse like a boy, and at your age," Mother had fussed.

To Jadene's way of thinking, one store and a few houses did not quite make a town, but Mother was not to be argued with, although Mr. Biladeau was quite used to seeing Jady astride a horse and wearing dungarees.

She remembered their first meeting, some three years earlier. The echo of hammering had led her and Pa to discover a sizable building rising on a level shelf overlooking the river just five or so miles east of their home place.

"Reckon we're gettin' business-minded neighbors," Pa had observed.

"Reckon sayin' howdy needs doin'?" Jadene had asked.

"Reckon it does," Pa had nodded and she had gone flying down the slope.

When she loped up, the man directing the builders had laughingly said, "Don't run me down, young feller."

Jadene had turned bright red and stammered so she couldn't get a word out.

Fortunately, Pa had been right behind her, his smile crinkling the corners of his eyes. "No danger of that," he had assured their new neighbor. "Your confusion's understandable, considerin' the way she rides and the way she's dressed, but yore talkin' to the youngest daughter of your neighbor, Gideon Box. Ah keep assurin' Jadene's mother it'll get easier for folks to see she's a proper lady—just hasn't happened as yet."

Today, Mr. Biladeau had been sitting in the shade on the front boardwalk, hoping to catch a breeze from off the river when Jadene rode in sidesaddle, wearing a simple dress of pink and white gingham.

"Why, Miss Jady," he had chuckled. "Either you're making good on the Captain's prediction to Mrs. Box, or it is too dang hot for your usual dungarees."

The light gingham dress was a bit cooler than dungarees, Jadene had to admit as she rode homeward on the wagon road that curved along the river.

The turnoff to the Box Ranch was just coming into sight when a stray gust of air billowed Jadene's skirt, exposing her bare legs.

"So much for being ladylike," she murmured, "Good thing no one's a—."

Her voice trailed off.

In the shade of the willows, right at the lane leading to her home, sat three riders on red horses. Jadene batted down her skirt as she quietly whoaed Soldier and Dustdevil.

Recognizing neither the horses nor their riders, she tilted her head curiously. They were a good quarter-mile away, but she could see each man was armed with at least one gun—two wore holstered revolvers, and two had rifles in scabbards.

In the rough Owyhee country of southwest Idaho Territory, guns were as common as red horses—two sorrels and a bay in this case. Her father almost always packed both a rifle and a pistol, as did his crew. For that matter, if Mother hadn't objected, Jady's own little carbine would have been tucked into her scabbard.

The strangers appeared to be deep in conversation and unaware of her approach. The man on the bay and packing only a rifle seemed to be pointing at the oddly shaped little mound her family called Humpy Hill.

Despite the heat, an icy shiver ran up Jadene's spine. Feeling exposed and vulnerable, she swung her right leg over Soldier's neck to sit astride and was modestly tucking the hem of her gingham skirt around her legs when the men noticed her.

The two who were riding sorrels instantly wheeled their horses and faded into the willows, but the man on the bay reached as if he were going to pull his rifle from its boot. He gave her a long look before following his companions.

Jadene shivered again and gathered up her horses. At her cue, the pair sprang forward and ran as if they were yoked together, swinging smoothly off the wagon road and cutting through the sagebrush on a beeline toward home.

Jadene kept them stretched out until they rounded Humpy Hill. At the old stone house, she slowed them to a walk, taking care not to raise dust as she neared the fine woodframe house the Captain had built for Mother when he brought her home from the East two decades earlier.

"My heavens, Jadene," Faye Box scolded from the veranda. "What devilment have you been up to this time?"

Jady bit her lip and silently handed over the paper of pins, the spool of cotton thread and the letter from Darlene. Her father made a practice of shielding her mother from anything that might worry her so

4

Jadene did not mention the strangers she had seen, but she couldn't help sounding anxious when she asked, "Did Pa get back yet?"

"The Captain! Call him the Captain," Mother scolded. "Get cleaned up before he sees what a mess you have made of yourself."

"Always see to the horses first, the Captain says," Jadene demurred.

"So he does," Mother sighed. "Well, be quick about it."

As Jadene rode toward the barn, Sarge Hankins straightened from scratching the ears of a big gray tomcat and hobbled inside the barn, muttering as he went.

When Jady jumped off Soldier, Sarge reappeared, a bottle of liniment in hand.

After rubbing down both horses, Jadene took out a sketchbook and pencil and began recording what she had seen, although the men at the river had been too far away to see their features clearly. "Wish I could draw as good as Pa thinks I do," she sighed.

"An' Cap wishes he could sing as good as you think he does," Sarge chuckled as a flat baritone reached their ears.

Singing his usual coming home song, Cap Box rode in on the tall black gelding that was his favorite mount.

"... *Ye who are weary, come home*,"[1] he finished as he swung down from SoBig and shook his head ruefully at his youngest child.

"Ah see yuh found somethin' thet needed doin', Baby, but yore shorely overdressed fer it," he said in a drawl that testified to his boyhood in Texas. "Imagine what yore mother'll say."

---

[1] Chorus of *Softly and Tenderly*, written by Will Lamartine Thompson, 1880

"No need to imagine." Jadene smoothed the skirt of her soiled dress. "Mother sent me to Biladeau's for a couple things."

"Explains the dress," her father observed.

Jady nodded. "I made the best of it—ponyed Dustdevil—"

"Go easy with that baby, Baby," Cap chided.

"Yes, sir," she nodded. "Mother had me ridin' sidesaddle, so I sure enough kept to a walk. Pa, there were three strangers where our lane turns off from the wagon road. I straddled Soldier and cut for home. Dusty kept up real easy."

Cap's face hardened. "Wha'd they do thet made yuh run?"

Jadene shrugged. "They just gave me the willies."

She described the encounter, sketching as she talked.

"Hmmm," Cap mused. "Likely nothin'. But if they spooked *you*—might take a look after supper."

Jadene beat the dust and horsehair from her clothes as they walked up to the house.

Her oldest sister, Serena, was idly setting the table, ignoring her toddler son's attempts to help, while Mother franticly packed a carpetbag.

Waving Darlene's letter, Faye cried, "Jadene might not get to attend the Academy—we must leave for Boise City at once!"

"Calm down, Faye," Gideon yawned. "Ah wrote, they're expectin' her and classes don't start 'til along in September."

"They have set new standards," Faye cried. "Incoming students have to be interviewed in person before they are enrolled. With Jadene's tomboy ways, who is to say whether they will accept her at all—you should have seen the way she came back from the smallest of errands. I just do not understand that girl!"

Mother was sure enough right about that, Jadene thought, but her father just said, "Wal, ah do, Faye. Ah already talked to 'er 'bout it."

Serena tousled her small son's dark hair. "Lincoln has more sense than his Aunt Jady," she sniped.

"More'n his mama, ah'd say," Cap drawled. "Let me read Darlene's letter while yuh get supper on."

After reading it he said, "Ah doubt there's any problem, Faye, but ah'll take the two of yuh to Silver City in the mornin'—put yuh on the stage. Yuh make shore ever'thin's squared away, then c'mon home—tell Darlene to come, too, she hasn't been back to the ranch in near three years and we'll have most of a week to visit afore school starts up."

Throughout supper Faye fussed about all the preparations that weren't done and how she'd much prefer to have the Captain drive them to Boise City, the buggy being so much more comfortable than the stage, and it having been a good four months since he'd last visited Grandmother Box.

"Sorry, m'love," Gideon kissed her lightly. "Hirin' for roundup's takin' longer'n it oughta. The gent Larry Sutherland recommended didn't show today and Buck's still not back from Steen's Mountain."

"Blaine is always late," Faye fussed. "He promised Jadene a surprise on her fourteenth birthday. Some surprise, ten days past and he has yet to put in an appearance!"

"He's more predictable than reliable," Gideon admitted, "but Buck's a good boy."

"A boy!" Faye sniffed. "He's twenty-eight years old and not half the man you were at that age. He's all flash—wasting his education chasing mustangs and showing off with that fancy gun of his."

"Ah'll talk to him again," Gideon sighed. Rising from the table, he added, "Reckon Baby and ah'll ride out fer a bit."

7

Jadene bolted for her room, changed to dungarees, grabbed the .32-20 Winchester her father had given her when she turned ten, and ran to catch up with him at the barn.

Sarge had fresh horses saddled and waiting.

"I hope the Academy won't take me," Jadene said as the pair mounted up. "I got all the book learnin' I need from Mother. I'd learn more of what's worth knowin' trailin' along with you, Pa, than goin' to school with Dar."

Gideon chuckled. "We've plowed that ground, Baby. Gettin' along with your sister's a tough trail, but ah'm thankful my father saw to it thet ah got a good education and you will be, too. B'sides, yore mother won't be satisfied 'til you learn to act like a lady."

"Bein' a lady oughta be good enough," Jady countered, "The way Mother thinks a lady should act doesn't suit me. Can I at least come home summers?"

"Fer shore," Gideon said. "Stayin' in town's Darlene's choice and ah don't like it a-tall. Whenever school's out, ah expect yuh to be right here, doin' what needs doin'."

"For sure," Jadene promised. "Summer and Christmas and—"

"Not Christmas," her father interrupted. "We'll all be in Boise City through th' holidays. Yore grandmother's countin' on thet and' Serena's set on takin' Lincoln to see his pa."

"Some mother, takin' her young'un into a prison," Jady scowled. "I surely don't know what Serena sees in that danged Jerub—"

"Watch it!" her father cut in. "Yuh won't have to visit Drake, but yuh'd best fix yore mind to acceptin' him. He's family, as yuh well know—yore brother's cousin even afore he married yore sister. Ah expect he'll come home to the Box, once he's done payin' for the mistakes he made."

"He took advantage of Serena!" Jadene objected.

"It was as much her takin' advantage, as him," Gideon sighed, "ah should'a seen it comin', but ah looked the other way. Only thing to do now is help Drake make it right—and don't call him Jerubbaal, yuh know he hates that."

"I don't give a da—uh—uh-oh. Pa, I didn't say that," she wailed.

Her father raised an eyebrow. "Yuh need to chew on some lye soap?"

Upon reaching the wagon road, Jadene pointed out where she'd seen the strangers. They had cut through the trees to the narrow strip of sandy clay that was exposed by the low summer flow of the river, and had headed west, toward Silver City.

"The left front hoof turns out a hair on the second and all three are due for re-shoein'," Gideon observed.

"Not takin' care of their horses means they're bad men," Jady declared.

"Doesn't speak well of 'em," Gideon agreed, "but ah wouldn't judge a man solely by the state of his hoss's shoes. Still and all, ah'll tell Leroy and Guy. This is likely nothin', but if these three are on the hunt, we won't be easy prey."

"They were kinda lookin' at Humpy Hill," Jady said.

Pa nodded and headed up the misshapen mound, watching for tracks and seeing none.

"I hope Buck brings me one of those Steen's Mountain duns, so I can leave Soldier here for Linc to ride," Jadene said.

"Leave Soldier either which way," Cap said. "Yuh've outgrown him and there's other hosses yuh could take—the bay yore ridin's not bad."

"No, but he's nothing special, either," she said, "Wish Dustdevil was grown."

"If wishes were hosses," Gideon chuckled. "Likely Buck'll be here when yuh return. We'll have three-four days together, then ah'll ride up with yuh the day afore your classes start. Need to see Warden McKay anyhow."

"Ridin' alongside you will make goin' to town almost tolerable, Pa," Jady sighed. "But I don't know how I'll stand bein' there once you leave."

"Be strong and of good courage,"[2] Cap quoted. "Afore yuh know it, ah'll be up servin' muh time. Twelfth Territorial Legislature'll convene along in December an' run right through Christmas an' likly well into th' New Year. Thankfully, yore mother's aimin' t' c'mon up with me this time, not havin' t' stay home ridin' herd on you. That'll make legislatin' almos' tolerable."

"You make the legislature sound like a prison, Pa," she teased.

"Near as bad," he drawled. "But movin' Idaho along toward becomin' a state and gettin' the vote for you girls and your mother needs doin'."

"I'm not so sure anything needs doin' bad enough to warrant livin' in town," Jady sighed. "Wish there was a way out."

"Only the way Serena took," Pa deadpanned, "but ah won't look the other way again."

"Humph," Jady snorted. "Any fella messes with me that-a-way will get acquainted with the business end of my carbine!"

"Day'll come," Gideon predicted, "you'll look at someone the way Serena looks at Drake and your mother looks at me—"

"Won't matter if I do," Jady cut in. "I'd want a man just like you, Pa, but he'd want a real beautiful lady, like Buck's mother was and my mother is, not a plain little thing like me."

"Oh, Baby," Gideon laughed, "if love were like thet, ah would be a bachelor. Ruth was a real head-turner, to be sure, tall and slim with cornsilk hair. She

---

2 Deuteronomy 31:6

10

and her sister could've had any soldier at Fort Hall—and not jus' th' soldiers, as Naomi proved—but ah was th' one Ruth wanted. Never figured ah would love another after she died, but then ah met Faye—petite, brunette, with a figure thet had every single man linin' up to fill her dance card. Never figured ah had a chance, but Mrs. Ethridge rigged th' place cards, and there was Faye, lookin' across th' table at me. It's always been th' eyes that got me—Ruth's were sky blue, yore mother's're velvet brown—but, oh, th' look in those eyes! Jus' wait, Baby, th' day'll come yuh'll look thet-a-way at a man smart enough to see how beautiful yuh are—even if yuh do favor your ol' pa."

"I favor trailin' along with you," she declared, "which is what I oughta be doin', Pa, 'specially now when there's bad men pokin' about."

Gideon chuckled. "Ah rode clean through Hell twice. Yuh really think ah need muh baby girl to protect me?"

"Sounds silly, when you put it that way," Jady admitted. "But if your trail ever takes another turn through Hell, I hope I'm ridin' alongside to make sure you don't set up camp there."

"And ah hope yore not, Baby," Gideon said seriously. "Ah pray yuh never find yerself on such a trail, but if ever yuh do, remember the psalmist says, even if yuh make yore bed in Hell, God is there—Psalm one-thirty-nine—another piece of scripture yuh oughta put to memory."[3]

The sky turned to indigo as they reached the hilltop and looked back to the north where the Snake River slid like a silver ribbon below the bluffs. As if with one mind, they lifted their voices in a slightly flat baritone and alto duet:

"When peace, like a river, attendeth my way,
When sorrows like sea-billows roll,
Whatever my lot, Thou hast taught me to say,

---

[3] Psalm 139:8

It is well, it is well with my soul..."[4]

* * * * * * * *

The sudden trip to Boise City was not something that had needed doing.

Grandfather Box had been among the Academy's founders and had continued to serve on the Board of Directors, until he passed on just days after watching Blaine graduate. Any child of the Box family was welcome without question.

Darlene claimed she'd had no idea the Academy's new enrolment procedure did not apply to her family, brushed off her father's order to visit the ranch, and objected fiercely to her younger sister's presence.

"She is a terrible embarrassment," she cried, "Surely she can wait a year!"

For once, Jadene agreed with Darlene, but Mother most certainly did not.

"Oh, my precious Darlene," Faye pleaded. "Jadene simply must have your shining example to follow if she is ever to learn to behave like a lady! I understand your concern, but I can assure you there will be absolutely no tomboy shenanigans. We spoke of nothing else all the way here—Jadene, tell your dear sister what you promised—."

"She will ruin my senior year," Darlene bellowed. "Even if, by some miracle, she manages to behave, she is still an embarrassment. Look at her—she does not own so much as one suitable ensemble. It simply is not fair—and after all the work I have done to ensure that I shall be the most splendidly attired girl in the entire academy—" With a flourish, she threw open the doors of her wardrobe, displaying a rainbow of frilled gowns.

"Oh, look, Jadene," Mother cooed, "your dear sister's talent with needle and thread is surpassed only by her beauty. I am not so unreasonable as to expect you to match Darlene's accomplishments, all I ask is

---

[4] *It Is Well with My Soul*, verse 1, H.G. Spafford, 1873

12

that you learn to comport yourself like a proper lady. If you just endeavor to follow her example..."

Before Faye finished speaking, Jadene fled to the garden, where Grandmother Box—who had heard every word through the house's open windows—was picking string beans.

"A proper lady, humph," Zelma Box muttered, sharply snapping a bean.

* * * * * * * *

Silver lined the eastern horizon as Gideon Box rode out in the cool of the morning. He had an urge to hitch up the buggy and head for Silver City, but that wouldn't get the stage from Boise City there any sooner. He could head for town when the sun reached its zenith, and still have time to talk some business before Faye and Jady arrived. He wished Darlene would come as well, but admitted to himself that wasn't likely.

The hymn he and Jady had sung together on their last evening ride came to his mind and to his lips:

"When peace, like a river, attendeth my way,
When sorrows like sea-billows roll,
Whatever my lot, Thou hast taught me to say,
It is well, it is well with my soul."
"Though Satan should buffet, tho' trials should come,
Let this blest assurance control,
That Christ has regarded my help-less estate,
And hath shed His own blood for my soul..."

He reached the final stanza as he approached a particular fold in the foothills.

"And Lord, haste the day when my faith shall be sight,
the clouds be rolled back as a scroll..."

Without a visible cue, SoBig turned into the secluded notch that yielded a sliver view of the Snake River.

"The trump shall resound and the Lord shall descend,
Even so...it is well with my soul. It is well, it is well ..."

The sun was just bringing reading light as Gideon stepped from the saddle. He removed a small Bible from his inner jacket pocket and finished the chorus as he opened the book:

"It is well, it is well, with my soul."[5]

---

[5] Ibid

CHAPTER 2

"A good omen," Hatch thought, when his target rode in right at shooting light.

He'd been told right.

"The Captain makes a point of bein' reliable, not predictable," his source had said. "But you can catch him alone if you set tight where I said. Might take a day or three, but he'll come to you. Chances are you'll hear him singin' as he comes."

Day three, and here the target was, singing as he dismounted from a tall black horse. Hatch brought the cocked rifle to his shoulder and lined the iron sights on the target's spine.

"Right about five-foot-six," the outlaw thought, "but a big payoff."

"*It is well...*" the words rose on the morning air, but did not register in Hatch's mind. *"with my soul."* Hatch squeezed the trigger, levered rapidly, and fired again.

Both rounds slammed into Representative Box's back.

* * * * * * * *

Gideon Box had been wounded twice on his rides through the hell of the Indian Wars and the War for the Preservation of the Union. This was worse, he knew.

His leg twitched spasmodically as corpses often do, but he wasn't dead. God willing, the shooter would ride away, Gideon would order SoBig home, Sarge would backtrack the gelding and Faye would nurse him back to health.

15

If not—"it is well with my soul," he thought. "Praise the Lord, praise the Lord, O my soul!"[6]

* * * * * * * *

Hatch had neither needed nor wanted the help of Snell and Tovey, but his payoff would be split three ways, just the same. Still, it would be a good stake for a man just ten days out of prison.

Having covered other possible ambush sites, Snell and Tovey now appeared, drawn by the gunfire.

Snell prodded the body with the toe of his boot. "You sure he's dead?"

"Sure as hell," Hatch growled.

Tovey drew his revolver. "Me, too," he grunted, as he casually pumped a slug into the back of the target's head.

The black horse spun, nearly knocking Hatch down, but the outlaw snagged a rein and held on. "Load 'im," he ordered. "We'll make it look like he run onto rustlers."

* * * * * * * *

It was Sarge Hankins who was waiting with the wagon, not Gideon with the buggy, when the stage returned Faye and Jadene to Silver City.

"The Captain should be here," Faye fretted. "He should be here."

"You know Cap," Sarge shrugged, "reliable, not predictable. He musta run onto somethin' that needed doin' right fierce 'cause he been countin' the minutes, Miz Box. When he didn't come fer the wagon, I figured he headed here straightaway, so I brung it myself so's ol' SoBig wouldn't hafta pack yuh home triple." He forced a laugh at his own attempt at humor and looked around hopefully. "Cap'n could ride in anytime."

But he didn't.

Nor was the Captain at the Box when they arrived after a tense, silent ride.

---

[6] Psalm 146:1

16

Faye didn't object when Jady changed to dungarees, grabbed her rifle, and ran to the barn where Sarge had saddled Soldier.

* * * * * * * *

The track was made by a couple dozen head being pushed by three riders on freshly-shod horses. It looked like the left front hoof of one turned out a bit.

Clear prints in the dust showed SoBig following.

"Movin' slow," Jady muttered, as much to herself as to the pony she nudged into a canter. "Trackin' three rustlers, Pa likely turned off just around that little hill to go get Guy and Leroy."

But when she rounded the hill, Jady saw SoBig nibbling at the sparse, dry, late-summer grass beside her father's still form.

Jady bailed off Soldier before he came to a stop, but it was obvious she was much too late.

Pa had stopped three bullets—two in his spine, one in his head, all fired from behind. He still wore his gun belt, but his pistol, rifle and scabbard were gone.

How, she wondered, had they shot him from behind when he was trailing them? And why wasn't there a considerable pool of blood?

She removed SoBig's saddle and used the blanket to chase off the flies before covering her father's body with it. She left the tall horse standing guard over his master and rode slowly home.

When Jadene stopped at the barn without going to the house, Faye left the verandah, lifted her skirt and ran down. Jadene had never before seen her mother run. She wrapped her arms around her mother, buried her face against Faye's shoulder and sobbed.

Faye choked out a strangled, "No," pushed her youngest daughter away and fled back to the house.

Hankins had kept the wagon ready and silently drove where Jady pointed.

When they returned with Gideon's body, Faye was packing.

17

Artie Shaw, oldest son of their nearest neighbors, stopped by to inquire about when the Captain would have some work for him. Learning of the killing, he offered to fetch Owyhee County Sheriff Louis Haney. Jady objected. Pa had no use for the man.

"We didn't vote for him neither, but Haney won," Artie shrugged.

"I'd rather have you go tell Guy and Leroy," Jadene said. "They're over east at Battle Creek, mending the sorting corrals for the roundup."

"I'll tell them after I tell the sheriff," Artie said. He left for Silver City at a gallop.

Night was falling when Lou Haney moseyed in, deputying for his father. "Ain't much of nothin' to do," he said. "It's too dark to see nothin' an' they'll likely be over the border into Nevada 'fore mornin'."

"Their trail doesn't run south," Jady said. "Get a posse ready to ride at first light and I'll show you."

"The Law don't take orders from no snot-nosed girl," Lou sneered, heading out the door.

"Mother," Jady appealed, turning to Faye.

"I cannot be here without the Captain," Faye sobbed. "Sarge, our trunks are ready. Bring the wagon and get them loaded. We are leaving for Boise City."

"No sense to that, Miz Box, ferry don' run af'er dark." Hankins stumbled out.

Faye crumpled into Gideon's leather-covered rocking chair. Lincoln crawled onto his grandmother's lap, and Serena knelt and rocked them.

Jadene caught up with Hankins as he hobbled back to the barn.

"Don't go crawlin' inside a bottle, Sarge," she pleaded, "Pa wouldn't like that. I need you—Pa needs you."

"Cap'n don' need no one no more," Sarge muttered. He rummaged in the oat bin, pulled out a jug of home brew, and barricaded himself in the lean-to off the barn that he preferred to the bunkhouse in summer.

Returning to the house, Jadene found Faye, Serena and Lincoln huddled together in Serena's big bed. When she tried to talk to them, her mother's moans became screams.

Jady retreated to her own tiny room, dropped to her knees beside the bed and buried her face in her hands.

"Dear God, what am I gonna do?" she prayed. "Oh Lord, show me what to do."

After Mother's moaning subsided into sleep, Jadene left a note on the kitchen table: "Gone to fetch Blaine." She didn't know exactly where her brother was, but figured if she headed toward Steen's Mountain, God would, somehow, direct her path.

She slipped out to the barn, where she tried vainly to roust Sarge. SoBig could cover the ground faster than little Soldier. She hoisted her own saddle atop the big black horse, substituting Pa's cinch for her own to encompass the gelding's greater girth, and slipped her carbine into the boot.

"Do what needs doing," she told herself, as she mounted from a fence rail.

* * * * * * * *

Jadene didn't even get out of Idaho Territory.

In the silvery light of dawn, she heard cattle bellowing in a box canyon less than five miles short of Silver City. Jady hadn't trailed the rustlers, but one look told her she had found them. They were the same men she had seen at the river.

Two of the men had wrestled a steer down beside a branding fire and were awkwardly blocking out Pa's brand—a G inside a box—on the animal's flank. The third, mounted on the bay, was attempting to hold the herd. He wasn't very good at it.

19

Jady pulled her carbine halfway out of the boot, thought better of it and shoved it back in. Regardless of who wore the badge, this was a job for lawmen.

As she backed away, the mounted outlaw let fly with a string of curses.

One cow had slipped past him and the others bolted after it. When the outlaw spun his horse to give chase, he spied the youngster on the big black gelding. Forgetting the beeves, he yanked from his waistband the Colt .45 he'd stolen from the corpse of his victim the previous day and charged.

"Lord Jesus!" Jady cried. She levered a shell into the chamber as she pulled her carbine. Before the muzzle of the little rifle cleared the scabbard, the outlaw came alongside and fired at her at near point-blank range.

The hammer fell on the cylinder Pa always left empty for safety. With a cry of disgust, the outlaw threw the handgun in the dirt, grabbed the barrel of Jady's carbine as it cleared the scabbard and attempted to wrest the gun from the girl's grip.

Jady's finger was on the trigger when he twisted the gun toward himself and gave it a sharp jerk. The bullet caught him full in the face.

Even before his body landed in the dust, his partners had their revolvers out and were flinging lead in her direction.

Jady reined SoBig to a stop, aimed carefully, and put a round through the nearest man's thigh. He screeched as he fell and the other man turned tail and ran for his horse, which was packing Pa's scabbard and rifle. Jady cut short the outlaw's flight by driving a slug through his lower leg.

She ordered the two outlaws to tie off their wounds with their bandannas, and saw that they did so, then she carefully gathered up their horses and their weapons—three rifles and three pistols, including those they'd taken from her father.

20

"Be ready to talk when I get back with the sheriff," she gritted.

* * * * * * *

Sheriff Haney was not pleased. He kept Jadene at the courthouse, asking and re-asking a raft of senseless questions, while his deputy son investigated her report. Two hours later, the younger Haney returned. He had found the three rustlers just where Miss Box said they would be, he claimed, but all three were dead. Each had been shot twice in the back and once in the head, same as Captain Box. The killing shots all came from behind, except for the one man who had caught a slug in his face. The other two also had minor leg wounds, he added.

"M'gawd," Sheriff Haney swore, "I know yore upset over yer daddy gettin' killed, but that don't give yuh no right to massacre folks."

"I didn't!" Jady protested, "I only shot each of them one time and the only one I shot from behind, I shot in the calf."

"Now yore sayin' yuh shot a calf?" the sheriff mocked. "Git yer story straight, young lady."

However, when the elder Haney viewed the bodies, he readily identified all three. "That there's Howie Hatch," he said, indicating the man with the bullet-mangled face, "can't be more'n a week or two outta the pen."

He rummaged through his desk drawer, extracted two posters, and spread them out. "Thad Snell and Roscoe Tovey—seems yuh made yerself six-hundred bucks on them two, Miss Box," he announced.

"I don't want any blood money," Jady cried. "I left them alive. They should've stood trial—should've explained why they killed Pa—nothin's right here."

"Right enough, Miss Box," Haney patted her on the head. "Yuh bagged three bad men. Yer daddy'd be right proud. Lou, keep an eye on her while I go over to the bank. Be right back with yer ree-ward money, Miss Box. You betcha."

Jadene rode in stunned silence, the reward money heavy in her pocket, as Deputy Haney escorted her back toward the Box.

* * * * * * * *

Sheriff Haney drained his fifth beer and repeated the tale to the growing crowd at the Silver Dollar, ending again with the comment, "She ain't even full growed, but Cap Box shorely raised hisself a back-shootin', bounty-huntin' lil' bitch."

Instead of the chorus of agreement he had basked in, Haney's comment was greeted with uneasy silence. The tipsy sheriff swiveled around.

A lanky blond gunman blocked the doorway. Blaine "Buck" Box got his height and his looks from his long-dead mother, and his ability with a gun from a magician, it was said. Haney blinked and missed seeing Buck's hand move. Three shots came in a single burst. The first bullet shattered the mug Haney held. The second smashed the butt of the gun that sagged on Haney's hip. The third removed his hat.

"Bad-mouth my baby sister again, Haney," Blaine growled as he topped off the cylinder of his Colt .45, "and I'll punch the buttons down the front of your shirt. *Comprende?*"

Haney's bladder suddenly failed to hold the beer he had consumed.

CHAPTER 3

Blaine caught up with his sister and curtly dismissed her unwanted escort.

"I'm sorry this fell on you, Baby," he said. "I should have been there—should have been with Pa, or at least should have been the one to find him and track his killers."

"I didn't track them, Buck," Jady said. "It wasn't at all the way Haney said it was."

"Of course it wasn't!" Blaine said. "Are you up to telling me how it was?"

Jadene related every detail, from her first brush with the strangers at the river to the shootout at the branding fire.

"Any chance you squeezed off some wild rounds without realizing it," Blaine asked, "Like when you get buck fever?"

"I've never had buck fever in my life," Jady protested. "I'll take the blame for killing Hatch, but not the other two."

"The only blame belongs to Hatch and his partners," Blaine said, "They reaped what they sowed, and no fault of yours, but if you didn't finish them off, Baby, who did?"

"I don't know, Buck," she replied. "There's a lot wrong here. Pa's too wary to ride into an ambush and nothing about this deal lines up right. Maybe they had another partner who feared they'd talk. Question is how do we go about finding out?"

"That's a job for the law, Baby," he said. "Give Haney a chance to sort it through."

She gave a derisive snort. "As if the Haneys will even try! I'll tell Sheriff Sage."

23

"Pa wasn't killed in Ada County," Blaine said, "Still, that's not a bad idea—Lowell Sage is a good man and a good friend."

Reaching the Box, they found headquarters deserted, except for Sarge who was passed out, face down in the corral. "Hell of a way to repay his captain," Blaine grumbled as he packed the old man to his bunk. "Pa gave him a home for life, crippled up as he is, but all he cares about is the bottle."

"Sarge got crippled stoppin' a bullet for Pa, as you well know," Jadene defended. She gently washed Hankins' face with a dampened flour sack. "He only drinks enough to cut the pain—I reckon losin' his Captain hurt him lots worse'n his leg does."

In the house they found a note written in Guy's scrawling hand on the back of a calendar that had hung on the wall, but now lay face down on the kitchen table:

"Blaine and Jadene—Mrs. Box has ordered us to take her and the Captain's body to Boise City, along with Mrs. Drake and Lincoln. We will cross at Mundy's ferry and ask Rev. Mundy to go with us to conduct the funeral. The Shaws will handle ranch chores until we get back. Hope to see you there." It was signed "Cpl Guy Glover."

Below, Leroy Stoops had printed: *"Sarge won't go. Tell Lem."*

* * * * * * * *

The two passed Biladeau's in the dark and forded the Snake by moonlight, Jadene riding SoBig, and Blaine on his grulla stallion, Steel.

As they rode, Blaine led out singing one song after another, each with a verse or two that spoke to their loss.

"O some-times the shadows are deep, And rough seems the path to the goal, And sor-

24

rows, some-times how they sweep Like tempests down o-ver the soul..."[7]

"Are ye weak and heavy laden, Cumbered with a load of care? Precious Savior, still our refuge, Take it to the Lord in prayer..."[8]

"...For I will be with thee thy troubles to bless, and sanctify to thee thy deepest distress..."[9]

All were songs Jadene had sung many a time with her father, but now the words caught in her throat. When Blaine finally paused, she asked, "Buck, do you ever think about maybe being a preacher, like your Uncle Elijah?"

"Preaching is not what I feel called to," he sighed. "Seems now I have a ranch to run."

"Pa was hiring for roundup," Jady said. "I don't know if he had a full crew yet, but you'll have Guy and Leroy, at least, and there's none better."

"Many younger, but none better," Blaine nodded. "I'll hire on the Shaws and pay them as if they weren't working their own stock along with ours."

"That's what Pa always does—did," Jady agreed. "Artie's gettin' pretty handy with a catch rope."

"You kinda like that boy, don't you, Baby?" Blaine teased.

"He's a good friend, but don't go thinkin' he's my sweetheart," Jady said.

"'Course not," Buck deadpanned. "Everyone knows Lem's your sweetheart."

"Lem's much too young for me," Jady said, repeating by habit a long-running family joke.

No one knew for sure how old Lemuel Walker was, but his hair was already gray and thinning when he made his mark on enlistment papers twenty-three

---

[7] *The Rock That Is Higher Than I*, verse 1, Erastus Johnson, 1871

[8] *What a Friend We Have in Jesus*, verse 3, Joseph Scriven, 1855

[9] *How Firm a Foundation*, verse 3, Rippon's *Selection of Hymns*, 1787

years earlier in order to ride alongside Lieutenant Box when the young officer rode east into a battle Walker had tried to tell him was none of their "consarned concern."

It was well after midnight when they reached the Bar None, but their adopted uncle wouldn't let them sleep until they had filled him in on every detail of the tragedy that had befallen his beloved captain.

* * * * * * * *

The mountains known as the Boise Front were silhouetted against the setting sun when they topped out on the bench overlooking the fertile valley, split by the tree-lined river. Brown foothills rose like rumpled velvet to blend into the blues and purples of the timbered mountains beyond. Lanterns marked the new bridge across the Boise River, and lamps shone in the homes of the city's nearly three thousand residents.

When Jadene and Blaine dismounted in the backyard of the tidy house on Hays Street, Zelma Box hurried out to hug the oldest and youngest of her grandchildren. As they settled SoBig and Steel into her tiny carriage-house, she told them they had missed their father's funeral and burial.

"Couldn't she even wait for us?" Blaine asked tightly. "Pa wanted to be buried on Humpy Hill."

Grandmother Box laid a calming hand on his arm. "Your father would want you to understand and forgive. Rev. Mundy read the one-hundred-thirty-ninth psalm—your father's favorite, and we sang that song he liked so much, 'It is well with my soul,' and we all know it was. But Faye's soul is in torment. You must not add to her grief."

Dressed in black, Faye perched on the stiff horsehair sofa, rocking herself. Jadene and Blaine knelt at either side of her, and hugged her gently.

"It's so awful," she sobbed, "I am glad you have come, but it is so awful."

"The men who did it have paid the price," Blaine said.

"It's so awful," Faye repeated, "so awful."

* * * * * * *

With school set to start the next week, Blaine and Jadene visited Ada County Sheriff Lowell Sage the next morning. Noting he had missed them at the funeral, Sage offered his sympathies. Thoughtfully twisting the tip of his mustache, he listened raptly to Jady's story, then told one of his own.

"Last time I saw the Captain was at a meeting of lawmen and legislators," Sage recalled. "Afterwards, we were swapping tales—odd things that happen—Norvil McKay told of a couple prisoners who each had half of a hundred-dollar bank note in their pocket when they checked into the penitentiary. One man was booked last winter, the other a couple years ago, not long after Norvil became the warden.

"Well, when McKay mentioned those torn-in-half bank notes, your father got real interested and started digging, like he was inclined to," the sheriff recounted. "Cap said he had seen that kind of pay-off promise before, when he was tracking down black-market gunrunners back in his army days. McKay was going to get him more information, and Cap was going to write to the military attorney he had worked with on it. That was in March, just before he headed back to the Box."

* * * * * * * *

Massive steel doors clanged open and closed when the sheriff took Blaine and Jadene to see Norvil McKay. The warden remembered the conversation with Representative Box, but had never heard another word from him about it.

McKay showed them the half notes. They were both from the same San Francisco bank, but the halves were not a pair, each being the lower half of a note. Each had been carefully folded in half the long way, and torn on the fold. The man who carried the second was found dead in his cell three weeks earlier, apparently having hung himself. The other man,

Howard Hatch, served his term and was released two weeks ago.

"That's the man I killed," Jadene gasped, "Sheriff Haney called him 'Howie.'"

"Who else knew about the Captain's interest in these half notes?" Blaine asked.

Sage and McKay had no ready answer. Several dozen men had attended the meeting, but they couldn't be sure who was in on that conversation—a legislator or two and, perhaps, Frank Lowry, chief of Boise City's new police department. But Chief Lowry later told them he didn't recall that discussion.

* * * * * * * *

Serena also visited the prison, but for an entirely different reason. She returned bubbling with the news that Drake was getting an early release—perhaps as soon as the following week—due to good behavior and the intervention of people in high places who were concerned about Representative Box's family.

"I will not have you taking favors we cannot repay," Faye fussed.

* * * * * * * *

Sunday afternoon, Blaine hugged Jadene goodbye before leaving for the ranch. She patted a lump in his shirt pocket curiously, and extracted a tiny derringer with walnut grips.

"You didn't bring the mustang I hoped for," she said, "is this my surprise?"

"Not quite," Blaine said. "I visited the Baker City gunsmith to order your surprise—a custom revolver in .32-20, to match your carbine. It wasn't ready when I stopped to pick it up, but I noticed this single-shot .22 derringer. It's not good for much of anything, but it didn't cost much so I bought it to add to my collection of unusual handguns."

"Wish I had that revolver now," Jady sighed, "Pray as I might, I get the willies whenever I don't have my carbine close at hand, and I sure can't be packing a rifle—even a short one—around town, much less to school."

"I'll pick up your revolver after roundup—have it to you by Christmas," Blaine promised. "But Pa intended to have Sheriff Sage hold it for you and spend some time with you at his target range back in the foothills."

"Pa was in on this?" Jady cried.

"My idea," Blaine said, "but he approved and helped pay for it."

"May I have the derringer for now?"

"It's a dangerous toy— has an accurate range of less than a yard, yet it could cause a mortal injury." He paused, considering her request. "Okay, if it will make you feel safer, Baby, provided," he teased, "you promise not to up and kill someone with it."

"That's not funny, Buck," she chided. "You've never killed a man so you don't know how it feels. I hope you never find out."

* * * * * * * *

For her first day as a senior, Darlene had fashioned a shimmering bright blue dress that emphasized her figure and highlighted her black hair and fair skin. She would not be dissuaded from wearing it.

Jadene wore the plain black of mourning.

Fifteen chattering laughing strangers filled the freshman classroom. "Do what needs doing," Jady told herself. Although the desks were arranged by size, with the smallest at the front of the room, she chose the rear seat nearest the open windows.

A tall, bony woman with a large bun atop her head wrote, "Miss Welch," on the blackboard.

Her cheeriness rang false in Jadene's ears as she directed each student to stand in turn, introduce themselves, and tell where they were from and something interesting they had done over the summer.

Jady sank deeper and deeper into her seat as she listened to boasts of city doings and fancy travel, so different from her life on the ranch.

The girl at the front of the center row used a cane to push herself erect. Several girls tittered and some boys openly guffawed. The lame girl smiled gamely.

"My name is Marian Copeland," she said with such obvious good-humor that Jady could not help but like her. "I was born in Boise City and have lived here all my life. I never do anything interesting, but I enjoy having others tell me about the interesting things they do, so I am sure I will enjoy having all of you interesting people for classmates."

When Miss Welch rapped her ruler on her desk and pointed at Jadene, Jady felt as if, for the first time in her life, she was having what her mother called "the vapors." She rose shakily and struggled to speak, but her voice came out in a broken whisper.

"Ja-Ja-Jadene Buh-buh-Box," she stammered, "fr-from O-Owy-Owyhee C-c-county. I—I ju-just, I just do—do what—do what needs—what needs—what needs doin'." She choked out the words and sank back down into the seat.

"What needs doing?" Miss Welch echoed sharply.

Jady nodded.

"Well, what needed to be done this summer in Owyhee County, of all places?" Miss Welch demanded.

Jady dropped her head. "Oh my Lord," she murmured.

"Speak up and stop slouching," Miss Welch snapped. "Stand up! Speak up!"

As Jadene shakily rose, the best day of the past year came to her mind. "Back in April, Pa and me—the Captain and I—we come—came—we came upon an old mare that was havin' trouble foaling." Jady's voice strengthened as she concentrated on speaking properly. "The Captain pulled the foal, but he couldn't save the

30

mare. We got another mare to nurse him some, but I mostly bottle-fed him. He's a dandy colt—prettiest little buckskin you ever saw. I call him Dustdevil 'cause a dustdevil ran right over us while he was being born. I shielded him from it, best I could. He's a dandy."

Miss Welch snorted contemptuously. "Miss Copeland," she said, "could you hear Miss Box, or shall I have her come up front and repeat her pathetic story?"

"I heard her just fine," Marian turned to smile at Jadene, "and I think it was the most interesting story of all. I shall look forward to hearing more about Dustdevil."

* * * * * * * *

Art class was nice. The other classes were bearable. School required concentration, which Jadene found actually helped her manage her grief.

When the closing bell rang, the students rushed out into the late summer sunshine. Darlene and two girlfriends whisked gaily past in a boy's fancy carriage.

Jady looked away, disgusted. Down the block toward town, she saw the girl who used two canes to walk. Marian was surrounded by a gang of taunting boys. One of the boys snatched a cane and sprang away. Marian struggled to keep her balance.

Jadene's face hardened. As she stalked toward the tormentors, she withdrew the tiny derringer from her pocket, hiding it among the folds of her skirt.

Unaware that Jadene was coming up behind her, Marian's annoyance turned to fear. She had hoped Billy Ellis would have outgrown this foolishness, but after eight years of teasing her, he'd only grown bolder.

Jadene was just a few steps away when Billy noticed her. He was well aware of what Representative Box's daughter had done the previous week. He saw the hint of a nickel-plated gun in the tiny killer's hand and heard her say, hard and cold and solid, "Give that back, or you'll need it yourself—permanent."

31

Billy Ellis swallowed hard, threw the cane at Marian and took off, his chums running with him.

"Good choice," Jadene muttered. She picked the cane up and handed it to Marian. "Walk with you, you don't mind."

"I would love it," Marian smiled. She was several inches taller than Jadene, with soft features and dark brown hair. "My new doctor thinks I need more exercise to strengthen my legs, so I am to walk to Daddy's bank each day after school."

"What's wrong with your legs?" Jady asked.

"I was born with my hip out of its joint," Marian sighed, "I have never been able to walk very well."

Jadene nodded thoughtfully. "Shouldn't be walkin' alone," she observed. "Those rannies trouble you in school, too?"

"I am used to it," Marian smiled. "I keep thinking they will outgrow it, but—"

"Won't be a problem, now on," Jady vowed.

She arrived early the next day, marched into the school office and ordered her schedule changed to match Marian Copeland's. When Headmaster Swanson objected, Jady shrugged, "I'll be sidin' Miss Copeland, regardless."

Instead of art, Jadene found herself in Miss Welch's choir.

"Go to art," Marian urged, "I am quite safe here."

Jadene was on the verge of agreeing, until she saw Billy Ellis in the room across the hall. Art was on the upper floor. "I sing the low part but I stand alongside Marian," she informed Miss Welch, with no trace of a tremble or stammer.

Miss Welch looked down her long nose at the tiny girl. Unblinking hard brown eyes met her gaze. The previous evening, Miss Welch had been given some disturbing information about her strange new pupil. She also knew who Marian's father was. She chose not to object.

* * * * * * * *

Friday, Jadene was handed a letter addressed "To the parents of Jadene Box." Billy Ellis's father had complained. Mr. Swanson wanted the two families to meet with him Monday after school.

"Mother's still in an awful state," Jady lamented to Marian, "I don't see as how I can even show this to her. What am I gonna do?"

Marian read the letter for herself. "We will pray about it," she said.

At close of school on Monday, Jady was worriedly chewing on her lip. Marian patted her arm comfortingly. "It will be okay," she promised, "I am going with you."

As they reached the office, a tall, impeccably groomed man with a handlebar mustache came alongside Jadene and gave her a quick hug and a wink. Jady couldn't keep from smiling as they entered the room.

Inside, Billy was trying to hide behind his father, William Ellis, Sr., who looked embarrassed as Delwin Copeland jabbed a finger at him, saying, "You are not the only lawyer in town, Bill, and I will not cut any slack for a boy who should have been raised better."

"Boys will be boys," Ellis mumbled. Looking up startled, he demanded, "Sheriff Sage, why are you here?"

"Jadene Box is my goddaughter," Lowell Sage informed him. "We will send for Chief Lowry if it seems necessary to file charges."

After the meeting, Sage asked to see the "pistol" Billy had claimed Jady threatened him with. He chuckled when she extracted the tiny derringer from her pocket. She carefully pulled back the hammer and twisted the action, opening the breech for safety, before handing it to him.

"How accurate is this?" he inquired.

"I can hit what I'm aiming at up to about two, maybe three feet away," she shrugged. "Farther than that, the bullet seems to stray real bad."

"That makes it potentially very dangerous," the sheriff warned.

"Yes, sir," Jady agreed, "I kept it aimed at the ground. Figured if I had to pull the trigger, the sound would scare them off and bring help. If I ever shoot someone with it, they'll have to be awful close and looking to do Marian or me some serious harm."

CHAPTER 4

Malcolm Grimm was perched on the corral fence when Blaine arrived back at the ranch. "Made a deal with Captain Box to lend a hand with the gather," the blocky stranger claimed. "When I heard what happened, I came straightaway."

The man had ridden in a day or two after Blaine and Jadene left for Boise, Sarge thought. It was a good thing, Blaine decided, when he learned they were a man short. Leroy Stoops had rolled his bed shortly after returning from the funeral, saying he wasn't taking orders from anybody but the Captain.

Hankins didn't know what set that off, but Leroy had been talking about having his own place clear back during the war and never stopped throughout the twenty years he'd been at the Box. Guy Glover said Leroy was going calling on a widow lady down in Nevada.

Within a week, Guy pulled out, too.

"Sorry, Buck, Sarge," he said, not meeting their eyes, "It's just time, that's all."

"You gonna run out on me, too, Sarge?" Blaine asked, as another hand who had been like family rode away.

"You ain't gittin' shut o' me, Bucko," Hankins replied. "Cap'n promised me a bunk 'til my dyin' day, so you're stuck with this good-for-nothin' gimp."

"You may not fancy climbing aboard a horse since that Confederate ball smashed your knee, Sarge," Blaine said, "but there's plenty you're good for when you're off the sauce."

* * * * * * *

Mal Grimm was a capable hand who quickly learned not to give Sarge direct orders. Blaine racked the unease he felt around the new hire up to the fact that he was used to working with the crew he had grown up with—a crew that would have followed his father through Hell—and had.

When Drake returned the next week, with his beaming wife and their child, he and Mal seemed to hit it off.

Mal was a forceful, take-charge sort. When Blaine grumbled, Drake shrugged, "So? You'n me've never run a roundup. Mal has. Uncle Gideon was always the boss—never let us do nothin' on our own but get in trouble. Job's gotta be done and I'm outta practice and you're all befuddled. Let Mal run the show 'til we get a handle on things."

Mal didn't do things quite like Pa had, but Blaine had to admit he was an able ramrod. The Shaws, who had always been thankful for work, may not have agreed. They barely hung on through the roundup before giving notice they would be too busy with their own place to help out at the Box in the future.

That didn't upset Mal. In fact, he bragged he would keep costs down by not replacing Guy and Leroy with year-round riders.

To fill out the crew, he demonstrated a talent for coming up with hands—some more competent than others—who worked a few days or weeks, and then drifted, often before the work was done.

"For the best," Drake would say, "wouldn't want to get stuck with that one."

Buck found himself enjoying having his cousin back. They had been a pair, these sons of Ruth and Naomi Blaine. Drake—who refused to respond to any part of his given name—was as dark as his full-blooded Bannock father had been, but tall and slim like his blond cousin.

Stephan Drake had taken a Christian name when he came to faith, and eventually married one of the missionary's daughters. They christened their son "Jerubbaal,"[10] honoring his Uncle Gideon, but everyone called the boy Jerry. After Ruth died of the fever when Blaine was three, the Drakes took Blaine in and the boys lived as brothers at the mission on the Fort Hall Reservation for nearly five years, until Gideon returned from the war in the east with his new bride.

For the next eight summers, Blaine Box's growing skill at trick-shooting and Jerry Drake's fancy rope handling attracted crowds all over southern Idaho. Men came to watch the boys, and stayed to hear their Uncle Elijah Blaine preach.

Jerry was sixteen when his parents died. Gideon fetched his nephew from the reservation. Rejecting his given name, the boy became just "Drake." He sulked about the ranch muttering bitter tirades, claiming his folks were killed by white men who couldn't stand to see a beautiful blond lady with an Indian.

Faye was terrified, but Serena, then barely ten years old, trailed Drake like a love-sick puppy. Gideon said she would outgrow it. She didn't.

Five years later, a grim-faced Gideon hauled the whole family to Mundy's for a sudden wedding, then escorted the groom to the sheriff's office in Silver City. Serena gave birth to Lincoln four months after Drake began serving time in the territorial prison for a short string of holdups he'd thought no one knew about.

"Wish I'd got a chance to thank him," Drake sighed as the cousins came over Humpy Hill one October sunset.

Blaine shot him a questioning look, and his dark cousin explained. "If Uncle Gideon hadn't stopped me, I'd be an outlaw or dead. Instead, I've got a second chance. And I've got Serena and Lincoln, and," he grinned, "likely another one on the way. Just wish the Captain was here to see it."

---

[10] Judges 6:32

"Amen," Blaine agreed. "It's good to have you back, cousin, but I would have you finishing out your jail term in the blink of an eye, if that would bring Pa back."

"So would I," Drake agreed. "So would I."

* * * * * * * *

With only four men working the ranch, Blaine found no time to collect Jady's revolver from the Baker City gunsmith before the snow got too deep on the Blues. He thought it just as well.

Visiting Boise for the holidays, he noted a troubling flintiness in his baby sister's brown eyes, although outwardly she seemed to be adjusting well.

Under the headmaster's and sheriff's watchful eyes, Billy Ellis was behaving.

Jady was back in art class and gaining fame for pencil portraits that were highly recognizable, yet very flattering to her subjects.

Gideon Box's insistence that his children learn scripture stood her in good stead for memorization assignments. In addition to Pa's favorite Psalm, she was steadily committing other verses, poems, essays and famous quotations to memory.

At school assemblies, with everyone listening and staring at her, Jadene stumbled through the passages in a barely audible whisper, but when the audience consisted of Blaine and Grandmother, she easily and smoothly recited piece after piece.

Jady was virtually living with Marian Copeland, daughter of Gideon's legislative ally, Representative Delwin Copeland, who was president of the First Bank of Boise and a member of the Board of Directors of the Academy.

Despite her handicap, Marian was extremely popular and led a young women's Bible study group. The other girls all did needlework as they discussed scripture. At first, they barely tolerated Jady, but she won them over with her sketches and they soon realized she knew her way around the Bible better than most.

Jady appreciated the red dun mare Blaine brought for her, especially because she had been borrowing a Copeland horse for use around town. She was hiding SoBig at the Copeland ranch on the bench southeast of town, the sight of Gideon's black gelding being unbearably distressing to Faye.

Jadene had organized a girl's riding club and was training a horse for Marian. Most of the girls rode sidesaddle. Jady found that so unsatisfactory that she had prevailed upon Darlene, who was a skilled seamstress, to help her make a Wyoming skirt—a divided riding skirt with a panel that could be buttoned in place to close the front when dismounted—and a matching bolero jacket so she could ride astride without being arrested either for indecent exposure or for wearing dungarees in town. That joint sewing venture was the only sisterly contact between the two girls, who moved in very different social circles.

Faye, by contrast, was not doing at all well. Grandmother Box confided that Blaine's stepmother walked to the graveyard and sat by Gideon's grave for hours every day, regardless of the weather. When not at the grave, Faye wandered the city streets, up one and down another, huddled in the sheared beaver coat she had brought with her from the east twenty years earlier.

Blaine's final evening in Boise he worked up the nerve to mention that Stoops and Glover had moved on, and the Shaws were keeping their distance from the Box.

"I cannot blame them," Faye said. "It is beyond me how any of you can bear that place without the Captain."

* * * * * * * *

March first, Faye surprised everyone by announcing she had rented a house on Franklin Street, about two blocks from Grandmother Box's. She and the girls would move there immediately.

39

"This house will seem so empty," Zelma protested.

"Dar can move with Mother, and I'll stay here so you won't be lonely," Jadene offered. Before Faye could object, Jady added the winning argument. "I think the Captain would like that."

"I am sure he would," Grandmother said, sealing the deal.

Helping Mother pack, Jadene found a small bundle tied up in a man's handkerchief. Opening it, she instantly recognized the contents of her father's pockets.

The Captain had carried three small jackknives— the newest was one she had given him the previous Christmas. It wasn't a quality piece, but she had bought it because it had a special blade for opening tins. The bundle also held his pocket watch in its hand-laced deerhide cover that also held a tiny tintype of Faye from their courting days, a sharpening stone, a small screwdriver and a large-headed screw, a silver dollar, a few coins, a tiny log-book and a stub of a pencil.

Checking the log, Jady recognized the last notation as a tally she had watched him record. There was nothing odd about Pa going several days without writing in the tiny book. But there was one item missing.

"Mother," she asked, "where's Pa's pocket Bible?"

"What is that?" Faye cried. "Oh, put it away—I can't bear it—put it away."

Jadene retied the bundle and stashed it in her own drawer.

Later, when they were alone, Jady asked Grandmother about the book Pa had always carried in his inner vest pocket, where he had also kept the little log book.

"I remember it well," Zelma said, "I gave it to him when he left for West Point. I don't believe he was ever without it, but it wasn't among the things the undertaker returned to us. Perhaps they missed emptying that pocket."

* * * * * * * *

Separating Jadene and Darlene was a relief for all of them. Without Darlene's sniping and Mother's criticism, Jadene stayed home more and found she actually enjoyed learning homemaking skills from Grandmother.

"When you find a keeper, like your grandfather was," Zelma chuckled, "you will see there is some truth to the saying, the way to a man's heart is through his stomach."

"I sure haven't seen a keeper yet," Jadene said thoughtfully, as she floured the glass she was using to cut biscuits. "I told Pa I wanted a man like him, but now—well, he'd still have to be uncommonly good, like Pa, but with a harder edge to him. I reckon there's no such a man, nowhere, so I'll do what needs doing my own self."

Grandmother shook her head. "You are talking vengeance, Jady, and that is a trail best left to the Lord."

"I know, '*Vengeance is mine, saith the Lord,*' [11] but Pa said God most always uses people to do what needs doing, so we should keep ourselves available. I pray He'll use me to settle up Pa's murder, with or without some man lending a hand," Jadene said.

---

[11] Romans 12:19

41

CHAPTER 5

The man who collected the ranch mail noted the letter from Jadene to Blaine. The girl had penciled "urgent" on the envelope. Away from Biladeau's prying eyes, he dropped it in the dirt and twisted the heel of his boot on it. The resulting tear would look like an accident, if he decided to deliver the message. He eased the letter out.

Easter vacation was coming and Jadene needed to talk to Blaine privately. She wanted him to meet her at Lem Walker's or at a mustang camp north of there, closer to Boise City. She would ride south from the city. The farther north Blaine met her, the better.

"Won't be Buck meetin' her," the man muttered. He hid the letter inside his shirt.

* * * * * * * *

A thin haze of smoke rose from the stovepipe of the cabin at north horse camp, seeming to welcome Jadene that Tuesday evening. She unsaddled and turned SoBig into the corral with a nice looking sorrel her brother must have added to his string over the winter. "Buck," she called, "I'm here."

A stranger appeared in the narrow door. "He had to take care of a horse," the man said. "Asked me to look after you 'til he gets here. Name's Al. You must be Baby."

"Jadene," she corrected. "Buck's the only one who still gets away with calling me Baby."

"No offense," Al smiled. "I see you're too grown up for that. Supper's ready."

Al was taller than Pa had been, but he looked to be about the same age and also moved like an old cavalryman. Jady followed him into the cabin, which

42

was comfortably warm after the chill of the early spring evening.

Ladling out a simple but tasty stew Al said, "You sure favor him."

"You knew the Captain?"

"Long time back," Al nodded. "Used to call him 'Mighty Warrior.'[12] I don't suppose he ever mentioned that."

"Oh, but he did!" Jady exclaimed. "It started as a joke at West Point because that's what God called the Gideon in the Bible. So you went to school with him? Tell me about it."

"You first," Al said. "I hear you found his body."

Jadene had thought she'd talked it all out with Buck and Marian and Grandmother, but Al was a sympathetic listener, and the words flowed, until she had told all she knew—and all she puzzled over. He held her gently when she cried. She rested her head against his chest as she used to do with Pa, and he stroked her hair as Pa used to do.

"Don't worry your head about it anymore," Al comforted. "News of the Mighty Warrior's passing was real slow getting to us, but ol' Jonathan sent me along, quick as we heard."

"Jonathan?" Jady echoed. "Oh! Are you from Pa's old friend, Mr. Ethridge?"

"You got it," Al grinned. "Might say I'm his right hand man, here to take care of everything. Now, I believe it must be past your bedtime, Baby."

"I reckon it is," she agreed, not objecting to the use of that name by someone who reminded her so much of Pa.

Al stepped into the night, saying he would bed down in the hay in the lean-to and keep watch. Jady changed to her nightdress and settled into the cabin's only bunk. The bar for the door had gone missing, but

---

[12] Judges 6:12

43

she slipped her derringer under her pillow and felt safe. She blew out the candle and dropped off to sleep midway through her prayers.

* * * * * * * *

Leaving his boots outside, Al eased the door open just wide enough to slip in. He smiled coldly as he dropped his dungarees. Jadene screeched when he flipped her blanket aside and ripped away her nightclothes, but he was strong and experienced in quickly mounting and pinning a resisting girl.

"I was real disappointed to miss the pleasure of doing for that damned self-righteous Gideon Box," he swore. "Turning you into a woman will almost make up for it, Baby, the more you fight me, the harder it'll be on you—and the more I'll like it."

She bucked like a bronco, trying to dislodge him, all the while screaming out, "Jesus! Lord Jesus!"

"Made you cuss," he crowed. "That'd really gall the Mighty Warrior."

She managed to jam a knee up, hard into his groin. "Bitch," he swore and slugged her in the jaw. She sagged back as if dazed, twisted sideways and clutched at her pillow.

Al rocked back on his haunches, grabbed her right knee and pulled, rolling her face up and opening her legs. "I want you watching while I make a woman of you, Baby," he exulted. "I'm gonna screw you till you're dead, if it takes all night."

"Lord Jesus," Jadene said, but she was no longer screaming. The derringer was in her hand as she raised her arm in a smooth steady arc. Without hesitating, she thrust the muzzle of the tiny gun into Al's ear and squeezed the trigger.

* * * * * * * *

Jadene was still working on digging a grave in the center of the round pen when Blaine rode in midday Wednesday.

44

He had never seen her letter—perhaps Mr. Copeland failed to mail it for her, he suggested. He did not recognize her dead attacker—probably some passing drifter who attempted to take advantage of a seemingly helpless girl.

Pure coincidence had brought Blaine to north horse camp. Mal had mocked the idea of checking for mustangs at a camp so far from the ranch. Annoyed, Blaine had just told Mal he was headed for Boise City. He hadn't mentioned stopping at the Bar None to visit Lem, which put him on the trail past north horse camp.

To Blaine's surprise, when he finished out the grave and laid the dead stranger's body in the bottom of it, Jadene stalked out with her Bible in hand. Without opening the Book, she recited a single verse:

"Surely thou wilt slay the wicked, O God: depart from me therefore, ye bloody men. Psalm one-thirty-nine, nineteen."

Once the grisly corpse was buried, deep and with no marker, Blaine took an oiled canvas bag from his saddlebag and handed it to his sister, saying, "I reckon it's a bit late to say Merry Christmas."

The bag held the long-promised .32-20 revolver, the last gift Jady would ever receive from her father.

"If I'd had this," she sighed, "I could've made that sidewinder talk instead of havin' to kill him."

"If you think that," Blaine said, "I am thankful you did not have it. If you had given that man fair warning, as close as he was to you, he would have taken your gun away and used it on you. Remember Pa's advice, never kill a man if you can avoid it, but if it needs doing, do not play games. Do what needs doing to keep yourself alive."

"But I'm sure Al knew who killed Pa and why," Jady protested.

"Pa was killed by rustlers," Blaine said softly. "Let it go, Baby."

Jadene fished a scrap of paper from her pocket, and showed it to Blaine. It was the bottom half of a hundred-dollar note from a San Francisco bank.

"This was in Al's shirt pocket—he knew Pa by name an' called 'im 'Mighty Warrior.' He said Jonathan Ethridge sent 'im, so don' be tellin' me there's nothin' more to Pa's death than we know," as she spoke, the pure Texas drawl of their father grew stronger. "In time, ah'll find out who had 'im killed an' why, with or without you sidin' me. Ah'll ride through Hell if thet's whut it takes, Buck—an' don' yuh ever agin call me Baby."

* * * * * * * *

In late May, Faye and Darlene were among the guests at a mother-daughter tea for graduating seniors. As a member of the freshman cooking class, Jadene was among those assigned to serve.

Jadene was surprised when her mother and sister suddenly rose and started to leave before the program. She hurried to catch up to them.

"You have ruined my senior year," Darlene fumed.

"You are a terrible embarrassment to your father's memory," Faye scolded.

"What?" Jadene asked, perplexed.

"Everyone is whispering about how you murdered those men," Darlene raged.

"I thought the sheriff caught them—or maybe Blaine," Faye anguished, "but, no, it was my own little girl! Your father would have wanted those men to stand trial, but you shot them down—shot them in the back!"

"That's not how it happened," Jady protested.

"And then you threatened poor little Billy Ellis with a gun," Faye continued. "You are a terrible embarrassment. I fear you will end up dead or in prison."

Skipping Darlene's graduation ceremony, Jadene left for the Box as soon as she completed her final examinations.

* * * * * * * *

The Box was strange without Leroy and Guy and Artie. Mal's bossiness didn't set well with Jadene, worse yet, he took to calling her the most offensive of names.

Drake was a further annoyance. Jady still hadn't forgiven him for taking advantage of her oldest sister, especially since—never mind that they were now married—he had obviously done it again. Serena was glowingly expecting a second child.

Jadene gathered her things and moved from the main house to the old stone house. Built by Pa in the days when renegade Indians were raiding, it had three-foot-thick walls and slits for windows. When Gideon had brought Faye to the Box, the first order of business had been building what Mother called "a proper house"—the house now taken over by Drake and Serena.

Jadene had been born in the new house, but the stone house had been her special fortress for as long as she could remember. She liked the dim light and the slightly musty aroma and the even temperature which made it seem refreshingly cool on hot days, and comfortably warm in chilly weather.

The Captain's military trunk sat in one corner, reminding Jady of childhood play when she used to dress up in his old uniforms—much to Mother Faye's dismay. Opening the trunk the first evening, she was thrilled to find that Serena had added some items, clearing them out of the main house after Pa's death. Atop the uniforms were Pa's papers and his Bridgeport belt.

Gideon Box had not been a gunslick, but he was a careful man. When he read about the device being patented earlier that year, he had declared it "ideal for legislative sessions an' political doin's," and promptly ordered one.

47

The belt looked much like a man's regular dress belt but it had a slotted metal plate riveted to it. Recalling the screwdriver and screw among the contents of Pa's pockets, Jadene knew they had been there so Pa could easily remove the hammer screw from his 1873 Colt Single Action Army revolver and replace it with the large-headed screw. That big screw head slid into the Bridgeport's slot, resting securely in a notch at the end. The gun could then be fired from the hip as quickly as the wearer could swivel the muzzle upward, or could be slid off the plate much faster than a man could draw from a regular holster.

The Bridgeport rig did not protect a gun as well as a full holster, so it was not well-suited to use on the range, but worn under a frock coat, it was not nearly as obvious as a belt and holster, making it discrete for town use.

After confirming that the large-headed screw worked with her own revolver, Jady used a leather punch to add holes to adjust the belt to fit her tiny waist. Then she packed it away to take to Boise in the fall, and began reading the Captain's papers.

The next morning, Jady set out, riding SoBig and ponying Dustdevil. Atop Humpy Hill she recited Pa's favorite psalm, then made the rounds of places on the ranch that had been special to him.

Ten months of scouring wind, drifting sand, winter rain and snow had passed since Gideon Box dismounted in the sheltered notch overlooking the river—yet Jadene felt his presence. Since his death, singing had been a struggle, but she suddenly and freely lifted her voice and sang out every word of "*It is well with my soul*," hearing in her mind her father's flat baritone mingling with her alto.

The yearling colt beside her pawed the ground impatiently. Jadene gave a schooling tug on the lead rope, looked down and saw something black, unearthed by Dustdevil's hoof. Jady swung down. The book was ruined, but there was no mistaking her father's pocket Bible, its pages stuck together by his dried blood.

"This is where they killed Pa," she told Blaine when she got him to follow her there late that afternoon. "They moved him to make it look like he caught them rustling cattle, but it wasn't really a robbery or they would have taken his watch and knives, or at least the coins he had in his pockets."

Blaine studied the scene thoughtfully. "I think you're onto something, Jady," he agreed, "something worth reporting."

"To Haney?" she said bitterly.

"No," he grimaced, "I talked to Haney—some lawman! He's up for another term—I aim to see he doesn't get it. I'll get Dan Leinert to take a look at this."

Leinert, who was running against Haney in the upcoming election, gave the site a thorough going-over, but the trail was too old and the shooters were long dead. Still, he put Gideon Box's death to good political use, traveling the county promising he would lead a posse when needed and wouldn't leave his work to be done by little girls.

Jadene didn't hear Leinert's campaign promises. Avoiding Drake and Mal, she spent most of the summer across the river—Sundays with the Mundys and weekdays with Lem Walker and his dogs, old Tracker and young Tipper, at the Bar None. Lem helped her with Dustdevil's training, cheered her daily revolver and rifle practice, and fussed when she usurped his dogs' dishwashing duties.

When Blaine visited, Jadene demonstrated her progress at wielding the pistol.

"I don't shoot near as straight as with my rifle, but I am gettin' faster," she said.

"You're drawing and shooting faster than you can aim," Buck coached. "Get your aim down first. Speed doesn't count for anything if you don't hit your target."

CHAPTER 6

"Couldn't stand being away from me no more, huh, lover?" Mal teased when Jadene returned to the Box in late August.

"Keep callin' me that and I'm liable to plug you," Jady threatened. "I just came to help Serena, so keep your yap shut."

But he didn't. Jady put up with it until Lincoln's new baby brother, Grant, was a week old, then announced that Sarge would have to handle the cooking until Serena was up to it, because she was headed back to Boise City.

"You don't need no more schoolin', lover," Mal objected, "I hear you turned fifteen a couple weeks ago. That's old enough for me. Let's get hitched."

"Stop it!" Jadene cried. "Even if I hadn't promised Pa I'd finish my schooling, I wouldn't have the likes of you."

"I'll wait," Mal grinned. "Man shouldn't get married afore he's forty, anyhow. But see you tell them schoolboys not to come sniffin' round, 'cause you're spoke for."

"Buck! Make him stop," Jady appealed, but Blaine and Drake were both doubled over with laughter.

"Oh, Jady," Serena tittered, "If you had any sense, you'd play along."

"Well," Mal grinned, "seein' as how you're set on it, lover, I'll see you to town."

"The devil you will," Jady growled.

"Actually," Blaine interrupted, "I need to talk to Mother Faye about something and I have not had a letter from her or Grandmother Box all summer."

50

"So you'll run out on your work here?" Mal grumbled.

"Better me than you," Blaine smiled.

Within the hour, Jadene had her pack loaded on the red dun she called Sunrise and was bridling SoBig. Blaine hurriedly stuffed his saddlebags while Sarge tacked up Steel.

They were barely on the trail when Jadene said, "Right after Pa died, you said you had a ranch to run, Buck. I wish you'd take hold and run it and send Mal packing."

"Drake and Serena wouldn't like that," Blaine deadpanned. "They hope Mal will be part of the family."

"Then they'd better get Darlene to marry him," Jadene growled. "But I'm serious, Buck, sometimes I think maybe Mother's right, you're all flash."

She regretted her words as soon as they left her mouth and stammered an apology.

"No," Blaine said. "I had that coming. I should have told you, Jady, last year my trip to Oregon took so long because I went all the way to Eugene. You'll remember, when I graduated from the University of Oregon six years ago, I talked about becoming an attorney, but they didn't have a law school. I could have read law under an attorney—Pa offered to write to his friend, Jonathan Ethridge—but you know me, I stalled. When I visited my old roommate last year, he told me the university was about to add a law school."

"And you signed up!" Jady cried.

"We rode clear across the state and got our names on the list to be in the first class—for once, I was not going to be late," Blaine said bitterly. "I rode into Silver City just grinning at how surprised and pleased Pa would be. When I came past the stage station, Sam Owings flagged me down and gave me the news."

"But you should go now," Jady said. "Pa would want you to!"

"Law school doesn't come cheap," Blaine said. "Without the Captain, the ranch is just breaking even. I intend to ask Mother Faye to give up her rented house and move back in with Grandmother—we need to cut expenses wherever we can and without Dar, the Hays Street place should be roomy enough for the three of you."

"Of course it is," Jady said. "I'll help you convince Mother."

Having spent the night at Lem's Bar None, the pair reached Boise City shortly after noon the next day.

Blaine and Jadene were surprised when Mother Faye hurried out to meet them when they rode into Grandmother's hedge-rimmed backyard.

"About time you came," she scolded. "When I wrote, I hoped you would come right away instead of dawdling away the entire summer."

"Wrote what?" Jadene and Blaine asked in unison.

"Why, that your grandmother was knocked down by a carriage," Faye said. "It has been nearly two months. She is somewhat recovered now, no thanks to you, but she is still quite frail and I fear she always will be."

* * * * * * * *

The Captain had been right. The years did pass quickly.

Jadene divided her time between the Hays Street house and the Copeland ranch. The girls' club rode often and Marian found new freedom atop Sweetpea, a gentle gray mare Jady trained to lie down on command for Marian to mount.

Jady continued to practice daily with her .32-20s, sometimes using Delwin Copeland's small range, other times shooting with Sheriff Sage or some of his deputies.

In the girls' junior year, Copeland ran for and won a seat in the Territorial Senate, besting William

Ellis, Sr., by several hundred votes. Mother Faye even did some volunteer work on the campaign, resuming her interest in women's suffrage.

Returning from seeing Marian home one winter evening, Jadene was accosted on the bridge by Billy Ellis. She was riding with her right hand inside her sheepskin jacket for warmth, with her revolver in the Bridgeport Rig on her left hip, butt forward for safety.

"Well, if it isn't Miss Ugly," Billy taunted. "You think you're so smart, but you're not going to even graduate from the Academy. Before the end of this school year, you'll be dead and buried and rotting alongside your stinking father."

Jadene's eyes narrowed and her hidden hand gripped her revolver. "You figure to put me there, personal?"

"You're not worth dirtying my hands on, you back-shooting bitch," Billy jeered, "Long before I leave for Princeton, worms will be eating your insides."

Jadene nudged Sunrise. The little mare lunged forward, sending Billy reeling. She crossed the bridge at a reckless lope.

Reaching home, Jadene spied a thin wire stretched across the gateway, positioned to trip a horse. She mightn't have seen it at all had she not been delayed on the bridge long enough for frost to form on it. Her hand was still on her revolver. A single shot broke the piano wire, the bullet burying itself in the frozen ground.

Police Chief Lowry berated her for "reckless discharge" of her weapon in the city, and claimed she had destroyed any evidence that might have revealed who strung the wire, but it was likely just a prank. He dismissed Billy's threat as post-election sour grapes.

After Lowry left, Faye fussed once again, "You are such an embarrassment, Jadene. I surely do not understand you."

"Then I reckon it's time I tried explaining," Jady said. "The Captain ran onto something suspicious five-six months before he was murdered. He wrote to his lawyer friend in California about it, but I don't think he got an answer. His body was moved to make it look like he tangled with rustlers, but he was really ambushed at one of his private devotion places. I've talked to Sheriff Sage and Warden McKay and Sheriff Leinert about it. I don't have it figured out yet, but I know enough that someone's taken a couple passes at me."

"But you are just a little girl," Mother protested.

"What suspicious thing did your father encounter?" Grandmother asked.

When Jadene described the mysterious hundred-dollar note halves, Faye gasped, "I can't believe it."

"Well, you should," Grandmother said.

"But it has been nearly 30 years!" Faye cried. "When the Captain and I were courting I watched the entire trial—that wretched man gave his minions half of a bank note as a promise that they would be paid for some devilment. Gideon was magnificent on the stand— Colonel Ethridge said there would have been no case without him." Jadene stared gape-mouthed as Faye added, "The Colonel never replied when I wrote right after we lost the Captain. That is very unlike him, I believe I will write to him again."

"Don't," Jady commanded. Remembering what Al had said but unwilling to tell her mother about that encounter, she just said, "Considering that things went wrong right after the Captain wrote to Ethridge, I'm thinking maybe he had a hand in the Captain's killing."

"Colonel Ethridge would not be involved in any such thing," Mother protested, "He was always a very dear friend, as well as a highly ethical gentleman. Why, he is now a federal prosecutor! You might remember, the Captain and I visited him in Sacramento about five years before—"

"Maybe so," Jady gritted, "but letters always seem to buy us trouble. Fact is I'm through writing anything important to anyone, not even to Blaine and Serena at the Box."

CHAPTER 7

The Copelands invited Jadene to spend the summer of 1886 traveling with them, but Jady opted to head for the ranch. True to her word, she did not write telling anyone she was coming.

Blaine and Drake were battling to keep a hundred steers headed northeast when Jadene met them north of the Bar None. Their only helper was a pale, round-backed stranger who struggled to stay atop his mount and was more hindrance than help.

"Mal was supposed to be with us, but he got cocky—thought he was a squeeze chute and caught himself a horn so he's laid up," Blaine explained. "We have to deliver these beeves to some hungry miners at a place called Gimlet." Indicating the strange rider, he added, "This is all the help we could find on short notice."

"It's just Sarge and Mal at the Box, and Mal's stove up?" Jady asked in surprise.

"Yeah, you better rush on down and give yer lover a hand," Drake jibed.

"Not likely," Jady gritted. "His fault, runnin' a short crew like he does."

"Saves money," Drake argued. "Mal always comes up with a drifter or two when we need 'em—no sense keepin' extra men on when we can get by without."

"Doesn't look like you're gettin' by just now," Jady drawled. "Reckon I'll put off visitin' Lem until we're on the way back," she said, falling in with them.

That evening, the drifter drifted rather than take his turn as nighthawk, watching the stock.

* * * * * * * *

Located high in the Sawtooths above Hailey, Gimlet was a long, hard drive from Owyhee County.

"A strange deal," Jady said.

"Lucky Mal put it together, 'cause we need the cash," Drake said. "Now shed that gun rig, 'cause we don't need no trouble, hear?"

Jady bristled, but she switched to the Bridgeport belt and positioned her revolver on her left hip. Butt forward, it was hidden under her jacket.

As Blaine, Drake and Jady drove the long-horned steers toward the holding pens, they noted an enclosed wagon in an open field.

"Hey," Blaine called, "Uncle Lije is here."

Once the steers were penned, Drake went to collect from the buyer and Buck made a beeline for where Elijah Blaine was setting up to hold a camp meeting. Jady had hoped to quickly change clothes, but someone needed to tend to the horses first and she was the only one left to do it. Gimlet was such a rough-sawn town, it probably didn't have an ordinance prohibiting females from wearing men's clothing, she told herself. Just the same, she tucked her braid inside her jacket, pulled her hat down and hoped no one would realize she was a girl.

Rounding the evangelist's wagon, Blaine found his uncle facing a belligerent lawman. "Gimlet don't allow preachers," the town marshal bellowed. "Pack up an' git."

Kindness softened Elijah Blaine's rugged face. "With all due respect, dear brother," he said earnestly, "prohibiting the free exercise of religion, abridging freedom of speech, and denying the right of the people to peaceably assemble would violate three of five tenets of the First Amendment to the Constitution of the United States of America—the highest law of the land."

"Highest law!" Marshal Witt roared, "I'm the highest law in Gimlet and I don't allow no preachin'."

"You present me with a choice of honoring the laws of men or the laws of God," Elijah said, calmly opening his Bible. "A circumstance very like Peter and John faced, as recorded in the fourth chapter of the Book of Acts."

Swearing foully, Witt reached for his gun.

Blaine spun his uncle to the left, out of the line of fire, and stepped in, jamming the muzzle of his Colt into Witt's belly before the town marshal's gun cleared leather.

"No shooting, Buck, no shooting, Marshal," Elijah commanded, fearlessly separating the two armed men.

Witt seemed to relax, dropped his half-drawn weapon back into its holster and stalked away, disappearing around the tailgate of the wagon.

Blaine holstered his gun and hugged his white-haired uncle.

Gun drawn, Witt stepped clear of the wagon and began firing. Blaine's big Colt thundered in response, quickly silencing Witt's, but the exchange left the spring grass turning blood red beneath two men.

Blaine knelt beside his fallen uncle. "Hang on, Uncle Lije," he begged, trying vainly to stop the spurting blood.

Elijah whispered Stephen's prayer[13]—and then he was gone.

Rough hands dragged Blaine away, removed his gun belt and locked him in the jail cell in the office that had been Witt's. Hunched on the pallet, he buried his face in his bloody hands.

"Buck," Jady whispered. He looked up to see her, still dressed in her trail clothes.

"Baby," he cried.

"I'm so sorry, Buck," Jady whispered. "I saw it coming, but I couldn't get there quick enough. I wanted

---

13 Acts 7:59-60

you to never know what this feels like, but now you do—I'm so sorry—but you shouldn't be locked up. It was self-defense!"

"It's not your fault, Baby," Blaine said. "It will come out okay, but that man was wearing a badge, so they have to hold a trial. Think you can round up an attorney?"

"You bet, Buck," Jadene said. "I'll be back before you know it." As she rushed out, Jadene nearly collided with six stony-faced men—Gimlet's mayor and town council. Claiming to have witnessed the shootings, Witt's deputies made Blaine out to be the killer of both the marshal and the traveling preacher.

"Damn killer sent that kid for help to bust him out," one deputy claimed.

"You got a scaffold up already," Mayor Wilbur Frey rasped, "Hang him quick." Four councilmen nodded. The fifth rolled his eyes but said nothing.

There was no trial. Within the hour, Blaine was standing on the gallows with a noose around his neck, a burlap bag over his head, his hands tied behind him. Through the burlap, he could make out a crowd of gawkers gathering before him.

Swallowing hard, he prayed softly, "Lord, I'm not nearly as ready to see you face to face as Uncle Lije was, but if this is my time, I commend my soul into your hands, and ask you to forgive my sins, and Lord, please, oh please, Lord, keep Jady safe."

A volley of gunshots rang out across town. "Amen," Blaine said, as he felt the platform shudder.

The crowd scrambled for cover as the bellowing herd rounded the corner. The stampeding beeves filled the narrow street, wide horns banged hitch rails and hooves raised a veil of dust.

Another burst of gunfire sounded close by just as the mayor tripped the drop. Blaine felt himself falling, felt the rope go taut around his neck, felt it snap, and then he landed on his feet. A sharp blade sliced the cord that held his hands. He whipped the bag off his head and followed Jady, who was reloading even as they snaked through the crowd to where Drake waited with the horses.

They turned the herd, driving the maddened steers back into town, spun their horses and left at a gallop.

Not until Alturas County was behind them and they were well into the wild lava breaks of Logan County did they stop to rest their horses in a secluded hollow.

"Thought you was a goner, cousin," Drake grinned. "Lucky the rope broke."

"No luck," Buck said. "I am blessed with a baby sister who can shoot, and for that I thank the Lord God Almighty."

"God a-mighty," Drake jeered, "I better circle back an' get ol' Lige's wagon so's you can take over his preachin'."

CHAPTER 8

"Get the job done?" Mal demanded from the bunkhouse doorway when Drake rode into the Box alone.

"Got the herd delivered and the money in my pocket," Drake replied. "Jady joined up with us, then Buck run into some trouble. Our uncle was there—got hisself killed in a shoot-out with the local law. Buck stepped in and dropped the lawman. Almost got hung for it, but him and Jady took off."

"Damn," Mal swore, "Can't nothin' go right without me ridin' herd on it? Where are they?"

Drake shrugged. "They sent me across the Snake alone when we got to Glenn's Ferry—said they were gonna rest their hosses, visit a spell and decide where to hole up. The Glenns are shirt-tail relations, y'know, so they might still be there, or maybe they swung over to the Bar None, went to chasin' mustangs around the Bruneau dunes or—"

"Shut up," Mal growled.

* * * * * * * *

After dark, Dan Glenn ferried Blaine and Jadene across. Riding all night, they reached south horse camp the next morning. On their home range, they were close to the Duck Valley Indian Reservation and the Nevada border, if they needed to make a run for it. The camp had a good cabin with a deep well, but Mal and Drake weren't likely to come by at this time of year.

Jady was elated to find Dustdevil running with a band of mustangs there. The three-year-old eagerly answered her nicker and seemed to welcome a

60

thorough brushing, and readily lifted each hoof for cleaning.

However, when Blaine sharpened his knife and remarked it was long past time to geld the colt, he was greeted with laid-back ears and bared teeth.

"Don't you dare try to cut my sweet little Dusty," Jady ordered.

"You intend to ride a stallion?" Buck shook his head.

"You do," Jady shot back, and she soon had the young stud under saddle.

Buck cringed when, after a brief workout in the round corral, she prepared to climb aboard. He quickly jumped off the fence to hold the beast, but Dustdevil reared and struck at him when he approached.

"Get away," Jady screeched.

Blaine returned to his perch. Dustdevil calmed down. Jady swung up. Dusty shivered his skin. Jady calmly sat still until he was done. When she leaned forward and clucked softly, Dustdevil carefully walked out. Amazed, Blaine watched horse and rider circle the corral, alternating between a walk, jog and lope, without so much as a crowhop.

"He's a dream," Jadene sighed when she dismounted.

"A dream?" Blaine laughed. "I expect I'll have nightmares about that devil."

A month later, Jadene slipped into Box headquarters, after spying to make certain Serena and the boys were home alone. "We haven't heard a word," Serena assured her. "Drake thinks it's all blown over. I mean, they have to know it was self-defense, don't they?"

* * * * * * * *

As summer drew to a close, Jadene reluctantly prepared to head back to school. She brushed Dustdevil until he shone, kissed his velvet nose, and turned him loose.

61

Jadene was again riding SoBig, while ponying Sunrise as a packhorse, when she and Blaine forded the Snake River. They reached the Bar None that evening.

"Ol' Tracker's slowin' down," Lemuel Walker observed, as his dogs cleaned up the supper dishes. "I been mostly leavin' him to home when Tipper an' me're out workin' stock. I don' think the ol' feller sees much a anythin' no more an' he ain't got no more choppers'n me."

Jadene knelt to pet the aged dog. "His tail still works," she smiled as Tracker beat a drum roll on the floor. She gathered up the dishes, knowing Lem would grumble at her for wasting water, but determined to boil them before breakfast just the same.

* * * * * * * *

Two days later, Jady and Buck rode on into Boise, pausing to leave SoBig at Copeland's at mid-day, although Marian and her parents were out.

Crossing the bridge over the Boise River, they met an acquaintance who returned their friendly greetings with a nervous twitch. Riding up Ninth Street, they nodded at a city policeman walking his beat. The officer startled and stared, then rapidly walked away in the direction of the police stationhouse.

"What the hey?" Blaine puzzled.

The flintiness returned to Jadene's eyes.

They nudged their horses to a fast walk and soon turned into the Hays Street alley, then into the backyard of Grandmother Box's house.

Mother Faye rushed out, a worried look on her face. "Blaine! Whatever possessed you to come here in broad daylight?" she cried. "Oh, never mind, come kiss your grandmother goodbye and then go quickly, before someone sees you."

Zelma Box was propped up on the couch in the front room, her Bible open on her lap. She reached out a trembling hand to grasp Blaine's steady, strong fingers.

"The Lord will bring out the truth, Blaine," she rasped, "You should not be risking your life to visit an old lady, though I cannot say I am sorry to see you once more. Now, go with God, Blaine. As we said in our letter, we are praying without ceasing for your safety and your deliverance."

"Another lost letter?" Jadene asked sharply.

"It likely reached the ranch after you stopped there," Blaine said. Turning to Faye, he asked, "What did it say?"

"Oh, Blaine, it is awful, just awful," she sighed. "Your uncle, Rev. Blaine, was murdered in June and Chief Lowry is accusing you—he put your name on the poster."

"What does the poster say?" Blaine asked, knitting his brow.

"It says someone called Buck Blaine is wanted for the murder of the Gimlet town marshal and the reverend," Faye said. "There is no picture, but the man is even taller than you are. They have offered a hundred-dollar reward—dead or alive! Of course, we know it was not you—"

Blaine hugged his stepmother. "What happened was," he began.

"I'll do the tellin' later," Jady cut in, "Mother, pack him some food, and be quick about it—we were seen comin' in."

"I'll head north into the foothills," Blaine said, "Cross the county line, then swing west and cross into Oregon."

"When you get someplace safe," Jadene said, "get someone—a woman if you can swing it—to write out an envelope for you to put a letter in. Don't send it here— send it to Marian—better yet, send it to Mrs. Copeland. Let us know where you are. We'll write back the same way. We've got to get clear of this mess so we can get on with trackin' down Pa's killers."

Blaine took the grub-sack Faye handed him and tied it on, then ran inside to give his grandmother a parting hug and kiss. Jady had a halter and lead rope on Sunrise when he came out. "Take her, too," she offered, "so you can trade off when Steel tires."

Blaine hugged her, "Thank you, no, she's too small for me and her bright color shows up too far away, besides, there's no way she can keep up with Steel. I will be fine—he can outrun and outlast anything they have and I can hide easier with one horse than with two, if it comes to that."

Jady grabbed a handful of mane and jumped on the little mare as Blaine gave Faye a final embrace. Checking the alley, she found it was clear, but she rode to the east end and saw two mounted policemen approaching. "Cut through there," she hissed, pointing a route through the across-the-alley neighbor's yard that would bring him out on Fort Street, with the foothills just beyond.

When the officers entered the alley, they found a slip of a girl struggling with a wild red dun. After Sunrise settled down, Jadene claimed she had accidentally dropped her saddle, spooking her mare. In answer to the officer's questions, she said the man she had been seen with was a stranger she encountered on the trail and chatted with because he resembled her brother. The officers looked for tracks in the alley, but the struggle with the spooky mare had wiped out all other sign.

Faye greeted the officers at the door, broom in hand. She and Zelma both insisted that Jadene was alone, coming to town for her final year of school.

"Why would you be looking for Blaine?" Jady asked, with wide-eyed innocence.

When they stated their suspicions, she became irate, stormed downtown to the police station, and ripped the poster off the wall. "This description doesn't even fit my brother," she raged. "Blaine was with me when this happened, and he sure enough didn't do what this says. You put his name to this again, and you'll be talking to our lawyer."

Returning home, Jadene carefully flattened the poster. A line at the bottom added a twenty-five-dollar reward for a boy about 10 years old, called "Bobby," who had aided the murderer's escape. She chuckled, remembering that Buck had called her, "Baby."

"Do you think this has something to do with the Captain's death?" Faye asked.

Jadene knit her brows, considering. "I don't see how it could," she said, "but we sure are running into more than our share of trouble."

"Only such as is common to man,"[14] Grandmother quoted.

* * * * * * * *

The few places where a rider could safely cross the Snake where it forms the Idaho-Oregon border were all being watched. Hiding by day and riding at night, Blaine worked his way southeast to Mundy's Ferry, arriving shortly after midnight on Saturday.

Despite being awakened from a sound sleep, Titus and Lydia Mundy responded to their young friend's story with much prayer and encouragement— plus a nourishing meal.

Titus was well known for operating his ferry on a strict eight-to-eight schedule, six days a week. On Sundays he collected no fares and only transported people coming to hear him preach in the small chapel he had built beside the river.

At three o'clock Sunday morning, Titus Mundy deposited Blaine Box on the Owyhee County side. "You know the country, Buck," he said, "may the good Lord help you to pass through it without being seen, may He guide you and fill you with His wisdom, and deliver you from all evil, for His name's sake. Amen."

---

[14] I Corinthians 10:13

* * * * * * *

September first, Blaine reached Nevada's Ruby
Valley. A strong sense that he should go to visit the
Sutherlands had come over him after he left the
Mundys. The Sutherland-Box friendship dated back to
Gideon's early childhood, when his father moved the
family to Georgetown, Texas, to take a teaching position
at the University. Eager to learn all he could about
cattle and horsemanship, young Gideon had befriended
the Sutherland boys and hung around their father's
ranch right up until he left Texas for the Military
Academy at West Point.

A quarter-century later, Gideon and Lawrence
Sutherland had been pleased to discover they were
nearly neighbors, Larry having settled in northeastern
Nevada and Gideon in southwest Idaho Territory. Their
ranches were less than two days' ride apart, allowing
for fairly regular visits. Blaine had tagged along
regularly, until, when he was seventeen, he and Gideon
arrived at the Lazy S to find Nancy Sutherland married
to Steve Tanner, Jr.

Although Nancy was two years older, she was the
sort of girl a boy could feel comfortable around. Blaine
had imagined that she would wait for him to grow up.
He, of course, had never mentioned that to her, but
they had laughed together and rode together and he
had liked her and thought she liked him.

He had not known the man called Young Steve.
Steve Tanner, Sr., had been a neighbor of the
Sutherlands for several years before his son showed up
and essentially took over. A decade older than Blaine,
Young Steve was a hard-charger who soon transformed
his father's ragtag outfit into the second largest spread
in the valley.

It wasn't surprising that he caught Nancy's eye.
And it wasn't surprising that Nancy caught Young
Steve's eye, Blaine thought.

Fresh "No Trespassing" signs bracketed the lane leading to T-Bar headquarters, but he turned in, taking care not to stray from the lane.

Nancy had never known of his feelings for her. Fourteen years had passed. There was no reason not to spend the night and ride on to her father's Lazy S the next morning. He wondered whether she would even remember him.

Two girls, about ten and twelve were snapping beans on the porch.

When he said, "Howdy," they looked up sullenly but said nothing. "Is Mrs. Tanner about?" he inquired.

"Maw," the older one bawled, "you got an admirer lookin' fer yuh."

Blaine turned red. As he waited for Nancy to appear, he thought to be troubled by the girl's disrespectful way of addressing her mother.

A worn woman shuffled to the doorway. Her face was grayer than her hair and she looked at him with weary colorless eyes. She was shorter and slighter than Nancy had been. Blaine thought that Old Steve, who was a widower, must have remarried.

He tipped his hat politely. "Pardon me, ma'am, I'm headed for the Lazy S and it is getting late. I thought I might be able to get some supper here and sleep over in the barn."

The woman shook her head negatively. "The mister wouldn't like it, Blaine," she said, "You shouldn't've come. My folks'll be pleased to see you, so hurry along. I'm sorry, but please go—go quick."

Blaine spun Steel to hide the shock he knew must be plain in his eyes. As he lifted the stallion into a canter, he heard the taunting voices of the girls, "Maw had a caller—we're gonna tell—we're gonna tell—Maw had a caller."

CHAPTER 9

"Yore shore 'nough welcome," Lawrence Sutherland said, after Blaine explained his need to lie low while Jadene finished school, "but things ain't real good hereabouts, neither, Buck. We been losin' so much stock to rustlers, ah badgered Sheriff Granger into sendin' down a range detective.

"If ah'd'a knowed you was acomin', ah'd'a give yuh th' job," he added. "Thet son-in-law o' mine might've took it better'n muh bringin' in this Ice Cole fella. Speakin' of which, he's a sorry excuse fer a range detective, but he's pure poison with a gun. No way can Granger be payin' gunslick wages, but it seems as how Ice is th' sort thet'll pack a badge as a ticket to hunt bounties. He don't much care who's payin' an' he ain't known fer bringin' no one in upright in th' saddle. Ah shore wouldn't let on to 'im yore on the dodge, Buck."

"The dodgers on me are pretty far off," Blaine said. "They give my name as Buck Blaine, exaggerate my height, underestimate my age and there is no picture. Best of all, the reward is so small I doubt it will catch your man's interest."

"Wouldn't call 'im muh man," Sutherland grumbled. "Showed up atop a crazy race horse, scared stiff o' cows—give the boys a good chuckle. Ah'm hopin' he don't stay long 'cause he shore don't earn his keep. Keeps pushin' fer a set-down talk—camped out on muh porch first night he wuz here. About gave me th' willies—ah tol' 'im straight out ah ain't got no time fer his kind an' Lonnie already tol' 'im all there is t'say."

"I'll be glad to help any way I can," Blaine offered.

"'Preciate thet, Buck, but, like Lonnie tol' Cole, it's kinda been took care of," the rancher swallowed hard. "Couple days afore Cole showed up, Old Steve an'

Young Steve caught Jimmy Evans changin' brands on some T-Bar steers."

"Jimmy Evans?" Blaine interrupted. "The son of James Evans, your range association president?"

"'Fraid so," Sutherland nodded. "His oldest—only ah'm th' range association president now, y'see."

"I remember Evans from when I used to come down to visit," Blaine said, "I cannot imagine any son of his becoming a cattle rustler."

"There's bad blood 'tween th' Evanses an' th' Tanners," Sutherland shrugged. "Started right after th' feller thet had a little spread b'tween th' T-Bar an' th' Buffalo Head pulled out, not long after Young Steve married my Nancy. They started pushin' each other— truth-to-tell, ah reckon it galled Young Steve, th' way folks looked up to Evans, him bein' near as big an' black as a bull buffalo, and married t' th' daughter of a squawman, b'sides."

"The Captain thought highly of that big buffalo soldier," Blaine said, "What does Evans have to say about the accusations against his son?"

"James Evans don't have nothin' to say 'bout nothin'," Sutherland said sourly, "rode his horse off a cliff a couple-three years back. Left Mrs. Evans with five young'uns—four now. Y'see, it weren't just accusations—dang it, Buck, Jimmy weren't but seventeen—they used his own rope."

"Hung without a trial!" Blaine cried. "That nearly happened to me on totally false charges. Even if they caught the boy with a hot running iron in his hands, it seems awful hasty."

"Yuh ain't th' first t'say so," Sutherland agreed, "but Young Steve says it's th' only way to stop th' rustlin'. Him and Old Steve said all along we didn't need no outside help—reckon they made their point."

The old rancher blew his nose. "Ah woulda give th' Evanses a steer or two, if ah'da knowed they was hard up. Not Young Steve. He's posted th' range 'round the T-Bar, says he'll hang anybody he catches nosin' 'round, no exceptions. He sure blew up when he come by today an' lernt th' sheriff sent us the likes of Ice Cole."

"Ice Cole," Buck echoed. "A known man?"

"Not t' me, but th' hand Young Steve had ridin' with 'im knowed th' bugger ri' off, dunno why Granger'd pin a badge to the likes a 'im," Sutherland said. "Ah been askin' 'im to send down a deputy fer a good two years, fine'ly got so desperate, ah wrote to Cap's ol' buddy, thet Ethridge fella—got no answer."

"After years of faithful correspondence, Mr. Ethridge suddenly stopped answering the Captain's letters, as well," Blaine nodded. "In fact, when Mother Faye sent notice of the Captain's passing, he never replied."

"If ah'd a knowed thet, ah wouldn't'a bothered writin' to 'im," Sutherland shrugged. "Now we got this wuthless Ice Cole critter from the local law. Looks to be about the same breedin' as Mrs. Evans—but it looks a whole lot better on her than on him. C'mon, ah'll introduce yuh—say yer name's Buchanan, jus' to be safe, William Buchanan from Texas."

He led the way to the Texas house—two log cabins connected by a single roof and separated by what they called a dog-trot, but future generations would call a breezeway. Sutherland opened the door to the cook shack side.

Lonnie Latham, who had been with the Lazy S since the beginning, whooped, "Buck! What brings you down?"

Sutherland grabbed his foreman's shoulder and shoved him outside. "Boys, say howdy to William Buchanan—visitin' from muh ol' hometown back in Texas," he announced. He stepped outside and slammed the door, leaving Blaine inside.

A short but sturdily-built fellow offered his hand. "Dermit, I'm the wrangler."

"Cookie," the man by the cookstove nodded.

70

Four others gave their names—Fish, Handy, Wyatt and "Bill, not William."

There was a long pause as the remaining man studied Blaine with ice-gray eyes, sharp as razor blades. He was slightly built, nearly as dark as Drake, with softly-curling red-black hair and exceptionally long fingers. When he finally spoke, all he said was "Cole."

Sutherland and Latham came in, nodding to one another, just as Dermit asked, "That grulla stud at the hitch-rail yours? Now that's a hoss!"

"Steel's th' best ever," Blaine boasted, deliberately mimicking Sutherland's Texas drawl. "Wait'll yuh see th' tricks he does. Ah give a hand sign an' he shakes, plays dead, rolls over—like an oversize puppy dog."

"Ah shore wish we could match 'im up with some of muh mares," Sutherland said.

"Steel's always willin'," Blaine chuckled, "but ah can't imagine yuh havin' any mares open this late in th' season—yuh always kept some nice stallions of yer own."

"Means you gotta stay through to summer," Latham grinned.

"Ah wish," Sutherland sighed, "but Buck's set on takin' off come spring—gotta go collect his gal."

"Figures a handsome bucko like you's got a gal waitin'," Latham chuckled.

"The gal's muh baby sister," Blaine shook his head. "As yuh might imagine, ah'm disinclined to introduce her to th' likes of this crew."

The men laughed, all except the gunman, who ate silently, left-handed, keeping his right below the tabletop.

Upon emptying his plate, Cole rose with the effortless grace of a puma. He was a shade shorter than the Captain had been and the gun that rode in the well-oiled, low-cut holster on his right hip was a Schofield-model Smith and Wesson .45—the sidearm made famous by the outlaw Jesse James, Blaine noted. A Schofield's cylinder could be easily swapped out, allowing a man to fully reload in the time it took most men to shove a single shell through the loading port of a Colt like Blaine carried.

"Not a man you would want coming against you," he muttered to Sutherland when Cole stepped outside. "Reckon I had best make a friend."

"Try to," Sutherland corrected, dryly.

Cole was leaning against the bunkhouse end of the Texas house, next to the open door, lighting a sweet-smelling cigar when Blaine stepped out into the dog-trot.

"Nice night," Buck drawled.

Cole barely nodded.

"Sutherland tol' me 'bout the rustlin'," Blaine continued. "Ah'm well experienced with cattle and ah've dealt with rustlers before. Ah stand ready to lend a hand."

The pale eyes settled on the silver-plated, gold-inlaid, ivory-gripped Colt .45 in Blaine's fancy-tooled gunbelt. One corner of the gunman's mouth lifted in a sardonic half-grin, disconcertingly like Pa's smile had been when he found humor in odd places, but Cole said nothing.

"This is muh show rig," Blaine shrugged, "Ah do some fancy shootin' at fairs and such—quick draw, knock silver dollars out of the air—lost muh range rig awhile back."

Cole raised a skeptical eyebrow. "Lost?"

"Not a pretty tale." Blaine shook his head shamefaced. "Sutherland offered to replace it. Until then, this fancy piece works real well, if need be."

Cole drew on the sweet-smelling cigar and seemed to relax. "Expect it does."

Emboldened, Buck momentarily forgot the drawl as he said, "I just want you to know, if you need a friend, Ice, I'm your man."

Cole's jaw instantly tightened and his eyes narrowed. He ground out his cigar. "Blast," he said flatly, as he took a step to the side and one backwards. He disappeared into the bunkhouse without turning his back and closed the door in Blaine's stunned face.

* * * * * * * *

"Bunkhouse is near full, Buck," Lonnie warned. "Cole took over the rack closest to the door–threw his warbag on the lower bunk and his bedroll on the upper."

"Considering how he took to my offer of friendship, I might be better off sleeping in the hayloft," Blaine said.

"Danged if I'll let that gunner run you out." Lonnie slammed the door open.

Cole was sitting cross-legged on the upper bunk, his warbag beside him. His eyes narrowed and he snapped a loaded cylinder into the Schofield he had been cleaning.

Buck managed a smile. "You're welcome to the lower berth, if you would prefer."

"It's all yours, showman," Cole growled.

Fish had his mouth harp out and several of the men were singing along. As Buck spread his bedroll, he added his fine tenor voice to the chorus:

"Swing low, sweet chariot, comin' for to carry me home..."[15]

Fish played several more old spirituals, with all the men—save Cole—joining in. When he paused for a dipper of water, Lonnie jibed, "Y'see what a fine crew I run, Buck? Ain't no cause to be chary of bringin' your baby sister on down."

"You have it backwards," Buck laughed. "Jay—" he caught himself just in time. He sure didn't want to risk putting the likes of Ice Cole on Jadene's trail if murderous people had, indeed, put a price on her head.

---

[15] *Swing Low, Sweet Chariot*, African-American spiritual, 1872

"Janey's the toughest tomboy you never met, I'm afraid you delicate gentlemen would not hold up."

When the laughter died down, Lonnie said, "Mebbe so, but I have met her—Cap brought her down once, she musta been eleven or twelve and built like a stick, but one tough little tomboy all the same. He said she'd outgrow it."

Blaine wished Lonnie would not mention the Captain when Cole was within hearing, but when he glanced at the upper bunk he was relieved to see Cole yawn, stretch out on his side with his back against the log wall, and close his eyes. "Pa was not often wrong," he said quietly, "but Janey has not outgrown her tomboy ways—at least not as yet."

"Man can have some fun with a tomboy," a leering voice said.

Buck spun, fists up, but couldn't tell which man had made the remark.

"Easy, Buck," Lonnie soothed. "He's just funnin'."

"Wouldn't be fun for anyone if Janey were here," Blaine growled. "She is not a girl to mess with. For all her tomboy ways, she's a lady, too—and quite ready to set straight any man she thinks is stepping out of line."

"Wouldn't none of us step out o' line with her," Lonnie laughed, as he poured some water in the wash basin and peeled off his shirt.

"Ah dunno," Blaine drawled, "Janey's picked up some peculiar ideas from the mother 'bout where the line runs. First time I noticed it, she couldn't've been more'n six years old. She wandered out to the barn one day while we were puttin' up hay. When she saw some of the boys had taken their shirts off, she stood there arms akimbo and announced, 'Menfolk shouldn't be nekkid around ladies.'"

Buck's attempt at impersonating a little girl raised howls of laughter from the whole crew, except Cole who appeared to be asleep.

"What'd Cap have to say about that?" Lonnie asked.

"It was one of the few times Pa didn't back her up," Blaine recalled. "He sent her off to do something that needed doing elsewhere, but, to this day, Lonnie, if Janey were here and you shed yore shirt like you just did, she'd give you what for—mind you, her bein' a lady doesn't keep her from wearin' dungarees around the ranch. The mother, of course, is scandalized, but Janey claims Romans 7:6 trumps Deuteronomy 22:5."

"Say what?" Dermit puzzled.

"Deuteronomy is the Old Testament legal code," Blaine explained. "It prohibits women from wearing men's clothing, and men from wearing women's clothes, but the New Testament tells us Jesus' death and resurrection released us from those laws."

"Janey was wearin' dungarees that time she came down here," Lonnie recalled, "At first glance, we all took her for a boy."

"That still happens," Blaine laughed. "Last year, she and Sarge were tidying up around the barn when we rode up. A new hand who hadn't yet met her curled his lip and said, 'That kid moves like a girl.'

"Janey gave him this long, hard look, and said, 'I reckon you didn't mean that as a compliment, but that's how I'll take it.' We laughed so hard we nearly fell out of our saddles."

The bunkhouse again erupted into laughter, but Cole slumbered on.

* * * * * * * *

The next morning, Blaine saw what Sutherland had meant when he called Cole "a sorry excuse for a range detective." The man was still snoozing in his bunk when the crew rode out in the pre-dawn darkness.

"I told him he ain't cowboy enough to work for this outfit," Lonnie said. "Seems he's takin' me at my

75

word—never lends a hand. Danged if I know what he does."

"Well, the farther he does it from me, the easier I'll feel," Buck said.

* * * * * * * *

Two weeks later, Sutherland declared they were about ready to drive the herd to the railhead at Wells.

"Never have I worked such a lightly stocked range," Buck observed, eyeing the meager gather.

"Damn rustlers," Sutherland said. "Should've had three-four times this many. Musta been more'n just Jimmy Evans makin' off with 'em. Cole comin' along so late in the game shore didn't help none."

"Yeah, couldn't've been all Jimmy's doin'," Lonnie agreed. "But I don't see how Cole comin' sooner woulda helped none. He jus' bumbles around—last week he snuck up on me a time or three, askin' dumb questions 'bout the Evanses or Tanners or whoever—always ended up askin' 'bout you, Buck. I'm hopin' he's pulled out—he ain't come in for at least four days and good riddance to him. Dermit's the only one misses him— can't hardly see why."

Buck shrugged, "I don't see that they have anything in common except they are about the same height. Cole is built like a strip of spring steel. Dermit is built like a bull. My stories put Cole right to sleep. Dermit can't get enough."

"Noticed that," Lonnie grinned. "I think our wrangler's sweet on your little tomboy."

"Waste of his time," Buck allowed. "And we are wasting our time beating the sagebrush for stock that is not there."

"There's thirty head we gotta pick up yet," Sutherland said. "Ezra Peterson was by a few days back. His brother over to Winnemucca took sick so he asked if we'd drive his along with ours if he wasn't back when we was ready to head 'em up an' move 'em out. Said they're prime steers, hid out down in what he calls

76

Pinch Gulch. Lonnie, you an' Buck might's well go git 'em."

As they neared Peterson's Triangle Six, gunfire rang out.

"Sounds like a battle," Blaine said. "Let's check it out."

"I hate shootin'," Lonnie muttered, but he spurred his horse to the ridge overlooking Peterson's Pinch Gulch.

From that vantage point, they spied Cole in a nest of rocks at the edge of a brushy copse. There were three horses with empty saddles, plus two dead horses, one with an injured rider trapped beneath it. The other dead horse was providing cover for its rider who had a rifle and was peppering Cole's hiding place with lead.

Latham pulled his rifle from the boot. "Dang, I hate shootin'," he repeated.

"Look there," Blaine pointed, "one of them is working his way around our friend."

"Ain't real friendly to you," Lonnie allowed.

"I don't think Cole sees that fellow," Buck pointed. "Do what you can about the rifleman. I'll head off the flanker—and maybe get on friendly terms with Cole."

As Blaine worked his way downhill, he marked Cole's position and noted where his stalker disappeared into the brush. The rifle fire stopped by the time he reached the trees. Moments later, movement caught his eye—the stalker, seemingly taking aim at about where Buck figured Cole to be.

"Drop it," Blaine commanded. The man swiveled and pumped a shot toward him, then another, which came closer but, like the first, thudded into a tree. The plain Colt that Sutherland had given Buck felt good in his hand. He returned fire and the man dropped from sight before Buck could trigger a second shot.

Cautiously, Buck worked his way through the brush until he came to the spot where he had last seen

77

the outlaw. The man was still there and would never move again.

"You lookin' to get killed, showman?" Cole demanded, gun aimed at Blaine.

"Nope, just lookin' to keep yuh from gettin' shot in th' back, my friend," Buck countered, in a strong Texas drawl. "Thet's Lonnie up th' hill with th' rifle. Says he doesn't like shootin', but he took out th' rifleman who had yuh pinned down."

If Buck expected Cole to express gratitude, he was disappointed.

"No," the gunman gritted, "I had to drop the rifleman myself, and I woulda had this one, too, if you hadn't plugged him." He extracted two small black cigars from his vest pocket, put one between his lips and offered the other to Blaine.

"No thanks," Buck declined.

"Smoke it, Buchanan, or whatever the hell your name is," Cole ordered. "I can tell this ain't your first kill. Take care you don't get to likin' it." He puffed his cigar alight and held the match for Blaine, then demanded, "You on the run from a killin'?"

"Whut makes yuh figger ah'm on th' run?" Buck drawled to avoid answering.

"First off, you made up a phony name," the lawman replied.

"Ah did not make up no name," Buck evaded.

Cole eyed him speculatively, his look as sour as the cigar. "Why do you keep puttin' on that phony Texas drawl?"

"Jus' th' way ah talk," Blaine claimed, as he grudgingly smoked the cigar, which he found to be extremely bitter.

"Only when you remember to," Cole countered. "You do it pretty good, just not consistent."

Before Blaine could come up with an answer, Lonnie joined them and helped pull the dead horse off

78

the sole surviving rustler. The man screamed and fainted.

"Broken leg," Cole observed. He removed the man's gunbelt and emptied his pockets. "Let's get it set while he's out."

He vanished into the woods and returned with a small hatchet and a canvas sheet.

After splinting the leg, he tied the man's hands securely, while Lonnie and Buck loaded the four dead rustlers, face down, on two of the surviving horses.

The injured rustler came to while they were making a travois to transport him behind the third horse. "Ford?" he called weakly.

Cole walked over and stared down at him. "You're the last man alive," he gritted. "You wanna stay that way?"

"Ford's dead?" The injured rustler wailed.

Cole nodded. "All four you were ridin' with've checked out. You wanna gimme names for the markers?" He pulled out a small notebook and pencil and wrote down the names the captive gave. "And what d'you want on yours?"

"Richard Gwinn—G-W-I-N-N," the man shuddered. "I answer to Booger, but I want it right if I'm dyin'."

"Broke your leg," Cole allowed. "You'll live, Booger, if you play your hand right. Smart play'd be to tell me who sent you and your pards here."

Fear rose in Gwinn's eyes and he chewed his lip. "Need a drink."

Cole held a canteen so Gwinn could drink, but the man didn't seem real pleased that the drink was water.

"Who sent you?" Cole demanded again.

"We was jus' passin'," Booger claimed. "Been down on our luck. Heard them cows an' took a look. Seein' as how no one's about, we figgered on drivin' 'em up inta th' Rubies—figgered they'd bring a fair price at any minin' camp. It ain't like we's outlaws—jus' driftin'—our luck shore run out."

Gwinn screamed when Lonnie and Buck loaded him on the travois.

"I've got this under control," Cole growled, squatting to lash the man down. "I reckon you're here for Ezra's beeves. Get on with your business and leave me to mine."

They rounded up the steers and reluctantly moved out, wondering whether the injured man would reach town alive. They were surprised when they later learned that he had.

* * * * * * * *

When the Ruby Valley herd reached the railhead at Wells, Cole was already there, perched atop a loading chute, talking to two larger gents who Lonnie named as Elko County Sheriff Newsome Granger and a brand inspector called Chance.

"If I was you, I'd make myself real scarce, Buck," he advised.

Sutherland loped over on his blue roan and seconded that advice. "See how fast ol' Steel can get yuh back to th' Lazy S," he said. "As little stock as ah got left, ah'm payin' Handy, Wyatt and Bill off. Ah'll see if'n ah can't git Granger to cut Cole loose, too—no sense payin' a range detective when there's nothin' left to rustle."

CHAPTER 10

There was a nip in the air, but Steel moved out at an easy lope and Blaine relaxed as the miles stretched out between him and Ice Cole. Upon reaching the Lazy S, he pitched in, helping Cookie with the chores until Sutherland, Lonnie, Fish and Dermit returned a few days later—without the bounty hunter.

A pleasant month later a storm stripped the last leaves from the trees and coated the valley in ice. The crew put in a hard day checking the remaining stock and breaking ice on water holes.

Returning to the barn at dusk, they found a tall red horse munching hay in the corner stall—Ol' Blue's stall.

The barrel stove in the bunkhouse glowed a welcoming red. Buck had moved to a bunk farther from the door, but Cole hadn't taken advantage of the empties. He was sacked out on the upper bunk closest to the door, seemingly sound asleep.

"Danged if we're gonna tiptoe around so he can snooze," Lonnie groused. "Fish, get out your harpoon."

"My lips are about froze," Fish hunched over the stove. "Buck, tell us again about Janey and the Dustdevil, while I thaw out."

Blaine laughed and retold the tale of the orphan colt—it was the crew's favorite.

"How'd you get him broke for her?" Dermit asked.

"I didn't," Buck chuckled. "Truth to tell, I've never even tried to climb on the Devil. Janey's sure we'd kill each other."

"Happens," Fish allowed. "Bottle fed orphans tend to be outlaws."

"Janey won't tolerate anyone calling Dustdevil an outlaw," Buck chuckled. "She trained him herself and he's never taken so much as a crowhop with her on board. She calls and he comes running and hugs her with his neck. I pass by and he's all teeth and hooves."

"Sounds like my kinda gal," Dermit grinned.

"Mebbeso," Buck teased, "but you'll be hard pressed to convince Janey you're her kinda guy."

* * * * * * * *

The next morning, they awoke to torrential rains. "At least it's not freezin' so the water holes should be open," Dermit observed, as the crew dawdled over breakfast.

When full daylight dawned, the crew gave up on waiting for a break in the deluge, and headed out to check the stock.

A miserable day stretched into a week, marked by landslides and flash floods. "Weather can't get much worse," Lonnie grumbled.

But it did. As the days grew shorter, a succession of blizzards buried the valley. Every man from owner to cook pitched in to haul hay to the remaining cattle, chop ice to keep the water holes open, and clear snow from rooftops to prevent buildings from collapsing.

Every man except Ice Cole.

"Lucky you shipped ever'thin' you could, Larry," Lonnie said as they pushed the last of the day's hay ration off the sledge. "If'n we'd carried over more'n just some breedin' stock, we'd be in a world of hurt, considerin' how fast they're goin' through hay."

"Yeah," Sutherland nodded. "Wish ah'd've got th' cash from sellin' off all th' stock them rustlers ran off, but havin' th' herd pared down's fortunate. Could almos' say they done us a favor, which is more'n ah kin say fer thet wuthless gunslick."

Not only had Sutherland's blue roan been displaced from its corner stall, the previous evening Red

82

was wearing a heavy wool blanket that Larry had snuck out to the barn when his wife wasn't looking. He had stashed it in the tack room to drape over Ol' Blue, but Cole had taken it "without so much as a by-yer-leave," Larry groused.

"A man who takes good care of his horse can't be all bad," Buck teased.

"So Cap always said," Sutherland rumbled. "Still, Cole oughta lend a hand now and again."

"He stokes the fire," Dermit defended. "I'm right fond of comin' in to a warm bunkhouse."

"'Course it's warm," Lonnie snapped. "Most days, he goes to the barn, the cook shack and back to bed."

"Actually," Buck said, "I am quite certain he slips out, now and again. More than once, I've caught a glimpse of him, drifting across the frozen range like a silent ghost."

"What devilment you suppose he's up to?" Lonnie demanded.

"Devilment's what the mother always says Janey's up to," Buck chuckled, "Actually, I don't think Janey is ever really up to devilment, but the mother often doesn't understand the what or why of whatever she's doing—Pa seldom corrected the mother, but he did counsel against judging someone based on your own lack of understanding of their actions."

"So he did," Larry agreed. "But ah don' see thet gunner doin' nothin' good."

"Cole packs a badge," Dermit reminded. "He's a good guy."

"A badge is no guarantee a man is on the square," Buck allowed. "To my experience, badge toters run about fifty-fifty."

"Suppose that fool don't know rustlers're out of season," Lonnie jibed as he swung the team, backed them to get the wagon under the roof of the loafing shed—they had cleared it of snow that morning and needed to do so again—and dropped the traces.

83

When Latham lifted the collar off the near horse, Blaine stepped up to do the same for its teammate.

"Thet's what ah mean by lendin' a hand, an' it's much 'preciated, Buck," Sutherland said as he passed by, leading Blue into the barn.

"Well, looky there," his voice carried back. "Thet good-fer-nothin' gunslick's rode off somewheres. Ol' Blue's goin' in his rightful stall. Yessiree. Gonna get his blanket, too. We'll see how thet Ice Cole fella likes thet."

* * * * * * * *

They built up the fire in the barrel stove. By the time they finished eating, the bunkhouse was warm and they settled down to the winter chore of inspecting and repairing tack, sharing tales and songs to drown out the blizzard howling around the corners of the Texas house.

After Dermit finished lacing the final string on a saddle he had mended and oiled, he shrugged into his coat and collected his still damp boots from beside the stove.

"What're you up to?" Lonnie demanded.

"Friend of mine's out there," Dermit said. "He don't have nothin' but a slicker to block the wind. I'm warm clean through now. Least I can do is take a look around."

"You're goin' nowheres," Lonnie ordered. "God only knows where that city slicker's got off to and the way the snow's blowin' you'd get lost 'tween here and the barn if you let loose of the guide rope."

Dermit clenched his jaw. "If it was me, I'd want someone to at least try."

"I would go with you if we had any idea where to look," Buck soothed, "The way it is out there, we probably could not see him even if we looked right at him. Besides, Dermit, Cole would not appreciate our help."

"You don't know nothin' 'bout him," Dermit argued, but he put his boots back by the stove. "Buck,"

84

he pleaded, "would you at least say a prayer to keep him safe?"

Blaine dropped a hand on the little wrangler's shoulder, "Of course, although that is something you can do yourself, Dermit. Fact is, I pray for that man regular."

Weeks passed without Cole putting in another appearance. As snowdrifts piled up chest-high on a tall horse, Dermit continued to peer worriedly across the snow and often asked, "You're still prayin' for him, ain't yuh, Buck?" When Blaine assured him he was, Dermit would nod and say, "Me, too."

* * * * * * * *

Lonnie and Buck took advantage of a break in the snowfall to ride down to the little town of Arthur for supplies. The store shelves were nearly empty, but Lonnie collected the mail from the storekeeper, who also served as postmaster. A letter addressed to Mrs. Sutherland bore a return address and postmark that indicated Mrs. Copeland had mailed it from Boise City a month and a week earlier. As soon as they were out of sight of the store, Lonnie handed it to Buck.

Ignoring the cold, Buck quickly opened it. He was relieved to learn that life in Boise City was quiet. Grandmother Box, although still very frail, was resting comfortably. Reading further, he groaned aloud.

"Trouble?" Lonnie asked.

"When I wrote to Jady shortly after I got here," Buck said, "I didn't want to worry her so I so left out a few details, which I now see was a mistake—listen to this: '*We ladies have been praying that God would put the right helper in your path to resolve the difficulties we face. My heart leapt when I read of your friend, Cole, for he sounds like the very answer to those prayers.*'"

Lonnie shook his head, "If you're really prayin' regular for Ice Cole, like you told Dermit, I hope you're prayin' he's safely buried under a snowdrift."

But he wasn't.

85

Inside the Lazy S barn, Cole was mucking out the corner stall, as Red dozed under a custom-fitted, wool-lined, canvas blanket.

* * * * * * * *

The last half mile, a rising blizzard beat Buck and Lonnie in the face. They rode until they bumped into a stretched rope and followed it to the barn. Sutherland, Dermit, Fish and Cookie had just finished putting up the team.

"C'mon to the house," Larry called, "The missus is fixin' supper 'cause I needed Cookie."

Dermit was grinning widely. "Our prayers paid off, Buck. Red's in his stall. He's even wearin' a fancy blanket. Ain't seen Cole yet, but Red bein' here means he's safely back and the bunkhouse'll be toasty."

* * * * * * * *

Mrs. Sutherland had set out a huge tureen of ham and potato soup, a platter of thick slabs of fresh-baked bread and a dried apple cake, but she did not join the men at the table.

Nor did Cole. Dermit had slogged over to the bunkhouse to invite him, but came to the house alone. "He's there alright," the wrangler grinned. "Looks like he fed hisself and turned in. I threw another log on the fire. It's right toasty."

Blaine looked around the room as the men ate in silence. Lawrence's impressive collection of firearms still decorated the walls, along with his wife's prized chinaware, but the cheery hostess he recalled from his boyhood visits was now sad-eyed and reclusive. What, he wondered, had drained the love and laughter out of the Sutherland home?

* * * * * * * *

The crew followed the rope back to the bunkhouse where Cole was sacked out, seemingly dead asleep, in the upper bunk closest to the door.

"Bein' Ice, he's prob'ly scared he'll melt if he moves closer to the fire," Lonnie jibed. Hunching over the stove, he opened his coat to capture the heat.

Exhausted from the day's ride, Buck stretched out on his new bunk close to the fire. He was about to doze off when Fish asked, "Wha'd'ya think of the boss man's guns?"

"I'm surprised he hasn't added any new ones since I was here last," Blaine said. "He has a good collection, but I fancy handguns more."

"I wish he'd let me shoot that Sharps buffalo gun of his sometime," Fish said.

"It'll really hammer yuh," Buck yawned.

"Larry never let you shoot it," Lonnie said.

"No, but Jerry dragged one like it home most of ten years ago, and I haven't yet forgotten the feel," Buck replied, giving his shoulder a rub. "He fired it first, reloaded and handed it to me. That sucker really hammered, but I wasn't about to complain since he hadn't. Janey had tagged along—she was maybe eight and was beggin' for a turn, of course, so I hung a fresh bullseye while Jerry reloaded. I suspect he went a bit heavy with the powder. When he handed it to her, I stepped over behind her, knowin' what was comin'. That gun was longer than she was tall but she snugged the butt up to her shoulder, aimed, and squeezed the trigger. Boom! It kicked her over right into my arms. She didn't mind—laughed right along with us. And that target had a hole dead center."

"Bet that Sharps ain't too long for her now," Fish chuckled. "I bet she's growed up to be a long drink-a-water, like her brother."

"You lose." Blaine yawned again. "Janey doesn't even come up to my shoulder—she's not much to look at—real plain and kinda flinty—she's a flash of fire—definitely not a girl to mess with."

"Don't tell me she handles a gun like you do," Dermit cried.

"Close," Blaine chuckled. "She's too shy to put on a show, but she is a whole lot quicker than you'll ever be and I can scarcely recall the last time I saw her miss a shot."

The men's chuckles faded into silence and Blaine nearly dropped off to sleep before someone softly asked, "She still usin' the Sharps?"

Not realizing the source of the question, Blaine replied sleepily, "Nah, Pa got her a Winchester Model 73 carbine in .32-20 when she turned ten. I got her a revolver to match when she hit fourteen."

Cole dropped from the top bunk nearest the door, landing lightly on the balls of his feet. "Awful light load," he said, tilting his head curiously.

"It's right for her," Blaine countered. "She generally gets the job done with one shot."

The gunman went rigid. "So Jane has a taste for killin'?"

"Not hardly!" Buck leapt to his feet and totally forgot the Texas drawl. "Janey enjoys hunting and takes pride in making a clean kill. It is important to her not to cause undue suffering and to damage as little of the meat as possible—she reads Deuteronomy as saying venison is a gift from God."[16]

As Blaine was speaking, Cole drew his left hand across his face, from temples to jaw, his long fingers seeming to wipe away his icy expression and replace it with puzzlement. "You said that once afore," he said. "Some kinda legal code, you said. Doo-ter—what?"

"Deuteronomy," Blaine repeated. "The fifth book of the Bible—Janey links the list of wild game in the twelfth chapter to a verse in the fourteenth about wild meat such as deer and antelope being a blessing from the Lord."

"Never heard that afore," Cole wondered.

---

[16] Deuteronemy12:15; 14:4-5

"Buck knows lots a stuff me and you never heard afore," Dermit laughed. "That first night when the blizzard hit and you didn't make it home, I was right concerned. Lonnie said God only knows where you'd got off to, so me and Buck've been prayin' for God to look after you—'bout all we could do, seein' as how Lonnie was scared we'd get lost ourselves, so he wouldn't let us go out lookin' for you."

"Go out lookin' for me?" Cole did not sound pleased.

"Sure," Dermit admitted. "You was out in a blizzard with nothin' but a slicker."

"Blast," Cole muttered. He hooked a thumb toward the end of his bunk where a heavy wool coat hung like a liner inside his slicker. "I been dressin' myself for awhile now, Dermit," he growled, then he aimed a long accusing finger at Blaine, "As for you, Buck, didn't you learn nothin' at Peterson's? You bustin' in on me without so much as a by-your-leave is somethin' I can do real fine without."

Blaine sank down on the bunk and dropped his head in his hands. Knowing that Ice Cole harbored a grudge against him for getting in the way of his finishing off Richard Gwinn did not distress Buck nearly as much as the awful realization that on the countless nights when Cole had appeared to be sound asleep, the bounty hunter had actually been listening attentively. Blaine silently vowed to give the killer no more information about Jadene.

Cole took a deep breath, as if deliberately calming himself. He ran his long fingers through his dark, curly hair and then leaned his left shoulder against the bedpost.

"So, uh, Buck," he said mildly, "I bet you could tell stories about Miss Jane and her matched set of .32-20s all night long."

"Not likely," Blaine growled. He stretched out, face to the wall, and repeated, "Not likely at all."

* * * * * * * *

89

Through November and into December, Cole grew less and less predictable. Some days he was up and gone before the crew awoke, other days he didn't stir until they were out tending stock. There were evenings when they found him asleep in his bunk when they returned, and times when he was gone so late they never saw or heard him come in, yet he was there the next morning.

The only chore Cole could be relied on to do was to clean Red's stall.

"Roundin' up that last elusive turd," Blaine chuckled as he watched the man one mid-December morning. "Like Sarge, wantin' to keep the barn tidy as a cavalry stable."

Finished, the gunman mounted up, fixed his icy gaze on Sutherland and growled, "I don't mind Blue usin' this stall when Red's elsewhere, but if I come back and find it full of muck again, I'm liable to take offense."

The rancher was so taken aback that he was still sputtering incoherently when Cole and Red disappeared into the falling snow.

Although they weren't seen again that year, Dermit dutifully cleaned the stall daily, never showing the least worry about the vanished gunman.

CHAPTER 11

From her parlor window, Mrs. Sutherland waved a letter at Blaine when the crew came in one February evening. The snow was deep but the wind had been still most of the day, leaving the track of a sleigh visible where it had pulled up to the door.

"Much obliged," Buck said as he leaned over the porch rail to take from Mrs. Sutherland's hand what appeared to be a letter from Mrs. Copeland. She made no reply, melting back inside as he slipped the letter inside his sheepskin coat.

Continuing toward the barn, Blaine asked Dermit if he would tend to Steel.

"Why, sure, Buck," the wrangler said, "You feelin' poorly?"

"Not at all," Blaine smiled, "I just have something I am eager to read."

But when Buck opened the bunkhouse door, Ice Cole was sitting at the little table beside the barrel stove. He had been there long enough to get the bunkhouse quite hot. His back was to the wall, his left arm almost against the glowing stove, and he was artfully shuffling a deck of cards using just his left hand.

Blaine stopped like he had been shot.

Dermit burst past him. "Cole!" he whooped. "I seen Red and knowed you was back. Bet you had a fine Christmas."

Cole shook his head wearily. "Avalanche closed the pass. You're lucky bein' in this protected valley—rest of the West's havin' a hell of a time. Buildings caved in, tracks swept away, snow piled up fifty feet deep, maybe two-three times that in places. Trains backed up clean into the next county. Supplies not gettin' through. Folks on the prod. Granger took sick. There I was, packin' an Elko badge." He shrugged. "Only good thing—I refilled my money clip at Flora's."

Dermit laughed. "Flora's ladies're better known for emptin' a fella's pockets."

"Only ladies I'm interested in are the four queens in a deck," Cole claimed.

Recalling the gunman's interest in Jadene, Buck figured that wasn't strictly true. He backed out and retreated to the barn where Lonnie and Fish were still untacking.

"Soon as Dermit caught sight of that danged racehorse, he bolted for the bunkhouse, hollerin' for us to see to the horses," Lonnie said.

Buck stripped the saddle off Steel, rubbed him down and did the same for the stocky red roan Dermit had ridden that day.

When all the horses had been seen to, the men headed for the cook shack end of the Texas house. Cookie had dumplings simmering in a stringy stew made from an old bull that had been losing its fight with the winter. Blaine was pulling out Jady's letter to read over supper when Cole and Dermit entered. Knowing how eye-catching his sister's letters always were, he shoved the envelope deep in his pocket.

Buck ate quickly, left the others in the cook shack, returned to the bunkhouse, eagerly withdrew Jady's letter and slit open the inner envelope—just as Cole and the crew walked in.

"Didn't know you played," Fish was saying.

"Higher stakes than you can handle," Cole shrugged, "but I reckon I can go a couple hands with you."

"Just for matchsticks," Lonnie ordered, setting out a well-worn deck of cards. "I don't let my boys clean out each other's pockets. You in, Buck?"

"Suppose so, as long as we keep it to matchsticks," Blaine sighed and again returned Jady's letter to his coat pocket. "High stakes poker is the devil's invention."

"You got a citation on that?" Cole demanded.

"A what?" Blaine asked.

"Chapter and verse," Cole said. "Maybe somewheres in that Deuteronomy book you like so much."

"I never took you for a Bible scholar," Blaine said in surprise.

"But you are," the gunman countered.

"Deuteronomy's far from muh favorite," Blaine drawled, "and ah'd never claim to be a Bible scholar. However, ah do know thet playin' cards weren't invented till long after th' Bible was written, so there certainly is no citation regardin' poker, however..."

"Figured not," Cole cut in. "Rev Stanton would've beat me over the head with it if there was."

"You're friends with a minister?" Blaine asked in surprise.

"Know one," Cole shrugged. "Never claimed to be friends." He picked up Lonnie's deck, flipped the cards into the fire, produced a fresh deck and shuffled, again using just his left hand.

A couple hands was all it took for Cole to own all the matchsticks. "You boys're too blasted easy to read," the gunman muttered, rising. He left the matchsticks and the deck on the table and retired to his bunk.

Once the room grew silent except for the steady breathing of men asleep, Blaine sat up, pulled on the boots he had placed carefully beside his bed, shrugged into his sheepskin coat with Jady's letter in its pocket, and slipped silently out of the bunkhouse.

The night was black despite the white snow, and blacker still inside the barn. He groped his way to the granary and closed the door behind himself before scratching a match. He lit a hooded lantern that spilled

93

a narrow beam across the page. As was typical of Jady's letters, each sheet was a work of art, illustrated with precise drawings which surely would have drawn Cole's eye.

Grandmother Box was eighty-eight years old when she died peacefully in her bed the night 1886 ended and 1887 began. "You could not ask for a more peaceful passing," Jadene wrote. It was expected news, but Blaine grieved that he had not been there. He pulled out his handkerchief, blew his nose, wiped his eyes—and caught a slight movement in the shadows when Ice Cole tilted his head curiously.

"My grandmother died," Blaine explained.

"Your grandmother?" Cole's skeptical eyebrow rose and he reached for the letter, asking, "News from Miss Jane?"

Blaine nodded and quickly slipped the letter inside his coat. "Janey has been stayin' with Grandmother Bah—" he covered the lapse with a cough—"Grandmother Buchanan while going to school."

"Jane's alone now?" Cole sounded concerned, but Blaine was not fooled.

"No," he said, "Her mother is there."

"Her mother," Cole echoed, "But not yours? You're not blood kin."

"Half," Blaine corrected. "Same father."

"You quit tellin' stories 'bout her," Cole observed.

"They seemed to stir up inappropriate interest in her," Blaine allowed.

"Handy's the only one ever said somethin' inappropriate and he's long gone," Cole mused. "Dermit and Fish like tall girls, so they kinda lost interest."

"And you found it," Blaine accused.

Cole mixed a shrug and a nod. "Any interest I got tain't inappropriate—you said she's flinty, like maybe makin' meat ain't all she does with them .32-20s?"

"She has an edge to her," Blaine admitted, "but she does not go around shooting people, as you seem to imagine. I was referring to how Janey can set a man straight with just a look—like the time she came upon a gang of bully-boys tormenting a crippled girl. Tiny as she is, all it took was a look and a word from her to send them all running."

A half-grin softened Cole's face and crinkled his eyes in the way that was disconcertingly reminiscent of Pa. He extended his hand for the letter. "Let me see."

"This isn't about that. It's private." Blaine eased his words with a smile, but all the softness fled from Cole's face. For a moment Blaine feared the man wouldn't stop at murder to get that letter.

But Cole did stop. He gave his head a shake and faded into the darkness.

Blaine turned up the lamp, leaving no shadows in which Cole could skulk while he studied the rest of the illustrated message:

"The fierce weather has shut down the whole territory. I suppose it is the same where you are. There is talk that the whole cattle business will be wiped out. I do not know how the Box is faring. We have had no word, not even a Christmas letter, although a nice greeting came through from the Mundys.

"A young man comes by regularly to clear snow from the roof of the house, and also from the stable. He refuses any pay except to sit and have a cup of tea. At first, Mother thought it was very sweet of him. Actually, she thought he was sweet on me. Then he asked Mother where he could write to you to ask for permission to court me. He calls himself John Johnson, but I am quite sure he is the older brother, or perhaps a cousin, of one of Billy Ellis' chums.

"Mother told him she cannot imagine you would be anywhere except at the Box Ranch in Owyhee County. That is what we tell everyone who asks, and a lot of people do ask, even Mr. Swanson at school and some

of the shopkeepers. The policeman who walks this beat tries to flirt with Mother and claims to be concerned because there is no man about the house to look out for us. Chief Lowry even came by and said he is now convinced that you are not the person described on the Gimlet reward poster. He said we should send word to you to come home right away. Sheriff Sage and Sen. Copeland both say that is a lie and the reward has actually been raised.

"Until the snow came, my horse training business was going well. I have saved every cent I earned because we will need it to hire the very best attorney to clear your name. Sen. Copeland is eager to help, but, as you know, Mother will not abide our taking favors.

"I am disappointed to learn that Cole proved not to be a friend. By the by, is that his first name or last? I guess it does not matter, but you need to continue to be very careful about whom you trust.

"I know how much you want to see me graduate in the spring, but it is too great a danger. Please, Buck, do NOT come to Boise City. Everyone expects you and you must not make it that easy for them to capture you, or, worse yet, to shoot you down in the street. I could not bear that. What I would do would be a terrible embarrassment for Mother so you must not let it happen!

"These past years, I have ridden out from the Copelands' many times without anyone being aware. After graduation, I shall pretend to stay there, but will slip away down to Uncle Lemuel's. Marian will see to it that no one notices I am gone for at least a day. If I do not find you waiting for me at the Bar None, I will take the back trail south. I would like to visit the Mundys, of course, but the chances of being seen at the ferry are higher, so I will cross the river where you and I came across four years ago. I know you know the place I mean, Buck. I do not want to see Jerubbabel or Mr. Grimm, so I will cut around the east side of the Box and go on down to south horse

camp, where Dustdevil will be waiting for me if he weathers these storms, which I am confident he will. I hope you will be there waiting, too, if you are not at Lem's. If not, I will head for Sutherland's, but you better draw a map and send it to me so we do not take different trails and miss one another.

"I hope the weather is not too bad where you are. Stay away from cliffs and out of buildings that might collapse. You are always in my prayers.

Your loving sister,

Jadene

The letter's illustrations included drawings of John Johnson and the policeman, as well as of Dustdevil and Mother Faye. Beside her signature was the stylized letter J, enclosed in a box, with which Jady always signed her drawings.

Taking out his writing materials, Blaine inked a brief reply. He was not happy at the prospect of missing her graduation, but Jadene was right that his being there would be an unnecessary risk.

"I will make every effort to meet you at the Bar None," he wrote, "If I am not there before you arrive, I would prefer to have you wait there until I come. Under no circumstances are you to ford the Snake River alone. Fording that river is as much an unnecessary danger as my coming to your graduation ceremony. If you decide you must cross the river without me, have Rev. Mundy ferry you across discretely, and then stay at south horse camp until I get there. You must NOT try to come to Sutherland's. The bounty hunter, Ice Cole, is still lurking around and I have never met a more dangerous person, which is why I am NOT sending a map or directions."

The next morning, Blaine slipped the letter to Mrs. Sutherland who returned it disguised as a letter to Mrs. Copeland, but nothing was moving. The store at Arthur was stripped bare and ranch families up and down the valley were running out of food.

When Buck and Lonnie saw a starving cougar stalking a painfully thin doe, Buck dropped them both with his revolver before Lonnie finished pulling his rifle from the scabbard. Scavengers were snarling over the two gut piles even before the men rode out of sight.

Thankful to have fresh meat to cook, Cookie sliced thin fillets of cougar and fried them up. While the men chewed the tough treat, he chopped half the deer and set it to simmering, bones and all, in a big stock pot. It made a thin, strong flavored soup, but no one complained.

The next day, the rear haunch of the remaining venison half went missing. So did Lonnie's rifle—and Cole. Sutherland and Latham and Cookie all railed at the absent gunman for the obvious theft.

Mr. Arthur came by, headed north with his empty freight wagon on skids. He spent the night, resting his team. When he hitched up the next morning, Blaine entrusted the letter to him, and prayed for the miracle it would take for that letter to reach Jadene.

The Lazy S crew was in the cook shack, slurping more thin venison soup when Cole ambled in and ladled himself a bowl. Lonnie knocked over the bench getting up.

"Damn thievin' breed bastard," he roared, using much stronger language than Buck had ever heard from the man.

Cole's icy eyes flashed and his Schofield was suddenly level in his hand.

Lonnie froze mid-charge.

"I don't engage in fisticuffs," Cole warned. He took a long swallow direct from the bowl before adding, "so don't make me plug you, Latham"—he drained the bowl—"I understand James Evans counted you as a friend."

He holstered his gun and walked out, leaving Lonnie gape-mouthed.

* * * * * * * *

The hay was gone and April was half over before
the spring thaw pushed back the drifts of dirty snow,
exposing belly-deep mud.

Because they had entered the winter with so
little stock, the Ruby Valley ranchers were actually in
better shape than ranchers in most of the West, where
spring roundup was more like a burial detail, made
even more unpleasant by attempts to salvage some of
the hides off animals that had frozen to death.

"So much for breedin' stock," Sutherland
grumbled as he eyed his sunken-sided cows. The best
of them had scrawny sickly calves. Many had come up
open, while a distressing number deposited stillborn
calves in the clinging muck. Every bull had been turned
into stew.

There was little or no stock in the valley worth
stealing, and there had been no evidence of rustling
since Cole had wiped out the pack of down-on-their-
luck drifters at Pinch Gulch. Nevertheless, the gunman
still drifted the range aimlessly, disappearing for days
at a time, only to pop back up when least expected.

The only reason Blaine could imagine for Cole's
persistence was that the gunman was hunting
bounties, as Sutherland had warned him from the
start, and not just any bounties. He silently cursed
himself for having ever mentioned Jady's guns. Ice Cole
had immediately seized on that information—her .32-
20s were unusual enough that they must have been
described in the kill order issued against her, Blaine
concluded, and his fear deepened that the badge-toting
bounty hunter was aiming to collect that evil reward.

That suspicion was confirmed in mid-May, a
scant two weeks before the Academy would hold its
graduation ceremonies. Cole had been gone when the
crew woke the previous morning and was still gone
when Blaine awoke before sunup. Feeling pressed to
head north, he quietly gathered his gear and headed for
the barn. He was tacking up Steel by lantern-light, with

his bedroll tied on behind the cantle, when Cole led Red in.

"Nice horse, even if it ain't red," he said, as he began rubbing mud off his mount with a handful of straw. "You run 'im in this muck, he's liable to get hurt, Mr. Blaine."

"Blaine!" Buck echoed in shock. "I don't know where you came up with that, but it is not my surname."

"It's what the dodger calls you," Cole declared.

"There's no dodger with my name or mug on it," Buck insisted.

"There's no mug," Cole agreed. "Details might be a shade off, but it's you alright—who's Bobby? That what your sister goes by when she uses those .32-20s for something other than makin' meat?"

"You're loco," Buck growled.

"And you're a liar," Cole countered. "Lyin' about more than just that dodger, ain't you, Blaine?"

"I told you, that is not my name," Buck said heatedly.

"Not your surname," Cole nodded. "Shame you ain't played straight with me, Blaine—the truth would've served you better. Now you're all a sudden set to run, like mebbe you're up against time to meet Miss—is it Jane or Bobby?"

"Janey," Blaine corrected. "And I would not say time is short," he lied.

"Humph," Cole snorted. A knife flashed in his hand and Buck leapt forward to protect Steel, but the gunman just snicked the saddle strings. "You ain't to leave Ruby Valley afore I say to go, Blaine. Y'hear?" he declared, and he headed for the bunkhouse with Buck's bedroll over his shoulder.

Blaine stood in the dimly lit barn thinking. Even doubled, Gimlet's reward was too little to hold the attention of a high-stakes bounty hunter, he reasoned—but the suspected bounty placed on Jadene

100

by people who had arranged their father's murder might well be quite large. Blaine could not imagine any other reason for Ice Cole's obvious interest in his baby sister.

* * * * * * * *

"I talked too much and put that cold-blooded killer on Jadene's trail," he moaned to Sutherland. "Now, as long as Ice Cole is around, I dare not go to meet her for fear I would lead him straight to her. I must warn Jady. Would Mrs. Sutherland address another envelope for me?"

"You write thet letter an' we'll git it sent off," Sutherland replied. "And we'll git shut of thet durn gunner when th' range association meets," he promised.

"Make it soon," Blaine pleaded.

"Ah'm workin' on gettin' folks together," the rancher said. "Went up an' seen Einer Danner. He come through pretty good. Sold ever'thin' but a dozen bred Hereford cows thet he kept up at his barn. His calves're lookin' better'n mine by a long shot. Einer's kinda stallin'—his missus dropped a baby not long ago—their first, so Einer's wantin' to stick close for a bit. Said he'll come on down if we don't meet afore th' end of next week. Old Steve said him and Young Steve'll come whenever," Sutherland added.

"So you looked in on Nancy?" Buck asked.

"Nah," her father mumbled. "Just talked to Old Steve out by th' barn. Me'n thet girl had a big set-to 'bout her marryin' Young Steve. She ain't talked to me or her ma since."

"I'm sorry," Blaine said. "I didn't know. I—"

"Fergit it," Sutherland cut in. "What's done is done. Now th' other little ranchers this side of th' road ain't doin' so good, except mebbe ol' Ezra. He sold every last beef he had left and put th' money in th' bank. Says he's throwin' in with Danner to raise them Herefords—gonna take th' train back east and buy th' best bull he can find.

101

"That leaves the Buffalo Head," Sutherland continued. "They didn't ship nothin' last fall, but Lonnie'd been tight with James Evans so he went over and talked to Joey anyhow—Joey's th' only boy left—kid said they're outta th' beef business so he's got no cause to come."

* * * * * * * *

All the way down to the store in Arthur, later that day, Blaine watched nervously for Cole, hoping the killer would not turn up before he posted the letter to Jadene. He was headed back when Cole joined him on the road past the Buffalo Head.

He rode silently alongside for a ways, studying Blaine calculatingly. "Hard to believe, with a smart, educated gent like you, Blaine," he said at last, "but, what with how things've been atween us, it sorta seems like maybe you don't realize who I am."

"I know exactly who you are," Blaine spat. "Who and what!"

He saw something flash in Cole's eyes at his answer. "Didn't expect that," he muttered. They rode in silence a dozen paces, then the gunman said, "Would've been real helpful if you'd played straight with me, Blaine, 'stead of goin' back an' forth atween lyin' an' pushin' to be friends—'course, lie is all you done since—oh—well—is that why you're set on keepin' me from collectin' Miss Jane? On account of—of what I am?"

"Exactly," Blaine gritted. "I would sooner have you shoot me dead than let you anywhere near Jady!"

"Jady," the gunman echoed. "Jadene."

Blaine blanched, horrified at having slipped in what he called her, and even more horrified at how quickly the killer had turned it into her proper given name.

"You are wasting your time tracking me, Cole," he gritted, "I will ride through Hell and set up camp there before I lead the likes of you to my sister!"

102

"So that's how it is," Cole said bitterly. "Didn't expect that—not from you." He spun his horse and loped away.

* * * * * * * *

The crew was finishing supper the next evening when Dermit moseyed in with a big grin on his face.

"We was gonna go lookin' for you if you didn't show by the time we was done eatin'," Lonnie declared. "Where'd you get off to?"

"I checked the range over east, like you said—got real lucky and found my dream girl," Dermit grinned, as he filled a plate. "What with the mud'n all, she was havin' a bit a trouble with her hoss, so I helped out an' she let me see her home."

"Your dream girl?" Fish laughed. "You sure you didn't dream her?"

"If I did," Dermit allowed, "I don't ever wanna wake up. She's so purdy—about yay-tall"—he held a hand several inches above his own head—"with a wild mane of curly hair that would put a bay horse to shame and eyes big and black as a fawn."

"Meadowlark Evans!" Lonnie cried.

Dermit laughed, "She prefers bein' called Lark—I sure hope she'll be my girl."

"More likely, Mrs. Evans'll skin you alive and turn your hide into moccasins," Lonnie warned.

"If that's her plan," Dermit grinned, "she'll get her chance Sunday. She thanked me for helpin' Lark and invited me to supper."

He filled his mouth, then asked around the food, "Say, uh, Buck, speakin' of girls, when you come down, you said you'd be headin' back up to Boise City this spring when that baby sister of yours finishes school. I was wonderin', when's she gonna graduate?"

"If you're still interested in Buck's kid sister," Fish jibed, "I might be willin' to take this Lark gal off'n yer hands."

Dermit turned red, "You keep clear of her, Fish. I was jus' wonderin' how much longer Buck'll be around—might want him to stand up for me when Lark'n me get hitched. So, how about it, Buck, zactly when's Janey's graduation ceremony?"

Knowing he had never mentioned Boise City, Blaine felt certain that Ice Cole had put the wrangler up to asking the question. He did not like lying to Dermit, but he recognized the opportunity to buy Jadene a two-week head start on the killer who was determined to "collect Miss Jane."

Keeping his tone mild, Blaine said, "I doubt that you can get the young lady to the altar before I have to be gone, Dermit. Graduation day is always the second Friday in June."

That evening, Blaine wrote another letter, with this added information. Uncertain it would reach Boise before Jadene headed south, he wrote two copies. Remembering that Jady intended to avoid the ranch house, he had Mrs. Sutherland address the second letter to Mrs. Mundy.

CHAPTER 12

The polished cotton fabric was the color of new growth on sagebrush in springtime. Rows of neat tucks smoothly shaped the bodice which flowed into a gently flared skirt that pooled on the floor.

"It suits you well," Faye observed as she pinned up the hem to ankle length while Jadene pivoted slowly. "I must confess, you have learned to do a credible job with needle and thread—nowhere near the standard Darlene set, but—"

Jadene twirled happily. "Well, I must confess I do not really enjoy sewing, but I am pleased with how this dress turned out. In fact, I would like to wear it for graduation, as well as for the Mother-Daughter Tea."

"It is quite flattering," Mother said, "but I doubt that the other girls will consider it appropriate for the commencement ceremony, or the baccalaureate."

Mother was right. When the six girls of the Academy's graduating class of 1887 met, Jadene's motion to let each girl wear her favorite dress died for lack of a second. "Oh, Jadene," Marian sighed, "It is an Academy tradition for all the girls to wear white gauze frocks. We have all been quite looking forward to it."

Another girl moved that they all wear upswept hairdos, which was quickly seconded and passed on a vote of five to one.

On graduation day, Jadene's sage green gown stayed in her wardrobe, alongside a few other garments she had made and was pleased with.

The white frock Jadene wore had been made mostly by her mother, with Marian adding a few touches. No one could convince Jady it was the least bit flattering, but she allowed Marian to pin her hair up in a bun atop her head.

* * * * * * * *

Faye watched proudly as her youngest daughter accepted her diploma. She wiped away a tear of regret that Gideon wasn't there. He had been right the many times when he assured her that their little tomboy would grow up to be a proper lady, she thought.

Jadene even cooperated with the photographer the Copelands had engaged. Marian insisted that he take several portraits of the two girls together, as well as individually and with the whole class.

Faye determined to talk to the girl again about going to finishing school. Jadene had flatly refused to join Darlene back east, but Faye had read about a new school in California, with a good art department. Surely, she told herself, her little artist could be convinced to enroll there.

But Jadene declined to go home with her mother after the ceremony.

"I declare," Faye fussed, "you spend more time at the Copelands' than you do at home."

"I'll head home real soon," Jadene promised, kissing her mother's cheek. "I love you."

She abandoned Faye to walk the four blocks home alone.

A well-dressed, portly gentleman overtook Faye, revealing a bald pate when he tipped his hat. "Mrs. Gideon Box?" he inquired.

"Yes?"

"Simon Taylor, at your service, dear lady," he smiled. "I see my name means nothing to you, my dear, nor should it. Captain Box saved my life many years ago—a minor incident to him, I am sure—he likely didn't even remember it. I was at the ceremony because I am looking into the academy as a possible school for my nephew and I couldn't help but notice your daughter's name and how much she looks like the

Captain. I inquired and was told he passed on a few years ago—such a tragedy. May I have the pleasure of taking you and Miss Box to dinner? I presume she will be joining us shortly?"

"Actually, Mr. Taylor, Jadene is spending the evening with friends," Faye sighed, "but I am certain she will want to meet an old friend of her father. Perhaps tomorrow?"

"Delighted," he said. "I recall Captain Box had a son as well, perhaps he will join us?"

"Regrettably, no," Faye sighed.

"Ah, I sense a problem," the man probed, "May I be of assistance?"

"Thank you, no," Faye said, "I do not accept favors I cannot repay."

"Ah, dear lady," Taylor cried, "it is you who would be doing me the favor, if you were to give me some small opportunity to repay the great debt I owe to your late husband. Still, I quite understand why a beautiful woman such as yourself might hesitate to accept aid from a stranger such as myself. Perhaps you could assist me in contacting your stepson so I can offer my assistance directly to him. I have many connections throughout the West that might well be useful to him in establishing himself."

"You may discuss that with Jadene tomorrow evening," Faye offered, turning up the walk to her house.

"Six o'clock here at your home, then," he said, although she had neither stated a time nor offered to be the hostess.

At the door, he took Faye's hand and raised it gallantly to his lips. "Farewell, my dear Mrs. Box, until tomorrow."

* * * * * * * *

The girls talked half the night, Marian curled into an overstuffed chair with her embroidery and her purring calico cat, and Jadene sitting on the floor, carefully wrapping her possessions in oilcloth and packing the items in a pair of canvas panniers.

Jady had sold sweet docile Sunrise to a younger member of the riding club, and purchased a young pack mule. She had never worked with a mule before, but it was a handsome animal, the price had been right, and the trader even threw in a new lead rope.

Jadene fully expected to be on the trail south through the desert before Marian awoke the next morning, but her friend hobbled out in her housecoat while Jady was adjusting the pack on the mule.

"Oh, Jady," Marian cried, "Life is going to be so boring without you."

"I'll be back," Jadene promised. "You're the keeper of my secrets."

"You will be careful," Marian pleaded.

"Careful's the only way to get done what needs doing," Jady agreed.

"I will pray for you every morning and every night," Marian offered.

"You do that," Jadene said. "In fact, if you think of it, you might do a little praying in between as well. Wouldn't hurt."

"Oh, I will, I will," Marian promised. "You know what," she unclasped the gold locket from around her neck, "let's trade lockets as a remembrance of each other."

"I'll remember you even without your locket," Jadene said, but she went along with the exchange. "Now you remember not to let anyone know I've gone."

With that, Jadene swung into the saddle high atop SoBig, leaned down to plant a kiss atop Marian's head and cantered away leading the reluctant mule.

* * * * * * * *

A visit to Delwin Copeland's bank mid-afternoon left Faye in a panic.

"I am uncertain as to how to handle this," Copeland said, handing her a letter addressed to his

108

wife, but actually from Blaine for Jadene. "When I looked out my bedroom window at daybreak this morning, Jadene was riding south, leading that young mule she took on, with a full pack."

"Oh dear," Faye cried, "When Jadene said she would head home soon, I should have known she meant the ranch. I will hide this letter inside a note to Serena and send it on at once."

As she came out of the Post Office, it occurred to Faye that Jadene would not be at her home for dinner any day soon. "Oh dear, what am I to do," she muttered to herself.

"Do about what?" a friendly voice behind her asked.

"Oh, Blanche," Faye greeted, "an old friend of the Captain's is in town and coming to dinner tonight. I thought Jadene would be there, but I just learned she has gone back to the ranch. I simply cannot entertain a virtual stranger alone in my home!"

A mischievous twinkle lit Blanche Sage's eyes. "Not quite alone," she said, "I am sure you invited the sheriff and me to dinner, too. I will just stop by the courthouse and remind Lowell. What time did you say and what can I bring?"

* * * * * * * *

The man who called himself Simon Taylor arrived with a bouquet of spring flowers. He hid his disappointment when Faye explained that Jadene had left for the Box Ranch and would not be joining them. Introduced to Sheriff and Mrs. Sage, he announced that the flowers were to apologize that he could not stay. He claimed he had received a telegram and was having to catch the evening train to attend to business.

Faye was closing the door when he turned back. "Ah, my dear Mrs. Box," he murmured, "you promised to give me an address for Blaine."

"I made no such promise," she said tartly. Closing the door firmly, she turned to her other guests. "I am so sorry—"

"Don't be," Lowell Sage replied. "I'm not sure what his game is, but that man is not what he claimed. If he approaches you again, I want to know about it at once."

* * * * * * * *

Only Old Trapper greeted Jadene at the Bar None, sniffing and wagging and moaning happily when she gave him a good rubbing.

While waiting for Lem—and hopefully Blaine— she sketched Lem's bay colt, Brandy. The last letter she had received from her brother had said he intended to meet her at the Bar None, but she found no sign that he had been there.

"Late as always," she sighed.

She left the picture for Lem and rode on alone.

The mule had settled in nicely, but Jadene didn't intend to own it for long. She imagined some miner would pay well for the beast.

For sure she would include its uncomfortably stiff lead rope in the deal.

From the first time Pa had let her hold a leadline, he had warned her of the dangers of getting caught in a coiled rope and had shown her how to gather a rope in laps rather than loops. It was as basic as holding one's reins in one's left hand, freeing the right for work. But this rope lacked the flexibility to lap neatly or to dally smoothly on the saddle horn, making it a hindrance, almost a hazard—but not bothersome enough to ruin the otherwise perfect spring day as Jady rode south through the soft greens of new growth.

Springtime perfumed the air, tumbleweeds skipped before a stiff breeze and magpies, brilliant in their black and white plumage, raced cottony clouds across the vivid blue sky. Resisting the urge to stop to paint, she rode without pausing, breaking into song from time to time as something brought to mind one hymn or another she had sung while riding with her father.

When she topped the ridge that overlooked the green velvet ribbon that was the Snake River, she sat for a long moment. Softly singing, *"When peace, like a river, attendeth my way..."* she intently scanned the countryside. The perfection of the river valley and the Owyhee range beyond was marred only by the absence of a tall rider on a grulla stallion.

"Guess we better head for Mr. Mundy's ferry, SoBig," she sighed, stroking the gelding's long neck, "'cause I sure don't see any sign of Buck and Steel."

Riding west along the north bank of the Snake, Jadene passed directly across from the Box Ranch. The trail climbed a small, low butte that pinched the river channel. The smooth dark ribbon of water roiled fast, deep and dangerous.

The Captain had crossed there once, long ago, fearing his first wife and baby were under attack in the then half-built stone house. Jady remembered the story and Pa's caution against anyone trying it again.

Pa had said he made it only because he was riding an exceptional mount and knew how to work with, not against, the current. He had followed a game trail down a fold in the bluff to the water, and had swum his horse across at an angle. He had come out downstream on a little beach where the river widened back out.

SoBig was surely exceptional, but Jady had no reason to attempt the hazardous crossing. Still, she recalled Pa's story as she passed the fold in the bluff.

Ahead, a willow thicket obscured the trail below where it dipped down off the west lip of the butte. Movement in the willows caught her eye and she yelped, "Buck!" The approaching rider was too far off to hear her, but the fact she could see the top of his hat told her he was a tall man on a tall horse.

Either Blaine had picked up a different hat, or—

Suddenly recalling her encounter with three strangers on the river's opposite bank nearly four years earlier, she cautiously pulled her Winchester from the boot and levered a shell into the chamber.

The willows parted to reveal a big stranger who immediately reached for his scabbard, as Hatch had when he first saw her. Jadene responded by pegging a warning shot right between his horse's front hooves.

"Hey," the big man yelled, "I just wanna talk, eh."

"I don't," Jady called back, quickly levering a fresh round into the chamber.

Having found his scabbard empty, the man pasted on a smile and began calling to her in a cajoling, friendly manner, all the while sidepassing his horse closer.

"Easy, now, li'l buddy," he said. "Didn't mean to spook yuh, eh. Jus' hopin' to get a line on a safe place to ford. Ferry's out, eh."

"There's a place to ford a few miles east of where you'll see Biladeau's store across the river," she called out. "You'll see the trail if you watch for it. Swing wide around me and keep riding."

"You don't sound real friendly, eh," he grinned, continuing his approach.

He was a big, handsome man, with an engaging manner, but an all-too-familiar icy shiver ran up Jady's spine.

"Back off," she ordered, but the man kept working his horse closer.

He openly laughed at her when she warned, "Stay away from me or else."

Jadene kept backing SoBig up in an attempt to maintain some distance between herself and the stranger whose smile reminded her of a coyote eyeing a calf.

She was relieved when her mule swung around, following the horse nose-to-nose and providing a buffer between her and the man.

She didn't see many options. She wasn't about to turn her back to him or to let him get near her. His

112

horse was even stouter than Steel. Could SoBig, who was no youngster, outrun it? Maybe if she turned the mule loose? To where would she run? The Bar None was too far, Lem hadn't been there and she wouldn't want to bring trouble to his door. The stranger was between her and Mundy's Ferry and he claimed the ferry was out. Might the Mundys and their ward, Johnny Lauchlin, be away?

Coming to a decision as she came even with the fold in the bluff, she slipped the safety loop over the hammer of her revolver, securing it in the holster, slammed her rifle into its boot and swung SoBig over the edge. Ignoring the stranger's startled cry, she played out enough rope to bring the mule into line behind her. She lost the dally on her saddlehorn but kept a firm handhold on the leadline.

They plunged down the steep trail and entered the green flow without pausing. The river bottom dropped away quickly, but SoBig calmly let the buffeting current carry him. The mule had no choice but to follow as Jady gathered the leadline into a couple laps that twisted into loops.

She started softly singing, *"When through the deep waters I call you to go..."*[17]

After the river propelled them out of the narrow slot, SoBig struck out for the southern bank, still angling with the current. When Jady felt his hooves strike solid ground, she relaxed, glanced up and back, and saw the stranger watching from atop the bluff.

A moment later, SoBig lunged out of the river, but the saddle he bore was very suddenly empty.

A waterlogged snag, floating inches below the river's murky surface, rammed the mule. The scream of the mule mixed with the crack of a rifle, but Jadene had no time to react to either sound. As if with a will of its own, the leadline had twisted around her wrist.

---

[17] How Firm a Foundation, Ye Saints of the Lord, verse 4, Keen, 1787

113

When the mule was jerked back by the impact of the snag, Jadene was abruptly popped out of her saddle.

As Jady plunged into the water, the unseen rifle cracked again. A bullet burned the mule's rump. The animal kicked and one of its steel-shod hooves opened a bloody gash behind the girl's left ear. A third shot clipped the mule's long ear and the panicked animal struck out wildly for the opposite shore, towing the unconscious girl. The long snag bobbed up between the girl and the mule and the troublesome leadline that connected the two caught on the root wad. As the snag rolled in the current, it took up the line like a reel on a fishing pole.

CHAPTER 13

As she drifted closer to consciousness, Jadene became aware of the nakedness of her body and the throbbing of her head.

She was struggling to mentally sort out the what and how of her circumstances, when the rough canvas in which she was wrapped was suddenly flipped aside. The cold morning dampness sent a shiver through her body, which set off an explosion of stabbing pains and loosed a moan from her lips.

"'Bout time you woke up, Miss M," a man said.

She forced open one eye. "Hurt."

"Expect so, eh," the big stranger grinned.

She fumbled futilely to cover her nakedness and asked, "Are yuh muh husband?"

"Hell, no! Where'd you get a crazy idea like that, eh?"

"Ah-ah'm not dressed," she stammered. "If we're not married, yuh shouldn't be seein' me like this."

"You got hung up crossing the Snake," he claimed. "Got kicked in the head and damn near drowned, eh. I had a helluva time gettin' you out. Had to take your clothes off to dry you out and patch you up, eh."

"Ah shorely don' remember any of thet but thank yuh kindly," she said. "Fact is ah'm havin' a hard time rememberin' anything much. Feels like muh brain's broke and all the pieces are rattlin' 'round in muh skull. Who am I?"

"How the hell should I know?" the man growled.

"You called me Em—Em who? Emma? Emily?"

115

"M's all I know," he shrugged. "Where was you going, hell-bent for trouble, eh?"

"Ah've no idea," she sighed.

"Well, someone t'other side was layin' for you with a rifle. You got a price on your head, eh?"

"No—maybe—wish ah knew," she stammered.

"You're worth something to someone," he said, "Where do I collect, eh?"

"Wish ah knew," she repeated, then asked, "Who're you?"

"Devlin Burke."

"Burke," she echoed the name, finding it familiar from her schoolwork. "Edmund Burke?"

"Huh?" he puzzled, dumping a bundle beside her.

"In school," she said, dredging up the memory. "Someone I learned about in school—Edmund Burke—a famous statesman."

"Famous, eh," he grinned. "Get dressed, you're slowin' me down."

She almost swooned when she sat up, but she pawed through the small pile, found bloomers and a camisole and managed to don them before he returned.

"Scrawny little thing," Burke grumbled as he finished dressing her in a chambray shirt and damp canvas jeans. His huge hands were rough and didn't take well to small buttons, but he twisted a large bandanna into a sling to support her right arm, which felt as if it had been nearly wrenched from her body.

"Thank you," she said. "Am ah hurt as bad's ah feel?"

He shrugged. "I sewed up the split in your skull, eh, got the bleedin' stopped. You got a helluva rope burn and your whole arm swolled up and turned purple but I don't think it's broke, eh."

"Thank you," she said again. "Are yuh a doctor?"

"Hell no," he laughed. "Ain't often a doc around when one's needed. Ain't the first time I done some patchin'. Ready to ride, eh?"

She looked around the rock corral that surrounded them, rising higher than Burke's head, and he was an exceptionally tall man.

Although sagebrush blocked her view, she pointed with her chin to where a seep had been dug out and rocked to make a small water tank. "Ah need some water 'fore anythin' else," she said faintly. "An' somethin' to eat."

"You know this place, eh," Burke said, handing her a tin can with no label. "This should do you."

She raised the ragged edge to her lips and sipped the syrup from canned peaches.

Burke strode away and returned leading a spavined paint gelding.

"*What* is that?" she yelped.

"Your horse," he smirked.

"Not *my* horse," she protested. "My horse is a buckskin—the most beautiful, most perfect horse that ever lived."

"Eh? A buckskin?" Burke appeared genuinely surprised. "You finally remember somethin', eh, and it ain't right. Well, with me you ride whatever's handy, eh."

He jerked her up and plopped her onto a cheap embossed saddle. She grabbed the saddle horn with her left hand and hung on until a wave of vertigo passed.

"I could tie you on," he offered. She shook her head. "Then let's move out, eh."

With its reins looped behind the horn, the paint followed Burke's stout brown gelding docilely. When Burke kneed Brownie into a trot, the paint lifted into a jarring jog. Clenching her jaw, the girl posted, lifting herself in the stirrups in time with each jolt.

"Cavalry as much as cowboy, eh?" Burke observed. "Rather lope?"

117

She managed to nod. The lope was a little better, but the paint's gaits were all rough, adding to the hammering in her head.

They rode in silence for nearly an hour, the paint steadily lagging and finally coming to a halt. Burke was a quarter mile ahead before he realized it wasn't following. Cursing, he rode back.

"Paint's lame," the girl said, "maybe we can replace him at the ranch t' other side of that rise." She pointed down a faint track leading off to the east.

"What ranch?" Burke demanded.

She gave a one-shouldered shrug. "Ah jus' know it's there."

He eyed her suspiciously, then pasted on a smile. "You're barely hangin' in the saddle, Miss M," he said, "Tell you what, I'll go have a look while you rest. There's a bit of shade by them rocks. You could lay down, eh. You'd like that, wouldn't you?"

She nodded gratefully, slid from the saddle and sank into the small patch of shaded sand.

"A hard man," she sighed, as he headed down the track with both horses. "Rescued me from the river—restrained himself from dishonorin' me—would take me home—if ah knew whar. Reckon ah've got no complaints comin', but ah'd be grateful if he'd ease up some."

Without knowing why, she whispered, "Amen."

* * * * * * * *

"Nap's over, Miss M." Burke's voice startled her awake. He was standing over her, silhouetted against the sky.

She smiled. "Considerin' how we met, please call me Emma," she invited, "and, if yuh don't mind, ah'd like to call yuh Devlin. It makes me feel more like ah know yuh, and since ah don't even know me, ah like the idea of at least knowin' someone. Yore Canadian, aren't yuh?"

She was rewarded by one of his charming smiles.

118

"You don't know yourself, but you know I talk like a Canuck," he chuckled. "Well, you talk like you're from down south, Miss M—er—Emma. Roll your bed now, time to move on, eh."

She sat up, wincing at the effort, then spied the bay. "Oh-h-h, he's wonderful, Devlin," she praised. "You have a good eye for horses after all."

"Better than your dream buckskin, eh?"

"Oh, no, ah told you, Dustdevil's the most perfect horse in the world," she said. "But this bay is very nice. Looks awfully young, though."

"Old enough to've been started, eh," Burke shrugged, "You remember how you are at riding a bucking bronco?"

"No," she admitted, "but even if ah'm real good at it, ah don't think ah'd last two jumps right now. Suppose yuh pony me."

"Just what I planned, eh," he grinned.

Compared to the paint, the bay was smooth. The colt did not object to carrying the girl, but Burke kept the rope short between them.

"He's a joy to ride, Devlin," Emma said. "Ah'll bet he cost yuh a good deal more'n thet paint."

Burke laughed. "No one's aboot. I left the paint, eh, and took the bay."

"But Devlin," she protested, "thet's stealin'."

Burke laughed harder. "So I'm an outlaw, Miss Emma. That paint was more than I give for most horses, eh."

They moved out at a fast pace, riding in silence until late in the day.

When they slowed to pick their way through a field of broken lava, the girl voiced a question she had pondered all day: "Why're yuh an outlaw?"

"What the hell should I be, eh, a damned dollar-a-day cowhand?" Burke growled.

"Ah think yuh could be anythin' yuh wanna be," she flattered. "Yore tall an' strong an' very handsome an' smart an' good at ever'thin' ah've seen yuh do—so why an outlaw? Ah was jus' wonderin'—"

"Got a bum deal," Burke shrugged. "Man don't get a fair deal, he's got a right to take it his ownself. That's what me'n Madden do, eh. We got a right."

"Who's Madden?"

"Damn fool kid brother," he swore. "Cut the ferry loose while I was across. Cost me a five-thousand-dollar haul, eh. Wound up with you instead—you worth five thousand, Emma?"

"Danged if ah know," she shrugged.

In the lead, he jerked his horse to the left when the faint trail forked. Emma rocked back in the saddle, halting Little Bay.

"There's a little hollow, good place to camp outta sight to the right," she said.

"Been watching for it," he said, turning back. "How'd you spot it?"

"Ah didn't spot it," she said. "Ah jus' know it's there."

Burke dismounted beside the remains of an old campfire and stripped the saddle from his horse before lifting Emma down.

"Ah'll gather wood while you see to the horses," she offered.

While she scoured the area, finding barely enough for a modest cook fire, he dug out a small skillet and a slab of bacon wrapped in oilcloth. Tearing off a scrap of the oilcloth, he used it for kindling. Once the fire was lit, he hacked off some chunks of bacon.

As the bacon released its grease, he dumped in some cornmeal, stirring it with the point of his knife as it started to blacken. "Add a little water," she advised. "Stir until it comes to a boil, then cover the pan with a plate an' set it aside for a few minutes."

"You figure to boss me around?" Burke demanded.

"No," she smiled, "but ah seem to know how to cook an' it looks like yuh don't."

When the pone was done, he dumped it on the plate and ate his fill, leaving her only what clung to the skillet.

"You were tellin' me how yuh got to be an outlaw," she said, as she scraped what she could off the bottom of the pan and licked the meager supper off her fingers.

"Got a bum deal," Burke repeated. "Had a pappy what got crazy when he drank, which he did a lot. He'd take after Mum and us kids with a butcher knife. Mum's brother give us a cabin on his spread and built this iron cage in the front room. When Pap started gettin' crazy, we'd lock 'im in. Mum had a passel a kids, but Madden and me's the only one's what growed up, eh."

"Uncle Amil made us go to school. 'Tweren't so bad for me, but Madden just couldn't make sense of letters. They made fun a him—I hadda fight 'em. 'Twas their fault, but I always got the whoopin', eh," Burke said.

"When I got to be sixteen, I moved into the bunkhouse and cowboyed steady—that's where I learnt to handle a rope good enough to get a line on you afore you drowned, eh," he said.

"Ah'm ever so grateful," Emma said. "Bein' sixteen, yuh musta graduated from grammar school. Bein' good at so many things, yuh didn't have to stay a cowhand, or become an outlaw, either."

"Shows what you know," he sneered. "Madden'd give up on school, eh, but Cora kept goin'. When she didn't show three-four days, Uncle Amil sent me to see. Pap was in his cage and Madden'd buried Cora by the others. The house just blew up—Mum run and tried to get Pap out—just got herself burnt up, too, eh. Took a couple days dyin'—made me promise to take care a

Madden. After she's dead, I bust him outta jail and we run for the border—" the outlaw's voice trailed off. "Now shut up—we gotta be movin' early if we're gonna make it to the hole by nightfall, eh."

Jadene scraped a hollow for her hip and rolled on her side in her blanket. The ground was hard, her body ached almost as bad as her head, but it was good to be lying down. A phrase surfaced in her mind, its source lost to her: "O give thanks."

"Devlin," she whispered.

"What?" he growled.

"Thank you for rescuing me from the river, and taking care of me, and telling me about yourself. I was right, you know," she added, "Taking care of your brother was the honorable thing to do, but you don't have to be an outlaw. You could be whatever you want."

He raised up on an elbow, stared at her, then gave a dismissive snort, but the next morning he treated her a bit gentler.

They rode hard all day and far into the night, headed east across a lava-pocked sagebrush plain that was no longer familiar to the girl.

Emma was barely hanging in the saddle when a small butte loomed against the starry sky, rising like a pillar from the Snake River desert.

Burke led the way into a brush-choked defile that opened into a hidden pocket. He deposited their packs and Emma in a tiny stone cabin before turning the horses into a corral where water from a spring raised a lush crop of grass.

Burke displayed an easy smile as they ate.

"Well now, Emma," he said, "I told you how I got to be an outlaw, eh, suppose you tell me how you got to be in the fix you're in, eh."

"I wish I could," she sighed. "I hope it's just 'cause my head's throbbing so hard I can't think, but I still don't remember much of anything—except some of the places we came through felt kinda familiar."

"Noticed that." He nodded thoughtfully, then asked, "How come you lose the drawl, now and again?"

"Lose what?" she puzzled.

"The way you talk keeps changin'," he said. "No matter, eh. I'll see what I can find out tomorrow, while you rest up, eh." He looked over at the lone bunk and grinned. "Bed's wide enough for the two of us, scrawny as you are, but don't expect me to warm you up, eh. You're about as pretty as a buzzard."

She turned bright red. "I may not know who I am, but I am certain I am not that kind of girl and I am very thankful that you are an honorable gentleman."

She was sound asleep before he quit laughing.

* * * * * * * *

"Get up, Em," Burke demanded, roughly prodding the girl awake. "I give you three days to rest up, now we got business to see to, eh."

She moaned.

"You're costin' me a bundle," he growled, "I missed one big haul pullin' you out of the river, eh, now I'm liable to miss another 'cause you slowed me down so I missed hookin' up with the pack. Don't know where they got off to, but you got some serious gear, let's see if you know how to use it, eh?"

Em's head reeled when she stood up.

"You remember how to use this, eh?" Burke held, out a small, revolver in a cutaway holster.

"Yeah," she muttered, clumsily buckling on the familiar gunbelt, "but ah'm bunged up so bad ah don' know as how ah can."

"Then use your other hand, eh," the outlaw ordered. "Best partner I ever had's even better with his left than his right—fastest man ever lived."

"Then get him to help you," she mumbled.

"He's servin' time," Burke said, "won't be out soon enough for this deal, eh."

"Servin' time," Emma echoed. "Pa talked 'bout servin' time."

"Figured you was an outlaw your ownself, eh, on the dodge, eh," Burke handed over a Bridgeport belt. "If you can't use your quick-draw holster, hang your gun on this for a left hand draw, eh."

Em needed no instructions, but she had never before shot left handed. He opened the cabin door, releasing a wedge of lamplight that illuminated a hitching post. "Make like that's a lawman aboot to shoot you, eh," he ordered.

Em tilted the barrel up.

"Trip the trigger," Burke commanded. She did, but the bullet sailed wildly off into the darkness. "Damn," he exploded, "I need a second hand and you're worthless. Not worth turnin' in to the law and not worth a damn with a gun. You owe me five grand, you ugly bitch. Gonna be ten. How're you gonna pay up, eh?" he raged, "Look at you—ugliest thing I ever seen. You tell me where you're wanted, I'll sell you quick, eh."

"I'd tell if I knew," she cried. "In time—"

"Time! We're outta time." Burke slammed her against the wall, pinning her there with his shoulder, her feet dangling far above the floor. With a wild fury, he stripped off her gunbelt and the Bridgeport, hurled them down, and tossed her on the bed.

She watched in horror as he unbuttoned, then he was on her in a flash, tearing wildly at her clothes.

"Jesus! Lord Jesus!" she screamed and she impulsively jabbed her index finger into his ear.

Burke stopped his wild attack, straightened, and shook his head.

"Hell! They're with the wild woman," he cried.

The girl desperately crabbed away from him. He grabbed her, growled, "Forget you," and flung her against the stone wall, as a petulant child would toss a rag doll.

124

THE TRAIL
OF THE SNAKE

PART II

*...though trials
should come....*

CHAPTER 1

Ruby Valley, State of Nevada, June 1887

Blaine "Buck" Box was stuck some three-hundred miles to the south of where he wanted to be—but dared not go.

Most of a year had passed since he had fired back when the city marshal of the remote mining town of Gimlet, in the mountains of Idaho Territory, had killed Blaine's unarmed uncle—and aimed to kill him, as well.

It was a clear case of self-defense, but the town officials had tried to hang Blaine for murder, without bothering with a trial. His tomboy sister, Jadene, had fired, breaking the rope as he dropped, and they had escaped in a cloud of dust.

Three months later, they had discovered Gimlet had issued a dead-or-alive reward for "Buck Blaine," charged with two murders plus an escape. When the Boise City police connected him to that poster, Blaine had fled to the Nevada ranch of their late father's friend, Lawrence Sutherland, leaving Jady in Boise to complete her final year at the Boise Academy.

Fortunately, no one was connecting Jadene with the "Bobby" named as an accomplice to Buck's escape from Gimlet. When they parted, the Box brother and sister had pledged to meet up after Jadene graduated in the spring, at which time they would resolve their legal difficulties—somehow.

Blaine had hoped for a peaceful winter, but Sutherland's Lazy S ranch had proven to be a dangerous refuge. A deadly bounty hunter had ridden in a day ahead of Buck, claiming to be a range detective sent to stop an outbreak of cattle rustling. To shield his young friend from the gunman, Sutherland had introduced Blaine as "William Buchanan."

The killer, Ice Cole, had instantly realized that name was an alias and had developed a dangerous interest in Buck.

Similar interest was rampant in Boise. Jadene had written insisting that Blaine not attend her graduation ceremony for fear he would be shot down in the street by people eager to collect the Gimlet bounty. Blaine had written back ordering Jadene not to come to Ruby Valley, for fear of Ice Cole. Instead, Blaine had promised to meet her at south horse camp, an out-of-the-way cabin on their home range—just as soon as he gave Cole the slip.

With every passing day, Blaine grew more anxious to slip away from Ruby Valley—without Ice Cole following him to the Box Ranch.

As spring approached, Cole had made it clear that he, too, had connected Blaine with the Gimlet dodger, and he had even guessed that the "Bobby" cited for having helped Blaine escape was the tomboy sister Buck had talked about far too freely. In fact, the gunman had stated straight out that he aimed to "collect Miss Jade."

Blaine had managed to trick Cole into believing Jadene would not graduate until the second Friday of June, rather than on the last Friday in May, but time was running out on that ruse, with Blaine no closer to being able to safely return to Idaho. He had, however, managed to warn Jady about the threat posed by Ice Cole. He had mailed letters, in envelopes addressed by Mrs. Sutherland, to the mother of Jady's dearest school friend, in Boise City, and also to Mrs. Mundy, whose husband operated the ferry on which Jady would have crossed the Snake River.

Blaine was confident at least one of those letters would have reached her by now. He felt certain Jady would have crossed the river and reached south horse camp, because she had been eager to reclaim her feisty buckskin mustang, Dustdevil, who she had left there.

The bitter winter had left virtually no cattle worth rustling in Ruby Valley—or elsewhere throughout the West. Sutherland, who was president of the Ruby Valley Range Association, was organizing a meeting, at which he promised to "send thet wuthless gunner packin'." Meanwhile, Cole continued to poke around and Blaine was steadily losing confidence that the ranchers could successfully fire the badge-toting gunman.

After warning Blaine not to leave the area without his say-so, Cole had rolled his bed and moved out of the Lazy S bunkhouse, but the deadly bounty hunter took pains to let Blaine know he was keeping an eye on him. Scarcely a day passed without the gunman appearing, close by or at some distance. Each time, Cole silently aimed a long finger at Blaine and gestured as if firing a shot. Blaine always responded with a curt nod, his thoughts a mix of thanks that the man was still stalking the Nevada rangeland—far from Jadene— and frustration that he, himself, was essentially trapped there.

* * * * * * * *

"First order of biznis is gonna be sendin' thet sorry excuse fer a range detective packin'," Sutherland, announced, when the ranchers finally gathered.

"Little late fer that," Ezra Peterson cackled, "Cole come by early yestidy, headed up inta th' Rubies, hot on th' trail o' some big bounty—tol' me not t' expect 'im t' pass this-a-way agin anytime soon."

"Yup," Collins agreed. "Seen 'im day b'fore that— said he'd done all he could fer us hereabouts an' had bigger fish t' fry."

"Told yuh," Old Steve Tanner crowed happily, poking a finger at his son. "Me'n TJ seen him with his bedroll an' warbag tied on, beatin' feet outta here, headin' west."

Blaine had heard enough. Cole had last aimed his long finger at him early the previous morning, perhaps on his way to Peterson's, he guessed. As he sprinted to the barn, he silently gave thanks for whatever it was that had distracted the bounty hunter. He saddled his big grulla, Steel, and led the stallion to the bunkhouse. Rushing inside, he was brought up short by the sight of a Gimlet dodger lying on his bunk. Across the top was a message, written in a very precise hand:

"Blaine, I will take care of this next—boss's orders. Get packed but sit tight here till I send the word to ride. Won't be long. Cohl"

"Cohl?" Blaine muttered aloud. "Odd spelling— even odder that he expects me to wait around to be turned in or gunned down."

He quickly rolled his bed, packed his saddlebags, and left at a gallop.

Once on the trail, he let Steel settle into a ground-eating lope. He shuddered at the thought of facing Ice Cohl in a gunfight. Blaine knew that Cohl had been right in calling him "a showman"—and Sutherland had been dead on when he had said Cohl was "pure poison."

Blaine leaned forward in the saddle and his big grulla lengthened its stride. Cohl's racehorse would not easily overtake Steel, he thought. Once he had a good lead, he could obscure his trail and hopefully lose the bounty hunter altogether.

* * * * * * * *

The Ruby Valley ranchers had quickly moved on to dealing with other business.

Peterson and Einer Danner laid out their plan to throw in together to raise Herefords, and invited the other shirt-tail outfits to join up.

Sounding hesitant, Collins started, "Maybe we could..."

Young Steve Tanner interrupted with a mocking laugh. "You're all ruint," he said. "Ezra and Einer'll go bust 'fore the year's out. Best thing for y'all is to sell

130

out. Hell, just to be neighborly, I'll give two-hundred apiece to whoever wants out."

Sutherland started to up the bid but Old Steve stared him down.

"I'd sooner sell to a rattlesnake," Peterson growled.

"Likewise," Danner declared.

The other four shifted nervously, then, one-by-one, they took the Tanners' cash and signed sale papers that Young Steve quickly produced.

"Looks like you had this planned ahead," muttered Collins, who was the last seller to sign.

Young Steve just grunted. He stepped out onto the veranda with the documents in hand, just in time to see a big grulla horse disappear northward at a full gallop.

Young Steve stepped back inside, grabbed his father's elbow and hustled the old man away from the waiting buffet table and out the door.

"The boys are working and I just saw Buchanan ride out, headed that-a-way," he told Old Steve as they cinched. As soon as they were out of view of the ranch, they spurred their horses and thundered north.

* * * * * * * *

Blaine had put most of twenty miles behind him when he saw a crew pushing a dozen cow-calf pairs through a clearing—good Hereford cows with cross-bred calves, by the look of them. He raised his hand in greeting, but the moment the drovers saw him, they clawed for their six-guns and threw lead in his direction.

At the touch of Buck's knee, Steel pivoted back to the scant cover offered by a grove of junipers. Blaine dismounted, pulled his rifle from the boot, signaled Steel to lie down behind a hummock, and worked his way through the copse until he found a log that provided fair cover and a view of the clearing.

The cattle wore Danner's brand and were exactly as Sutherland had described them, but Danner most certainly would not have a crew driving them away from his place at this time of year. Nor would an honest crew react to a passerby as these drovers had.

Blaine counted five horses, but the rustlers had scattered to hide in the rocks and brush across the way.

Five to one. Even Cohl had needed a hand with such odds—though the gunman never admitted it. Cohl could not be expected to return the favor, Blaine thought. Despite the badge the man wore, he had shown no interest in apprehending rustlers—not in the past and certainly not now.

The closest help would be from the T-Bar, a few miles northeast, but Old Steve and Young Steve had both been at the range association meeting at the Lazy S. As far as Blaine knew, they still were.

This was not his business and he really needed to put more distance between himself and the bounty hunter, Blaine told himself, but he could not bring himself to turn a blind eye to cattle thieves. He hunkered down, studied the rustlers' horses, and grew hopeful. Not a single one packed a rifle scabbard.

Time dragged by. A rustler crawled from behind a clump of sagebrush and peered over the horses' backs toward the trail where Blaine had been. The other owlhoots joined the first, apparently conferring about the horseman who had crashed their party.

"You still there?" one rustler shouted in the direction of the trail.

Blaine laughed silently. By using their horses to shield themselves from anyone on the trail, the men were exposing themselves to him.

"Whoever yuh are," another rustler hollered, "show yerself 'fore we come huntin' yuh."

Blaine sighted his rifle carefully and removed the rowel from the spur of a rustler who was standing sideways to him. "Holy shit!" the owner of the spur howled.

"Hoist your hands or I will start picking lint out of your belly buttons," Blaine called.

When no one did, he fired again, restoring the spurs to a matched—albeit useless—pair. The wearer yelped and raised his hands above his head.

"Rest of you do the same," Blaine ordered. The other four complied almost too readily. Relieved, Blaine stepped over the log and strolled forward, shifting the rifle to his left hand and drawing his Colt.

As Blaine emerged from the brush, he passed a large cottonwood. Standing on the opposite side of the tree was a man who now aimed a cocked revolver at Blaine's back.

In the same instant that Blaine sensed the danger, an unseen .45 barked and the ambusher folded, his gun firing harmlessly into the earth as he fell. The men in the clearing dove for cover and opened up with their six-guns as Blaine leapt back into the brush and vaulted the log.

From near where the would-be ambusher's body lay, a hard voice spoke: "Tanner. This is Cohl. I just killed your boy. Buck is sidin' me. Step out and tell your men to surrender. Or join Steve Junior."

"Stevie?" Old Steve's voice quavered down the clearing. "That true? Are you dead, Stevie?"

"It's true, old man," one of the rustlers called out, "We seen him get shot—he's just layin' there. What do you want us to do?"

"Do? Do?" Old Steve wailed, "I want you to go to Hell. I want every damn one a you to go to Hell." He fired five wild shots at his own men, grazing one horse. "Dammit to Hell!" His anguished cry was followed by a final gunshot.

"Blast," Cohl swore, "Fine'ly hit somethin' and it was hisself."

Raising his voice to the men across the clearing, Cohl called, "Your bosses are both dead. If you don't want to join them, step out and drop your guns."

They did. "We was just takin' orders," one man whined.

"You'll come out better if you take mine," Cohl commanded, gun still aimed. "Load the Tanners' bodies on their horses. As soon as Danner collects his stock, we'll head for Elko, get you gents afore a judge so you can spill the whole truth about this blasted set-up."

Relieved to learn Cohl was interested in arresting rustlers, after all, Blaine whistled up his horse. He hoped to be gone before the man noticed, but the lawman's Schofield was instantly aimed at Steel.

"Can't you read, Blaine?" Cohl growled. "I told you to sit tight."

"I-I was just going to round up the stock," Blaine stammered.

"No need," Cohl said, glancing at the cows that had settled into grazing. From his breast-pocket, he pulled two small black cigars, as he had after the shootout at Peterson's the previous fall. He put one between his lips and offered the other to Blaine.

"No thanks," Blaine declined, "Those are too bitter for me."

"They ain't for enjoyin'," Cohl gritted, as he lit up. "Well, you might's well get these rannies trussed up— hands tied in front ready to lash 'em to their saddle horns—clean out their pockets while you're at it."

Danner, Collins and Peterson rode up before Cohl finished his cigar.

"Yuh shore called that one, Cohl," Ezra cackled, "Looks like it come out fine, even though Buck took off 'fore we could invite 'im to the party—can't say I'm sorry to see them coyotes face down over their saddles."

Cohl shook his head regretfully. "I'd've much rather had them upright afore a judge. Mrs. Danner okay?"

"Safe and happy with Mrs. Collins," Einer grinned. "I took her and the baby there on my way down to the Lazy S."

"Good move," Cohl nodded. "Ezra, I reckon Danner and Collins can get these cow critters back home on their own. I need you to see to Mrs. Tanner."

"Thought you was gonna do that," Peterson said.

"I was," Cohl agreed, "but me and—uh, Buck and I got somethin' real important we gotta get to and we still have to deliver these snakes to the sheriff.

"Mrs. Tanner'll count it as good news," he assured Peterson. "Get her and those girls safely down to the Buffalo Head. Mrs. Evans is expectin' them and we don't want to leave them at the T-Bar where more sidewinders'll likely crawl in. I'll have Granger send someone down to handle that."

CHAPTER 2

All the way to Wells, Blaine listened in amazement as Cohl pried from his prisoners a stream of information about the Tanners' long-running campaign to control Ruby Valley. Nothing the outlaws said seemed to surprise the lawman, in fact, Cohl knew each time one of them tried to whitewash some detail, and he sternly corrected them.

Blaine was appalled to learn that Young Steve had taken Nancy Sutherland by force years before, to get a claim on the Lazy S. Although her father forced her into what had been a horrific marriage, Nancy—who was an only child—had preserved Lawrence's life by convincing her husband that she had older brothers back in Texas with large families, who stood to inherit if her father died. In more recent years, Young Steve had murdered his neighbor, James Evans, making the former buffalo soldier's death appear accidental, and had killed Evans' oldest son, Jimmy, when Jimmy caught Tanner altering brands on Buffalo Head stock.

* * * * * * * *

As they approached the depot in Wells, a train was starting to grind forward. "Hold up," Cohl shouted, as he raced Red up to the engine.

Blaine and the captives all laughed at the absurdity of someone expecting to halt a train once it started pulling out of a station, but the engineer instantly shut it down. Steam whooshed out around the wheels and the whistle emitted a long blast. Red was the only horse that did not go to pitching wildly. Buck easily stayed atop Steel, but the rustlers would have all hit the ground had their hands not been lashed to their saddle horns.

Railroad stockmen quickly loaded Steel and Red in a boxcar, along with the five live captives, while Cohl gave the stationmaster orders for handling the Tanners'

136

bodies and the seven T-Bar horses, plus a couple messages he wanted sent out by telegraph wire.

All the way to Elko, Cohl kept busy writing down the prisoners' confessions, detailing their crimes and those of their dead bosses.

Sheriff Granger met them at the station and escorted the group directly to the courthouse where the judge and prosecutor were waiting.

Cohl quickly laid out the case and recommended that the judge sign the T-Bar over to Mrs. Evans and Mrs. Tanner, equally, the two women having been friends before Tanner stole Nancy.

"Mrs. Evans is raisin' her youngsters right," Cohl told the judge. "Her son never stole anything. He just had the bad fortune to catch the Tanners in the act. Mrs. Tanner was a victim of this business and I expect she'll need all the help Mrs. Evans can give her to straighten out those two girls she's left with."

"I appreciate your advice on that, Mr. Cohl," the judge nodded. "But first we have a trial to get through. The defense will likely raise some questions."

"They won't. The defendants are pleadin' guilty and will answer all questions honestly"—Cohl shot a hard look at the five men—"'cause I won't take it kindly if I have to come back to correct them."

"You're leaving before the trial?" The judge looked incredulous.

"Mr. Box and I have pressing business in Idaho," Cohl said.

Blaine was dumbstruck at Cohl's use of his correct family name, but he followed the lawman's lead, tipping his hat to the judge and heading for the railroad's livery yard. At the rail station, Cohl paused just long enough to send another telegram before they reclaimed Steel and Red.

As soon as they were on the road north, Cohl demanded, "With Gideon Box for a father, how'd you come to rate a dead-or-alive dodger?"

137

"How could you know who my father was?" Blaine puzzled.

"It sure ain't your looks," Cohl snapped. "You don't look nothin' like him—don't look or act near your age, neither. And you're a liar like he never was. If I was half the field man he was, I woulda had you that first night, but I got hung up on you callin' me 'Ice' and then you took to workin' agin me most every step of the way. I didn't get past that till you as much as said Blaine's your first name—that fit with something Mrs. Evans had said and then Mrs. Tanner confirmed it—said you'd stopped by the T-Bar."

"Actually," Blaine corrected, "my full name is Gideon Blaine Box, but I have always gone by Blaine— at least until Jadene tagged me with Buck. I take after my mother's side of the family for looks. Jady is the only one who looks like the Captain—except for the color of her eyes."

"Her eyes aren't blue?" Cohl responded.

"Brown," Blaine replied. "So you knew the Captain?"

"Only by reputation—and that's considerable," Cohl said. "Boss don't tell me everything, so I missed him when he came to visit. Seein' as how that dodger you're runnin' from's got your name wrong—why'd you make up an alias, Mr. Box?"

"Mister? My friends call me Buck."

"I don't generally have friends," Cohl growled.

"You have one now, Ice," Blaine laughed.

Cohl's eyes narrowed. "Quit callin' me that, Box."

"Cohl, then," Blaine said contritely. "And I owe you an apology. When I reached the Lazy S last fall, Lawrence Sutherland told me you were a bounty hunter, and a crooked one at that. He said one of Tanner's hands knew you and he said his son-in-law really blew up when he learned the sheriff sent the likes of Ice Cohl."

"Which hand?" Cohl demanded.

"He didn't say, but we were both convinced—
that's why Sutherland gave an alias when he
introduced me—he was trying to protect me," Blaine
said. "Now that I know the Tanners were rustlers—well,
I apologize for believing their slander."

"Sutherland's a fool," Cohl growled. "Took
Tanner's word over his own girl. Wrote the boss for help
but wouldn't set down and talk when I showed up. Day
later, you blow in fakin' a Texas drawl, lyin' about your
name, callin' me 'Ice' an' gettin' in my way every time I
put somethin' together—you got no idea how much the
boss an' me'd been lookin' forward to gettin' Young
Steve afore a federal judge."

"But rustling is not a federal crime," Blaine
puzzled.

"Nope," Cohl agreed, "but Young Steve'd been
around—was in on an Army payroll heist way back,
escaped from the federal pen at Leavenworth—no
surprise he had a rider who knew me as 'Ice,' that bein'
a moniker hung on me by—well, let's just say they ain't
friends. Blast—I shoulda braced you right off as to how
you come up with that—whole case shoulda taken
less'n a month—coulda moved on to the Gimlet deal—
cleaned it up an' spent the winter watchin' out for Miss
Jade—now we gotta ride hard to get to Boise City in
time to see her graduate."

"Actually," Blaine admitted, "you scared me so
bad, I lied about that. The Academy's graduation
ceremonies are always held on the last Friday in May."

"Near three weeks ago!" Cohl cried. "Whaddaya
mean, I scared you? You think a dirty bounty hunter'd
bother with a two-bill dodger he'd have to haul clean up
north to collect?"

"Actually, I was certain he would not," Blaine
confessed. "I feared you were hunting Jadene."

"'Cause she's the Bobby at the bottom of the
dodger and worth fifty bucks up to Gimlet?" Cohl
challenged.

"Not for that," Blaine sighed. "Jady is convinced our father's murder was something other than a cattle rustling gone bad. There have been some incidents that suggest she may be right and that whoever was behind the Captain's murder is determined to stop her from raising questions."

Cohl's face went grey. "She's in danger and you run out on her and I'm not there," he breathed. "You know where Miss Jade is right now?"

"I expect she is waiting for me at south horse camp on our ranch up in the Owyhees," Blaine said.

"I know where the Box Ranch is," Cohl said. "The boss showed me on a map. We gotta collect Miss Box from the Box and get on down to see the boss."

"What interest would Sheriff Granger have in this?" Blaine wondered.

Cohl gave a contemptuous snort. "I don't take orders from the likes of Newsome Granger!"

"But you wear an Elko County badge," Blaine said.

"Wore," Cohl corrected. "Checkin' in with the local law is standard professional courtesy—'less he's crooked. Granger ain't real sharp, but he's straight. Like you said, rustlin's not a federal crime so I pinned on a local badge—just for a time."

"You're a U.S. Marshal?" Blaine questioned.

"Huh? No!" Cohl shook his head. "You still ain't put it together? Why'd you lie when I asked straight out if you realized who I am, when you don't?"

"I thought I was answering honestly," Blaine said. "I was certain I was talking to a bounty hunting killer who was after my baby sister—now I know better, but—"

"But you still ain't put it together," Cohl said with great frustration, "Not even after I wrote it out for you! Buck, how many folks you know spell their name C-O-H-L?"

140

"Actually," Blaine said, "until your note, I had never seen that spelling—I know some immigrants from Germany who spell it K-O-H-L, but I presumed yours was the usual C-O-L-E."

"But the boss wrote you folks about me," Cohl argued. "Cap'n Box wrote sayin' you were all lookin' forward to havin' us visit—then we didn't hear nothing from him for a long spell. When Sutherland wrote an' asked for help, he said, 'in mem'ry of our late mutual friend, Gideon Box.' Not the sorta case I usually handle, and it kinda smelled like a trap, but the boss told me to mosey over and see what I could learn about his passin'. Figgered if Sutherland was on the square, I could clear up his range problem along the way, only he flat refused to talk to me—never even let me give him my letter of introduction."

"My Lord!" Blaine gasped. "Are you Jonathan Ethridge's ward?"

"I kinda outgrew the ward business," Cohl said.

"Hold on, now," Blaine said, "I was not privy to everything Mr. Ethridge wrote, but I do recall that his ward is from Texas—now, my Texas drawl may be forced, but you scarcely have one at all."

"Spent less'n two years there afore the boss got me out," Cohl shrugged. "You really don't know nothing—don't know anything about me, do you?"

Blaine thought a minute. "Ethridge calls you I.C.?"

"I mostly go just by Cohl, but, yeah, the boss calls me by my initials now and again," he nodded.

"You do field work for him," Blaine remembered.

"Try to," Cohl agreed, turning the lapel of his vest so Blaine could see the badge pinned to the lining.

"Special Agent United States Department of Justice," Blaine read. "I was not aware there was such a thing."

"Mr. Ethridge swore me in—lifetime appointment," Cohl said with pride. "He's the lead

141

federal prosecutor west of the Continental Divide—you oughta know that."

"I am aware of that," Blaine said, "I was away at college when Ethridge came west to California, but the Captain mentioned it when I came home for the summer. He said Ethridge had taken on a ward he called 'I.C.' We had some fun guessing what those initials might stand for—I suggested 'Ichabod Crane,' after the Headless Horseman of Sleepy Hollow."

"I'm no more likely to answer to Ichabod than to what Mamma wrote down when I was born." Cohl gave his head a shake and added, "I surely wish you'd answered to what your folks wrote down—if you'd said the name 'Box' even one time last fall—"

"You were not exactly forthcoming yourself," Blaine countered. "If you had corrected the misperception that you were Granger's man or had mentioned Mr. Ethridge, I most certainly would have immediately introduced myself."

"I ain't *supposed* to be forthcoming," Cohl emphasized. "Blast—reckon Gideon Box would've seen it right off—the boss always says I'm a sorry excuse for a field man, compared to him."

"A sorry excuse?" Blaine choked. "That is not the impression the Captain got from Mr. Ethridge's letters, and certainly not what I have observed, but believe me, I know how it is to be measured by the standard set by Gideon Box. Early on, I decided to concentrate on the few things where I could outshine him."

"Which are?" Cohl demanded.

"Riding broncs, showing off with a Colt, and telling tales," Blaine confessed.

Cohl responded with an eye-crinkling half-grin.

Blaine had a sudden sick feeling. He couldn't imagine the Captain doing anything dishonorable, but if there had been a woman—maybe before Pa married Ruth, or after Ruth died and before Pa met Faye—well— maybe the woman died giving birth and Pa gave the baby to Ethridge to raise.

142

The more he thought on it, the more Blaine felt that he just might be riding alongside his half-brother. A son of Gideon Box might look like Cohl looked, if his mother were Indian or Mexican, Blaine thought.

"Now, Buck," Cohl said, "you've stalled long enough, get on with givin' me a full report—everything you know about Gideon Box's murder, the Gimlet deal, and on along to your runnin' off to Sutherland's, leavin' little Miss Jade to fend for herself."

"Her name is Jadene—Jady for short." Blaine corrected "No one calls her Jade."

"I do," Cohl said.

* * * * * * * *

A steep, narrow, rocky passage made talk difficult. When the trail widened so they could again ride side by side, Cohl heard Blaine softly singing, "*Fear not, I am with thee, O be not dismayed...*"[18]

"Trail ain't all that bad," he allowed.

"It is not the trail that concerns me," Blaine confessed. "I have been remembering the last time I kept Jady waiting for me this long."

"That was when?" Cohl asked.

"Four years ago, come September," Blaine replied. "I had gone to Oregon to see a college friend. We corralled some mustangs at Steen's Mountain and then I—well, I had promised to be home by Jady's birthday, but I got sidetracked. It was nearly three weeks later when I rode into Silver City—a friend flagged me down, walked me over to the undertaker's and told me what had happened to the Captain."

"Details," Cohl demanded. "I take it he'd been gunned down?"

"Yes," Blaine replied, "but I never got to see the Captain's body. Mother Faye had him taken to Boise City and buried before Jady and I got there."

"Then why the undertaker's?" Cohl asked.

---

[18] *How Firm a Foundation*, verse 2, quoting Isaiah 41:10

143

Buck reluctantly recounted the story, telling how Jadene had stumbled upon their father's killers, killed the first man in self-defense and wounded the other two to hold them for the law.

"Good girl!" Cohl approved.

"The thing is," Blaine continued, "all three of them were dead when the deputy got there. I looked the bodies over. In addition to the shots Jady admits she fired, they each had two slugs in the back and one in the head—all fired from behind, same as they had done to the Captain. Jady swears she did not do that, but there was no one else around."

"How'd the sheriff handle that?" Cohl queried.

"He insisted on paying off on the two she insists she left alive," Blaine replied. "They were all known men, but the one was fresh out of prison so there were no current rewards on him. Then Sheriff Haney went over to the saloon and started running off at the mouth. I walked in and heard him calling Jadene a back-shooting, bounty-hunting bitch."

"And you didn't drop him!" Cohl sounded incredulous.

Blaine shook his head.

"If she was mine—" The gunman left the words dangling.

"There are other ways," Blaine allowed. "Sheriff like that is not a real lawman—gets his size from strutting around with a badge, belly hanging over his belt, acting important. The next November, Haney lost that badge."

"Didn't know you was—uh, you were political," Cohl said.

Blaine shrugged. "The Captain was serving in the Territorial Legislature."

"You put in a better man?"

"One with less belly and more spine," Blaine drawled, "Campaigned promisin' he would lead a posse when needed and wouldn't leave his work to be done by

144

little girls. So far, I reckon Leinert's kept that promise. An' he don't see no resemblance 'tween me an' no dodger," he added, with a grim grin.

Cohl responded with one of his eye-crinkling half-grins. "Doesn't," he said. "You ought to set a good example, being educated and all, help me put words together by the rules like—well, like someone used to do who you kinda remind me of, just a bit."

"You remind me a bit of someone, too," Blaine ventured. "Drake—you've heard me call him Jerry—he's my cousin actually—and my brother-in-law. Anyway, he's half Bannock. I was just wondering—no offense— might your mother have been Indian, or maybe Mexican?"

Cohl replied with a negative shake of his head. "That C-O-H-L spellin's French. Mama's father answered to 'Frenchy Cohl,' or so she told me—he was nine months dead afore I came along. Mama had skin like cream, chestnut hair—all I got from her's the gray eyes and hair that won't lay flat. The man was half Kiowa, I reckon."

Before Blaine could figure out if he felt relieved or disappointed, Cohl asked, "Is not knowin' who finished off Cap'n Box's killers what makes Miss Jade think they were something other than cattle rustlers?"

"It goes deeper than that," Blaine admitted. "The man Jady killed—the one fresh out of prison—turned out to be the same man who had had some torn-in-half bank notes in his pocket when sent to prison. When the Captain had learned of that, it had piqued his curiosity."

"Piques mine, too," Cohl allowed.

"Well, you may get Jady to tell you more about bank notes," Blaine hedged. "There are things I don't really know—I was not always there."

"Seems you make a habit of that, Buck—a bad habit," Cohl growled. "Still, you must know some of it."

145

CHAPTER 3

Twilight was fading and Blaine was hoarse from answering Cohl's questions. He whoaed Steel at a good campsite he knew, where a small corral straddled a seasonal stream in the headwaters of the Little Owyhee River, and watered himself even before unsaddling and watering his horse.

Cohl directed him right back to the story of Uncle Elijah's death and his own narrow escape from a hangman's noose, as they set up camp and prepared supper.

"How's Gimlet connected to Cap'n Box's murder?" he asked.

"It isn't," Blaine said.

"How can you be so certain?" Cohl challenged."

"No one could have planned it out," Blaine said. "A lawman friend of ours did some checking and learned that Uncle Lije had not planned to stop in Gimlet—he was just passing nearby when one of his team threw a shoe. Since he had to stay over to get it replaced, he started to set up to do a camp meeting—that was like him, he never passed up an opportunity to share the gospel—and no one could have known Jady and I were headed for Gimlet, much less when we would roll in. The buyer expected our foreman to deliver those steers, but I took his place at the last minute because he was laid up. As I told you, Jady chanced upon us along the way."

"Chance," Cohl murmured. "Those torn-in-half bank notes don't turn up by chance—they're promises of payment, most often for a killing. They're used by a loose network we call the cabal—they'd pay up on a pile of them if you were to drop a fella they call 'Ice.' Ethridge's files on those notes take up a whole cabinet. Don't know how Cap'n Box's letter got past me, but it likely landed there. Just when'd he write?"

"March of 1883," Blaine recalled. "In August, or maybe September, Mother Faye mailed a notice of the Captain's death. We never received a reply from Mr. Ethridge to either letter."

Cohl's jaw clamped and a frosty look came to his eyes. After a long silence he said, "We were—otherwise occupied about then." After a longer silence, he added, "Last two-three years, Ethridge has sent a raft of letters to the Box Ranch."

"None reached me," Blaine said, "but we have had so much mail go missing, we quit writing."

"Miss Jade wrote to you at Sutherland's," Cohl corrected.

"Yes, each envelope was written by the mother of a friend of hers and addressed to Mrs. Sutherland," Blaine explained. "I wrote back the same way."

"Clever. Her idea?" Cohl asked. Blaine answered with a nod. "Let me see what she wrote."

Blaine thought a minute, then retrieved the thin packet from his saddlebags.

Cohl spent so long hunched close to the fire studying the illustrated pages that Blaine offered to read them aloud. Ethridge's agent shook his head negatively. "I read fine, Buck," he said softly. "It's all that's b'tween the lines that takes time to sort out."

"Jady is quite the doodler," Blaine chuckled.

When the firelight failed, Cohl started to slip the packet into his own inner pocket.

"Those are a loan, not a gift, I.C.," Blaine chided.

Cohl reluctantly handed them over.

"I was really countin' on gettin' to see Miss Jade graduate," he said.

"Sorry, I.C.," Blaine sighed, "I was counting on it, too, but, as you saw, she uninvited me most emphatically. I wrote back and told her to give no further thought to visiting Ruby Valley—there was this crazy bounty hunter hanging around." That remark did not produce the grin Blaine expected.

Cohl stared out into the blackness of the night. "What I see," he muttered, "is a grown man so worried about his own skin, he run out on his kid sister—left her alone with cabal killers likely on her tail."

"Jady told me to go," Blaine said lamely.

"She gives you orders?" Cohl countered. "What is she, ten-twelve years younger'n you?"

"Fourteen," Blaine replied. "And I would not say she orders me around, but I must admit, I am inclined to go along with whatever she wants. When she was born, I already had two sisters and was praying hard for a brother, but God knows, my disappointment was short lived. I swear, I.C., I would not trade that baby girl for a dozen brothers."

"You hit the jackpot when you were fourteen," Cohl observed. "Can't say the same for Miss Jade."

"No, not for Jadene," Blaine nodded sadly. "She found Pa, shot dead, just a few weeks after her fourteenth birthday."

"Few weeks after my fourteenth," Cohl started, then went silent for a long minute, before very quietly adding, "Mama was fourteen when she had me—I was fourteen when she died."

He dug one of those bitter black cheroots out of his vest pocket.

"Man who killed her had some of these in his pocket, so I took them," he said. "First night on the run, I smoked one. Bitter as hell, but I smoked it down to the end. Whenever it comes to killin'—I smoke another one, to keep the killin' from bein' a sweet taste in my mouth. Be careful of that, Buck, don't let yourself get to where you like the taste of killin'."

"I thought that a man in your business *had* to like it," Blaine responded.

148

"Just what business do you think I'm in?" Cohl said defensively. "I told you, I work for Ethridge. I investigate things. I solve puzzles."

"Well," Blaine said, "You are very good at it. That business with the Tanners—I never would have guessed."

"Takes more than a guess to win in court." Cohl aimed a long finger at Blaine. "I would've wrapped up the Tanner case at Peterson's last fall if you hadn't come bumblin' in."

"Bumbling?" Blaine countered, "You would likely be six feet under if Lonnie and I hadn't saved your bacon!"

"Like hell," Cohl growled. "If you and Latham hadn't crashed in without so much as a by-your-leave, I would've had three of them alive and talkin'. Why d'you think I dropped their horses instead of them?"

Blaine's jaw sagged. "But," he managed weakly, "that bunch wasn't in on the Tanner operation."

"Like hell!" Cohl repeated. "Once I got Gwinn alone, he laid it all out—it was prit'near what Peterson suspected—but thanks to you, I had only one witness, and a dirty witness at that. The Tanners would've walked if I'd taken them to court. Best I could do was ship Gwinn over to the boss. Ethridge has been putting the prison break case together for trial ever since. Then you bumbled in again and fixed it so I had to drop Tanner, too, so now there's no one left for the boss to bring up on charges. He likely ain't much amused."

* * * * * * * *

As they tacked up at first light, Blaine again attempted to apologize for his "bumbling" at Ruby Valley.

"Bad habit you got into," Cohl nodded. "What's done's done—just don't get in my way ever again." He swung into his saddle and looked down at his much taller companion. "When you said you didn't want me anywhere near your sister on account of what I am, I thought you meant what Latham called me that time he

149

got mad at me for doing what he should've done—if your cousin's a breed that part don't—uh, that part doesn't track—so what is it? You hung up on my being a bastard?"

"Heavens, no!" Blaine cried. "I meant what I believed you to be at that time—a murderous bounty hunter. The Captain would have tanned my hide if I ever held a man's circumstances of birth against him. You did not choose your parents any more than I chose mine. My Uncle Stephan was as fine a man as ever lived and I'm crazy about my nephews, Lincoln and Grant. As the Captain always said, regardless of breeding, we are all equal in God's sight."

The sun peeked over the eastern ridge as Blaine mounted Steel. "Now suppose you explain to me, I.C.," he said, "what you meant about Lonnie having been mad at you for doing what he should have—he was upset because it looked as if you had stolen a haunch of venison and his rifle."

"Stolen?" Cohl echoed. "James Evans counted Latham a close friend—Evans gets killed and Latham never so much as looks in on his widow until he brings her oldest son's body to her—without his gun, I might add—and he never once comes back after that until he stops by to invite them to the get-together at Sutherland's. Even then, he just talks to Joey out by the barn and ogles Lark—never even asks how their mama's getting along."

"You shouldn't be so hard on Lonnie," Blaine interrupted. "He told me Mrs. Evans wasn't welcoming of visitors—she would scream like a mad woman and whip out a tomahawk and threaten anyone who stopped by."

"Only screaming and threatening Dove Evans ever did," Cohl corrected, "was when Old Steve showed up, not long after his boy killed her man. He went weaseling around while Jimmy and Joey were away from the house—said a fine looking lady like her shouldn't be sleeping alone. Dove picked up her kindling hatchet and told him to get gone or she'd geld

150

him. Latham never come by and never sent anyone to check on how things were over to the Buffalo Head. Tanner was running off every calf soon as it was weaned, just cleaning them out.

"Last winter they were near starving," Cohl continued. "There's Joey left with nothing but his pa's rifle, and it's all busted up from going over the cliff when Tanner shot his horse out from under him, and there's Latham with a real fine Winchester he can't hit the side of a hill with. I give—gave Latham credit for sending over the venison and the rifle, even though he kept mouthing off about me not being good enough for his crew. I never worked cattle afore, Buck, but Joey was grateful when I lent a hand—once Red got over being scared of cows, we got to be sorta useful."

"So that's where you were—" Blaine started.

"Some," Cohl nodded. "You might recall, I had some range investigating to do, now and again."

"So you did," Blaine laughed. "And now I am wondering—is it possible that you played Cupid for Lark Evans and Dermit?"

"Dermit likes tall gals and Lark's a reg'lar beanpole," Cohl shrugged. "I was about to pull out and Joey'll need a hand, now and again."

* * * * * * * *

Mid-afternoon, Blaine remarked that they were leaving Nevada. At dusk, he pointed down a side valley. "South horse camp," he announced. "Jady left her pet buckskin running free hereabouts. I expect Dustdevil is keeping her well entertained. We'll likely find her at the cabin, unless she finds us before we get there."

Cohl's face relaxed into more than a half-grin and he eagerly scanned the range.

Buck laughed. "You two are going to hit it off real well, my friend," he predicted.

Cohl shook his head wonderingly. "I never afore in my life had someone try to fix me up with a gal," he said, "much less with his little sister."

151

Blaine's face hardened. "Whoa, there," he warned. "I just meant you will be friends. Jady's still a little kid."

"I was just joking," Cohl lied to cover his embarrassment. "But she must be eighteen now."

"Not until the middle of August," Blaine corrected. "Regardless of age, messing with Jady is a good way for a man to get himself killed."

Cohl gave him a long look. "You're not up to that job, Buck—but I promise you, I will not be 'messing with' Miss Jade."

* * * * * * *

A band of horses was drinking from the tank when they rode into south horse camp. "Better than your average covey of broomtails," Cohl complimented.

"The Captain salted the range with some good studs twenty-some years ago," Blaine explained. "We still sell a fair number of remounts to the army."

There was no sign that Jadene had spent time at the cabin, nor did she ride in that evening.

"I wrote telling her to stay here—that I had been delayed," Blaine said.

"On account of that crazy bounty hunter," Cohl drawled.

"Most dangerous man I ever met," Blaine agreed, flashing a grin. "Perhaps she has been here but took pains to hide her tracks. I don't know, I.C.—she asked for a map to Ruby Valley so we wouldn't miss each other on the trail—you don't suppose—"

The look on Cohl's face indicated he was not supposing anything good.

"I suppose she could be at the Bar None," Blaine hoped. "We were going to meet there the day after she graduated—then I wrote and told her I would be a couple weeks late—if she got tired of waiting there, she was to come here."

"How far?" Cohl asked, reaching for his saddle.

152

"A ways north of the Snake," Blaine said. "I'll bet she came and collected Dustdevil and went back up. We'll get an early start."

They were up and moving at the first hint of dawn. Given his head, Steel set a faster pace, as if eager to reach his home barn.

Topping a rise, they encountered a herd of free-roaming horses. A compact buckskin stallion reared and pawed the air, trumpeting a warning.

"The Devil!" Blaine cried.

Cohl saw nothing amiss and said so.

"That's Dustdevil," Blaine yelled. "Something's wrong—Jady hasn't gotten this far."

He kicked Steel so sharply that the big grulla bucked and then leapt into a hard gallop.

Cohl held his sorrel back, letting the grulla pick the trail. Both horses were fully lathered when they slid to a stop in front of the main house shortly after noon.

"Wondered if you were going to run them to death," Cohl muttered.

But Blaine's attention was on Serena who came rushing out the door, drying her hands on her apron. "Oh, Buck, thank God you've come," she cried. "We've lost Jadene!"

CHAPTER 4

"Lost her?" Blaine leapt from the saddle, "What do you mean you lost her?"

"Two days after graduation SoBig came in with an empty saddle," Serena explained as they sank down on the porch step, "Drake and Mal back-tracked him to the river. Mother forwarded your letter down along with a note that said Jadene had left Boise City headed this way, leading a young pack mule. They found it washed up on an island downstream. They haven't found Jady—yet—you know how the Snake is—sometimes they never find them."

Blaine held his sister as she sobbed. "I should have ordered her to travel back with you," he said.

"Travel with me? Why, I didn't go in for graduation, Buck," she said, "can't you see that I'm in no condition to be traveling?"

He hadn't noticed, but it was obvious. "Got number three in the oven, have you?" he teased gently.

"Yes," she sniffed, "I was so eager for Jadene to get here. She's—she was—so good with the boys. You remember how, for all her tomboy ways, she always mothered the calves and the foals and puppies and kittens—she's like that with the boys, too. She was—oh, Buck."

Listening intently, Cohl gave no outward sign of how the news affected him. He loosened the cinches and allowed the horses just two swallows each from the trough. They wanted a long drink, but he walked them first until they were cooled out enough that the cold water wouldn't cause them to colic.

154

After Blaine and Serena went into the house, Cohl led the horses to the barn, unsaddled, and was rubbing Red down when a crusty old man gimped in.

"Who in blue blazes are you?" the oldster demanded.

"Friend of Buck's. Name's Cohl, I.C. Cohl. And I'll wager you're Sarge—Sarge Hankins, isn't it? Buck's talked about you some."

"You got me there," Sarge confessed. "Just don't go believin' ever'thing Buck told you. That boy gets to spinnin' tales, next thing you know, he's embroiderin' a bit."

"Appreciate your sayin' that," Cohl nodded, "I was havin' trouble buyin' anyone bein' quite as good a man as he said you were."

The old soldier stood a little straighter. "That right? The boy were braggin' on me? Well—"

"What I need to know now," Cohl interrupted, "is everything you can tell me about the disappearance of Miss Jadene Box."

"Yes, sir," Hankins said. "It was me as found ol' SoBig that evening. Poor feller were just standin' right there," he said, pointing. "I pulled the saddle off and hung it right where you see it now and started yellin' at Miss Jady for abusin' him, but she weren't here..." he repeated what Cohl had already learned from Serena, then added, "It was an evil day. They say bad happens in sets of three and that was surely the day for it."

"What else happened that day?" Cohl demanded.

"Well, we didn't hear until later, but early that mornin' the boy what was runnin' Mundy's Ferry up and killed poor Elias Bruning, cut the ferry loose and taken off on Elias's horse. Then in the afternoon, two hardcases held up the stage, didn't get nothin', but did get clean away. That evenin', SoBig showed up without Miss Jady—it was an evil day," Hankins ended.

"How long does it take to ride from here to where her horse came out of the river?" Cohl asked.

155

"Hardly no time a-tall," Hankins shrugged.

Glancing at the sun, Cohl said, "There's time for us to have a look yet today. I'll get Buck. You have fresh horses waiting for us—and a guide who knows where the track led and where the mule is, if you can roust one. Oh, and if her saddle hasn't been gone through, I don't want it touched until we get back."

Sarge Hankins hadn't accepted a direct order from any man since Captain Box died, but he snapped to attention, saluted, gave a sharp, "Yes, Sir," and hobbled off toward the paddocks.

When Cohl knocked on the house door, the bigger boy opened it. "You must be Lincoln," he said, "I'm your uncle's friend." The boy looked at him big-eyed, but stepped aside and let him enter.

Blaine held a letter in his hand. Seeing Cohl, he said, "She never got my message telling her about the delay. Mother Faye sent it on down so Jady would get it here, but—"

"The ferry was out that day," Cohl said.

"What?"

"And there were outlaws about," Cohl added. "Hankins is saddlin' fresh horses. Let's have a look."

* * * * * * * *

"*This* is where SoBig came out?" Blaine asked in disbelief when they reached the river.

"Seemed strange to me, too," replied Hankins, who had saddled a horse for himself, too, and painfully climbed aboard.

"Our usual ford," Blaine explained to Cohl, "is upstream nearly ten miles—a ways east of Biladeau's—the ferry I told her to take is about six miles downstream."

"The ferry was out," Hankins said.

"She wouldn't have known that," Cohl said. "Where's the mule?"

"On a little island 'round the next bend, 'bout a mile down," Hankins said. "Drake and Mal took the

156

skiff out and had a look. Said the river cleaned everything out of the pack. No sign of Miss Jady." Looking upland, he added, "Here comes that damn breed."

Drake was a dark copy of Blaine. Grant clung to his papa's belt loops, legs stretched wide across the rump of a dappled gray that looked to be part Percheron, while Lincoln rode alongside on a whitish pony he had nearly outgrown.

"You should've been here weeks ago," Drake said by way of greeting.

Pointing, he was giving his guess of what had happened when he interrupted himself to say, "Linc, stay back from that river. You want to wind up sturgeon food like your fool aunt?"

But the boy splashed into the shallows, bent down and triumphantly held up a small silver gun.

Blaine hugged him, "Good find," he said, taking the piece. "That's the derringer I gave Jadene. It would have been in her jacket pocket."

"So," said Cohl, "she made it almost to shore on this side." He tossed a stick into the river and watched its course. "So why didn't the mule?"

"Fool girl probably lost the mule midway and swam after it," Drake scowled.

"Jady would never do that," Blaine defended. "She is no fool and I will not have you calling her that again."

"And if I do?" his cousin challenged.

"Where's the skiff?" Cohl cut in. "I want to have a look at that mule."

"Nothing to see and it stinks," Drake growled, but he showed them where the skiff was tied. "I got work to do," he said, hoisting Grant behind himself and riding off, trailed by Lincoln on Soldier.

"Damn breed," Hankins muttered, as he pulled on the oars. Reddening, he glanced at Cohl and said, "No offense, sir."

157

"And none taken," Cohl said. "Myself, I don't know for sure what breed I am, but I do know that breed doesn't tell much about a man."

"Cap tol' me that more'n once," Hankins admitted. He propelled the skiff onto the sandy lip of the island and they fought their way through the willows to the north side where the mule was, indeed, stinking. The stench did not deter Cohl's examination, including cutting the carcass open to check the lungs.

Carrying the tattered pack and the remains of the leadline back to the skiff, Cohl asked, "Sarge, why didn't you tell me there was shooting here that day?"

"Shootin'?" Sarge echoed. "Wal, now you mention it, I did hear mebbe half-a-dozen shots along about mid-afternoon—thought the first couple were acrost the river, then it sounded closer. This drifter—feller worked for us a couple-three days—he said he seen some kids plinkin' at jackrabbits."

"Awful big for a rabbit," Cohl observed. "That mule's got a notch in its ear and got burned by a bullet across its rump. Not what killed it—drowned—prob'ly 'cause it got hung up in that snag—and that's not all that's wrong here. Mule's on the wrong side of the island if it went under close to the south bank. There's two ropes in the mix and they both been cut, not broken—lariat's a good line, but"—he held up the shorter of the two—"even after a couple a weeks in the river, this leadline's got a helluva twist to it. The panniers've been unbuckled but there's still some soggy books and papers and pieces of oilcloth in the bottom of one—nothing else."

"Doesn't add up," Blaine agreed. "Jady was big on wrapping things in oilcloth, and her books and papers always went on top so they would be out of the water if she forded a stream. Why is everything she would have put at the bottom gone, and things she would have put on top are stuck in the bottom?"

"It wasn't the river done that," Cohl nodded. "Let's work upstream along this bank and see what we find."

Above the bend was a sandbar, separated from the north bank by a narrow channel. "Pull up," Cohl ordered. He stepped ashore to retrieve a scrap of cloth that was clinging to a shrub. "Mean anything?" he asked, passing it to Blaine.

"Needlework," Blaine said. "Jady has never been much for fancy stitchery, but it might be something she had from our middle sister. Darlene is quite the hand with needle and thread—she's away at finishing school back east now."

The three men fanned out and scoured the sandbar. Hankins found the remains of a pencil sketch of Dustdevil. Blaine found the other end of the lariat, still dallied around a good-sized willow tree.

Cohl brushed at a slight hump in the sand and unearthed a burnt can. Sifting blackened sand, he came up with an odd piece of wire, crimped and bent back upon itself. "A woman's hairpin?" he mused, finding another and another, until he had nine in all. They still carried the faint odor of burnt hair.

"Jady never uses hairpins," Blaine said "She braids her hair or ties it back."

While they talked, Cohl extracted an envelope from inside his vest, placed the hairpins and the scrap of cloth in it, and penciled some notations on the outside.

Another pass the length of the sandbar turned up nothing more. As they headed back to the skiff, Cohl directed, "Sarge, get a crew out here tomorrow morning with rakes and shovels. I don't think we missed much of anything, but we'd best make double sure he didn't bury something besides his fire."

"He?" Blaine asked. "He who?"

"Don't know that just yet," Cohl said grimly. "But he's tall like you and that cousin of yours."

159

"How can you know that?" Blaine puzzled. "How can you be sure there even was a man here that day?"

"Rope on the tree matches the line hung up in the root wad of that snag—someone saw her in trouble and managed to drop a loop on the snag." Cohl pointed to the belay marks on the Willow. "Man Hankins' or my height would've belayed the rope lower."

"I see, I.C.," Blaine nodded. "He snagged the snag and pulled the mule up on this sandbar, then cut the rope and it drifted down to the landward side of the next island—so where's Jady?"

"Maybe buried here, maybe in the river," Cohl replied. "But maybe not. Could be he's some honest puncher headed elsewhere, just took her along. Likely banged up some—maybe knocked out cold. Could be, soon as she heals up, she'll turn up."

"He might be honest," Blaine observed, "but I doubt that a cowpuncher would cut a good lariat like that and leave it behind."

Cohl nodded thoughtfully, then, looking across to where Lincoln had found the derringer, he wondered aloud, "If she went in here, how'd she get there, in this current?"

Blaine shook his head. "This is not where she went in," he pointed upstream, "A game trail comes down to the water about half-way up the narrows coming through that pinched-in bend. It is a very dangerous stretch of river, but the Captain crossed from there once and came out right about where SoBig did. I was a baby at the time, but he told us all the story and warned against ever trying it."

Cohl wanted to see the game trail, but they were losing the light and Blaine and Sarge both advised it would be full dark before they could reach it, going afoot. It was a hard pull just getting back across to where their horses waited on the south bank.

Arriving back at the ranch at suppertime, Cohl was surprised to find Drake a genial host, gently

160

directing his boys as all three helped Serena ready the table.

"Sure was surly earlier," he remarked, as he and Blaine washed up.

"Drake tends to get owlly when things don't go his way," Blaine shrugged, "Serena makes him leave it at the door."

"It's a bad habit," Cohl said. "He should work on changing."

"It's just the way he is," Blaine shrugged.

"No excuse," Cohl said. "Me, I'm a bastard, but that don't—doesn't mean I have to act like one. Man sees where he can improve himself, he should work on it."

* * * * * * * *

After dinner, they showed the Drakes what they had found. Serena didn't think the scrap of embroidery was anything Darlene had made. Jadene had drawn hundreds of sketches of Dustdevil and could have lost one long before she went into the river. Furthermore, Serena agreed with Blaine that Jady did not use hairpins.

Drake scarcely remembered the drifter who had claimed to see some kids shooting at jackrabbits that day. "Was that the one didn't like diggin' fencepost holes—or the one who couldn't stop sneezin' when we was puttin' up hay?" he puzzled. "They come an' go—most ain't real mem'rable."

Checking SoBig's saddle that evening, they found Jadene's Bible, a small drawing pad and two pencils in the pockets of her yellow slicker, which she had rolled up and tied behind the cantle. Hankins had cleaned her Winchester the first night. He recalled there were three shells in the magazine, where Jady usually loaded six, and one in the chamber, which was rather unusual, but he couldn't say for sure whether it had been fired on that "evil day."

161

"Blaine, it's been nearly three weeks," Serena said gently, "We didn't want to believe it either, but it is time to let go. I had this published in *The Owyhee Avalanche* yesterday." She handed him the obituary page from the Silver City paper. "I expect the *Statesman* in Boise ran about the same today," she added.

The brief piece stated that Miss Jadene Box, daughter of the late Rep. Gideon Box, born August 15, 1869, died of drowning in the Snake River. The mishap occurred in Owyhee County, Idaho Territory, on May 28, 1887. It gave no hint that her body had not yet been recovered.

CHAPTER 5

"Wish I had more information for you," Sheriff Dan Leinert told Blaine and Cohl over beer mugs in the Silver City Saloon the next day. "I was busy with two crimes that day, didn't even get word about Miss Box going missing until Thursday."

"Tell us about the crimes," Cohl said, "in detail."

Noting Leinert's quizzical look, Blaine said, "There could be a connection."

"Not likely," the Owyhee sheriff opined. "I got word shortly after eight that Tuesday that the ferry was out, so I telegraphed over to Jordan Valley to put a hold on the bank shipment, then I rode down to Mundy's," he recalled. "There was a big puddle of blood soaking into the ground at the south landing. I learned later that the raft was bloodied up, too. Mundy pulled it out of the tulles, half-a-mile or so downstream, on the north side, which is why I figure it was over there when the kid cut the line."

"What kid?" Cohl asked.

"Johnny Lauchlin," Leinert replied. "Kid's an orphan—seemed grateful to the Mundys for taking him in, eager worker—then he goes and does a thing like this."

"You're sure it was him?" Cohl asked.

"Looks that-a-way," Leinert shrugged. "Folks at McDowell's Ferry pulled Bruning's body out of the river that afternoon. His throat had been slit with something real sharp. The Lauchlin kid is just starting to shave— has been showing off his new razor and strop. Never can be sure of them real quiet types.

"Bruning was bragging to everyone about winning big at keno, I figure he bragged to the kid and Johnny just up and slit his throat. He bled out a bunch, then the boy got him on the ferry, bloodied it up, dumped him mid-river, went on over, cut the line

163

and took off on Bruning's horse," the lawman speculated.

"Horse hasn't turned up yet," he added, "but it will—loud paint, mutton-withered, spavined—a cripple. No one who knows horses would take it, especially no outlaw who don't want to stand out—another reason I figure it was that boy. I put the word out, reckon we'll hear when the paint turns up."

"You tried tracking the paint?" Cohl asked.

"The Snake's the county line," Leinert said. "Besides, the ferry was out and in short order I had a couple holdup men to track right here in Owyhee County. I talked to Mundy once he got back in business and I sent word to the Ada County sheriff to watch for that kid on the paint, but I doubt he sent anyone down to look for tracks." He drained his beer mug and signaled for a refill.

"What about the stage holdup?" Cohl asked.

"Now that was a whole different matter," the sheriff said. "As I mentioned, there'd been a big bank transfer set to come through, headed for Boise City— put together on the quiet, but I think some shady characters got wind of it because two hardcases threw down on the Jordan Valley stage about two miles west of here. All it was carrying was the mail and Sam Owings, back from Carson City. Owings was sitting up top with Bates who was driving and, Buck, you know neither one of them boys is a pilgrim. Bates looks them owlhoots in the eye and says, 'We didn't bring no cash 'cause the ferry's out.'

"Sam's got a 10-gauge in his hands. He says, 'Better cut yer losses.' They went to cussin' each other out. Bates cracked the whip and kept rollin', went right past the stage station to my office. I had a posse out in less'n an hour, with Bates and Owings along so we wasted no time pickin' up the track. We trailed 'em 'til they crossed into Nevada."

"Any description on the holdup men?" Cohl asked.

"Not much," Leinert said. "Had their dust rags up. The one was pretty good-sized, six feet or more. Owings thought he saw a knife scar 'tween the hat and the mask, oh, and they said he talked like a Canadian. Other man was smaller, a Southerner—"

"S'cuse me, Dan," the barkeep interrupted, "did you say one o' them robbers was a big Canadian with a scar?"

"That mean something to you, Mike?" Leinert asked.

"Sounds like a man was in here the day afore," the barman replied, "matter-of-fact, it was while Elias was buyin' rounds. I felt kinda sorry for him. Never knew a Canadian wasn't a right nice feller, but this one had a knife scar that ran from here to here" —Mike indicated a line from his temple to jaw—"and another crossin' it, from the corner of his mouth to his ear, looked like his cheek had been sewed together. Gave his face a bad look, but he talked friendly. M'gawd—I told him Elias won a real big pot..."

"Easy, Mike," Leinert said, "this wasn't your doin'. Men lookin' to take thousands of dollars off that stage wouldn't bother with a drunk with a couple-three-hundred. And for sure, they wouldn't've cut the ferry line—that just derailed their plan."

"That transfer ever get done?" Cohl asked.

The sheriff eyed him warily before answering. "Week late and twice as big," he replied. "Didn't try to slip it through the second time. Had ten outriders plus three guards on board. They didn't have no trouble a-tall."

* * * * * * * *

Blaine and Cohl rode north to the Snake. Buck fired a couple rounds in the air. After peering through his new telescope and recognizing the blond rider, Mundy brought his repaired raft over, its deck stained with blood far more extensively than Leinert's report had led them to expect.

"Blaine, I have been lifting your family up in prayer ever since I learned of the tragedy that befell your dear sister," Mundy said.

"I appreciate that," Blaine said, "Please keep on praying—it may not be too late."

As he started the raft sliding across the water, Mundy said, "It is never too late for prayer, my boy."

"You been prayin'," Cohl cut in bitterly. "Buck's been prayin'—don't seem like God listens a-tall—He sure as Hell never does what needs doin'—"

"You have a poor understanding of prayer, mister—er?" the ferryman started.

"This is I.C. Cohl, Mr. Mundy," Blaine quickly inserted. "He is Mr. Ethridge's personal agent and my good friend. I.C. is investigating Jady's disappearance and has discovered evidence that suggests she did not die in the river."

"Praise God!" the ferryman cried.

Cohl threw up his hands in frustration. "Praise Him? She's lost and prob'ly hurt and in trouble and we don't know where she is and here you are, yammerin' on when I have questions you should be answerin'!"

"I will help all I can, Mr. Cohl, but Jadene has not visited us since last September," Mundy declared. "The best I can do for her is to continue to pray. As James tells us, the effectual fervent prayer of a righteous man availeth much[19]—and I can assure you, God knows exactly where Jadene Box is—alive here on Earth or alive with Him in Heaven."

"Well, He sure ain't been lookin' out for her," Cohl growled. "Now tell me—where were you the day she disappeared? Same day your ferry got wrecked."

"Mrs. Mundy is much in demand as a midwife," the muscular ferryman replied as he pulled the ferry northward. "I had accompanied her the previous evening when she was called out to deliver a baby. We

---

[19] James 5:16

166

returned home about half-past seven, which should have been well before the first run of the morning—I have livestock to care for and, of course, my highest priority is my prayer and devotion time, so I operate this ferry only between eight in the morning and eight at night, never later and never earlier and never on Sunday, except to bring folks over to worship—everyone around here knows that."

"Leinert talked like it happened earlier," Cohl calculated, "Not long after dawn."

"Quite possibly," Mundy nodded. "Our adopted son begged to be allowed to run the ferry if I was not back by morning. I gave permission, although I did not think he was up to it. Why Johnny made a run so early is beyond me, but when we arrived home, this raft was washed up on the bank about a hundred yards below the landing. It was soaked with blood and Johnny was nowhere to be found."

"This Johnny—Lauchlin is it?" Cohl cut in, "Leinert says he killed a hard-luck prospector and took off on his horse."

"As I told Leinert, that boy would not kill anyone," Mundy countered. "Johnny was a fine Christian lad."

"Then where is he?" Cohl demanded.

"Absent from the body is present with the Lord,"[20] Mundy quoted. "The fact that he was gone from his post causes me to believe that whoever killed Mr. Bruning also killed Johnny. It is a tragic loss, but the greater tragedy is that Mr. Bruning died in his sins."

Cohl gestured dismissively. "It's possible that whoever cut your boat loose might've rode east and ran into Miss Jade—how tall's this Lauchlin kid and how good is he with a lariat?"

"Johnny is no taller than you are, Mr. Cohl," Mundy replied. "And I have no reason to think he knows how to use a lariat at all."

---

[20] II Corinthians 5:8

"Not the man who pulled her out, then," Cohl mused, "but he could be who chased her into the river."

"Certainly not," Mundy declared. "That boy was no threat to Jadene Box—he could not possibly have harmed her."

"Anyone can turn bad," Cohl said cynically.

"We are all sinners, as the Good Book says,"[21] Mundy agreed. "But if you listened carefully, you would have noticed that I said Johnny *would not* have killed anyone, and that he *could not* have harmed Jadene. The fever that took Johnny's family left him weak. If you know anything about Miss Box—"

"Mr. Mundy is right," Blaine cut in. "Johnny Lauchlin would not have stood a chance against Jady. Besides, having lost his own folks, he was a comforting friend to her after the Captain died."

"Likely not the only thing Leinert's figured wrong," Cohl nodded, "Shame he didn't get over to check for tracks, don't suppose anyone else did, either."

"You suppose wrong," Mundy corrected. "As soon as I returned home and saw my wrecked ferry that is exactly what I did—two horses came off the ferry when it reached the north landing that morning. The lead horse was above average in size and weight, possibly part draft horse like that Percheron Mr. Drake rides. The other was a cripple—recently shod but likely spavined. They started north on the stage road, then turned back and went east along the river."

Cohl looked quizzically at Blaine, as the raft slid up to the landing,

Blaine grinned. "Mr. Mundy reads sign as well as he reads the Bible."

"Suppose that means he's good at it," Cohl allowed. "You got anything else to tell me, Mundy? And I don't mean a blasted sermon."

---

[21] Romans 3:23

168

"Well, for one thing," Mundy said, as his passengers led their horses ashore. "Leinert has an inaccurate understanding of the circumstances of my ferry being set adrift. The short line from the ferry to the overhead cable was not cut, as he assumes. Rather, the pulley assembly on the far side was broken so that the cable dropped in the river. When the line went slack, the current worked against it and swung it over along this bank and began working the raft downstream. If I had not returned before it reached the end of the cable, it might have been destroyed."

"So we have someone riding the ferry to this side of the river," Cohl calculated, "and someone else on the other side, puttin' it outta commission."

"Exactly," Mundy agreed.

"Shame you weren't here to see who," Cohl said.

"Actually," Mundy said earnestly, "I believe our absence was the Lord's protection upon Mrs. Mundy and myself—and I thank and praise Him."

"The Lord sure didn't extend his protection to Miss Jade," Cohl said bitterly. "Anything else?"

"Just this, Mr. Cohl," Mundy smiled gently, "if you object to hearing the Gospel, you came to see the wrong man."

Cohl gave his head a shake, tightened Red's cinch, swung into the saddle and moved out at a lope, following the trail east along the river, while Blaine was still talking with the ferryman.

* * * * * * * *

When he caught up to I.C., Blaine was singing, *"What a Friend we have in Jesus."* Groping for words he did not know as well as most hymns, he sang it as *"all our burdens He will bear."*

"You makin' that up as you go along?" Cohl jibed.

Blaine chuckled. "No—it's a new song—I'm not real sure of all the words."

169

"Well, you got 'em ass backwards," Cohl opined. "To my experience, friends don't bear burdens for you— friends *are* burdens."

"Not Jesus," Blaine said mildly.

"'Specially Him," Cohl growled. "How far to that trail y'figure Miss Jade took down to the river?"

"At least five miles," Buck replied.

"Blast," Cohl muttered. He put Red in a fast walk until the stench from the rotting mule reached their nostrils, then slowed to a creep, hanging off the right side of his saddle to study the ground.

The riverside trail wound through willow thickets and Cohl paused from time to time to note water-filled depressions such as might have been made by a large hoof weeks earlier.

"Three weeks," he muttered. "Might be tracks— might not be."

"We're coming up on it," Blaine called as the trail climbed a small bluff.

Cohl dismounted and searched the area thoroughly, finding nothing of interest on the small mesa and nothing but game tracks and scat along the cleft that led down to the water. Standing on the edge, he tossed in a dry branch and watched how the current tumbled it through the river canyon, then climbed back up to where his horse was waiting.

"Blast," he muttered, turning Red back toward the ferry.

"Presuming we're headed for Boise City," Blaine said, "there's no need to go back to Mundy's, unless you've decided you need that sermon after all."

Cohl gave him a dark look. "You got a shorter route?"

"Shorter, faster and it takes off right there," Blaine replied, pointing to a faint track leading off to the north-northwest. "It connects up to the stage road— we'll be across the desert by nightfall, if we push."

"What do you make of what we've learned today, I.C.?" Blaine ventured as they moved out.

"Someone pulled Miss Jade outta the Snake," Cohl replied. "The deal with the ferry makes no sense, but it messed up that heist and might've put someone in the right place to mess up the welcome home party the cabal set up—that'd be the shots Sarge heard and that no-name drifter who explained them away. Beyond that, I got more questions than answers. Don't know enough yet to say for sure if she's alive or—"

He left the sentence unfinished.

* * * * * * * *

A golden lance split a darkening cloudbank over the Boise Valley when Blaine and Cohl topped out on the bench overlooking the city.

Buck pulled up, stepped down and loosened Steel's cinch. "Not everyone in town's a friend, I better hold up until full dark," he said.

Cohl nodded and also dismounted and saw to his horse's comfort. "Made good time, like you said, but I take it that's not the trail Miss Jade would've taken."

"You asked for the shortest route, I.C.," Blaine said.

They watched the gold in the sky shift to magenta and deepen to purple as the sun dropped, darkly silhouetting the mountains to the northwest against the sky.

"The Boise Front is one of Jady's favorite backdrops," Buck said. "She puts that mountain ridge in a lot of pictures, 'though she did not much admire living in the city below it."

"Quite the view," Cohl nodded.

They rode in quietly, crossing the bridge over the Ridenbaugh fork of the Boise River and the new span across the main channel, which was lit by a lantern at either end.

"I don't like exposing myself," Blaine said, "but the house is on the north side, so there's no help for it."

171

"Fording near where there's a bridge would look suspicious," Cohl nodded.

Keeping alert, they continued up Ninth to the alley between Franklin and Hays, where they turned west for a block-and-a-half. A tall hedgerow of lilacs, forsythia, and red leaf enclosed the backyard of the third lot. Steel threaded his way through a narrow passage that doubled back to keep passersby from looking directly into the yard. Red followed.

There was a small stable, just two stalls, separated by a storeroom. Steel took possession of the stall nearest the alley, leaving the other for Red. Working without light, the men unsaddled and Blaine scooped a can of grain into each manger. Taking a coiled rope from a peg, he ran it out to a post, continuing around to turn the yard into a rope corral.

"Pretty slick," Cohl approved, "Red's gonna get spoiled."

When Blaine raised the pump handle to fill the water trough, it gave a dry squeal. "Have to oil that," he muttered. The backdoor of the house opened, spilling a rectangle of lamplight into the yard. "It's me," he said. The door closed, and the lamp was moved to the front room so they could enter in darkness.

Faye Box was a handsome, dark-haired, dark-eyed woman, who appeared much younger than her forty-nine years. As Blaine bent to hug her, she said, "It's so awful. I am glad you have come, but it's so awful."

When he straightened, she realized he wasn't alone. Cohl read the instant dislike on her face and wasn't surprised.

"This is I.C. Cohl," Blaine said, "He is a friend and an investigator. He's helping figure out what happened to Jadene."

"A friend? An investigator?" Faye raised a dubious eyebrow. "What happened to Jadene is what I always feared," she sighed. "I do not know why, out of three daughters, I could not have even one grow up to be a proper lady. I suppose you have heard Darlene has shamed the family name by going on the stage and now Jadene's tomboy ways have cost her her life."

"Maybe," Cohl said.

"She is lost in the river," Faye snapped. "There is no 'maybe' about it."

"We have run onto some things," Buck said, "There's a good chance she came out alive."

"No," Faye cried, "I will not listen to this. I, more than anyone, wish Jadene were here with me right this minute, but she is not, and she never will be again, and I will not have some—" she gestured toward Cohl "—some *investigator* stirring up false hopes. And you will not get one penny out of me, mister."

"Mother," Blaine admonished, "I.C. is a friend. He is not asking for money."

Cohl's eyes lit on a picture on the lamp stand. "Jade?" he asked.

Mrs. Box snatched it from his gaze and handed it to Blaine. "See how lovely she looked for her graduation? She even let Marian fix her hair."

"With hairpins?" Cohl interrupted sharply.

"Hairpins?" Faye echoed. "Well, one can hardly do a proper upsweep without hairpins, can one?"

"You know where to find this Marian?" Cohl directed the question to Blaine.

"Her father has a ranch east of town," Blaine said.

"You are not to bother the Copelands," Faye cried.

"Won't be no bother," Cohl said. "Pleasure to have met you, Mrs. Box," he tipped his hat politely. Shifting his eyes to Blaine, he added, "You have a nice visit with your stepmother. I'll meet you out back an hour afore sunup."

173

CHAPTER 6

They arrived at Copelands' long, low ranch house before dawn, but the kitchen was already lit. "Marian is crippled," Blaine said. "Born that way, I think. Copeland designed this place so she would have no stairs to climb."

He thought a moment and added, "Ought to warn you, you might have the same problem talking to Marian that you had with Rev. Mundy. She can be a bit preachy."

"You, too," Cohl nodded as they dismounted at a hitch rail outside the kitchen door and loosened their cinches.

A plump middle-aged Mexican woman stepped outside and eyed them suspiciously.

"We are here to see Miss Copeland regarding her friend, Jadene Box," Blaine said.

"She already heard about Miss Box," the woman replied. "And she never receives callers this early." She disappeared inside, but returned a few minutes later to announce, "Miss Marian says I should feed you while you wait."

"Obliged," the two men said as one.

The cook watched with growing approval as they cleaned their plates twice.

"More coffee and biscuits?" she offered, when they pushed back from the table.

Blaine allowed her to refill his cup.

Cohl said, "*Mucho gusto, Señora, pero no espacio.*"

174

"Humph," she said. "You don't speak Spanish well and you don't eat near enough to keep a grown man going. My Julio puts away more than the two of you together."

The tinkle of a bell interrupted her and she said, "Miss Marian is ready."

She put the coffee pot, their cups and the plate of biscuits and bowl of preserves on a tray and led the men down a wide hallway and into a richly appointed parlor.

A pale, dark-haired, soft-featured young woman was curled up in a large over-stuffed chair, a calico cat purring on her lap.

"Thank you, Mrs. Garcia," she said, as the woman refilled her coffee cup and left with her breakfast tray. Turning her attention to Buck, she smiled warmly. "How good of you to come, Blaine," she said, "I know it is hazardous for you, and Jady would not approve of your taking chances, but we do need to talk."

Blaine took the soft hand she held out. "I was not sure you would remember me," he said. "This is I.C. Cohl, he is our friend and an investigator."

Marian's reaction was far different than Faye's had been. After gazing at him for a moment with a steady look, she closed her eyes, bowed her head and put her hands together as if in prayer.

When she looked up, Blaine said, "Mother Faye has accepted Jadene's death and believes Jady would want me to get on with trying to clear my name, which I.C. is going to help me accomplish, but—"

"But, Jady is probably still alive," Marian finished for him, surprising both men. "More than once, she rode off into the desert saying she would be back in a few hours, and we did not see her again for days. When I chided her, saying she could have been dead for all we knew, she laughed and said, 'Don't you ever believe I am dead until you see my cold, stiff body.' It

175

was so annoying, but now I cannot help remembering and, Blaine, they have *not* found her body."

"We have found a few other things," Cohl said, drawing an envelope from his vest. "These mean anything to you?"

Marian held the tattered bit of embroidered cloth to her lips and closed her eyes for a moment. "Her mother made her a white dress and petticoat for graduation, like all us girls were to wear. Jady hated it. I added some embroidery to the petticoat so she would feel guilty if she didn't wear it." She pointed to a picture on the harpsichord, "As you can see, we all wore the same ensemble, and we had our picture taken together. Her dress is still in my wardrobe. She was going to take it, and then she was not, but she had already packed the petticoat in her reticule at the bottom of the pannier, so she left it there."

"You're sure that's a piece of it?" Cohl asked.

"I know my own needlework," Marian replied. "I cannot be as sure of the hairpins. Her hair was not trained to that fashion, so it took a lot of pins—at least a dozen—but a hairpin is a hairpin. I cannot be certain those are the same ones, but I can tell you her hair was still done up when she left here. Where did you find these? What do you think it means?"

After the men laid out what they had learned, Marian sat with closed eyes for several minutes. When she finally opened her eyes, she looked straight at Cohl and said, "The moment Blaine said you are an investigator, I knew God sent you in answer to my prayers. Jadene is alive and you will find her."

"I hope you're right," Cohl said, "but it's a cold trail and I've never once seen a prayer answered for any good."

"I have," Marian said, "I shall continue praying, morning and night and in between, as I promised Jady I would. Now, what can we do to warm up her trail?"

"I've gotta get out in the field, see if I can scare up someone who saw something," Cohl said. "It won't be easy, especially since there's been nothing in the papers to get folks looking for her."

"Then we will place big notices in every newspaper in the West and offer a reward for information," Marian said.

"Mother Faye will not stand for it," Blaine said. "We talked almost all night. Even if she thought there was a chance of finding Jady alive—which she does not—she is adamantly opposed to hanging private Box family business out in public."

"I know someone who might be able to change her mind," Cohl speculated.

"Not likely," Blaine said. "She was absolutely distraught."

"There must be something I can do," Marian pleaded.

"Start by telling me everything you know about her," Cohl said, seating himself on her hassock, facing her.

"Jady told me many things in confidence," Marian said, "I will not violate her trust, but I can tell you that Jady is very tough and self-assured when she is dealing with horses or guns or some hazardous circumstance, but she is very shy and insecure in simple social situations. If she is required to speak in public, she stammers and gets confused, but she will face down troublemakers smooth as ice. She is quite the tomboy, yet she is a lady—very modest and proper—even when wearing dungarees. All in all, she is the most puzzling girl you will ever find."

"Puzzles suit me," Cohl almost grinned. "And I do aim to find her. What did you two talk about?"

"Everything—school, theology, all her adventures, horses, art, music, her guns, my needlework, our families, our girlfriends," Marian hesitated, "boys."

"There was someone she was sweet on?" Cohl asked.

"Heavens, no!" Marian exclaimed. "She told me what was wrong with each and every one of them."

"What was she looking for in a man?" Cohl asked.

"Jady is not out looking for a man," Marian chided, "She often said she would never marry because she could not hope to find a man the equal of her father."

Marian chewed on her lip. "She said that even more after she met a man who tricked her into thinking he was a lot like Representative Box, but he turned out to be a very evil man."

"Tell me about him," Cohl coaxed.

Marian shuddered. "I cannot. I double promised Jadene I never would—I didn't even tell Daddy, and I probably should have. It does not matter, anyway."

She thought for a moment, then added, "Perhaps I misspoke when I said she is not looking for a man. Jadene is quite determined to find whoever was behind her father's murder. We debated the issue often—I suppose it was the closest we came to arguing."

"You didn't approve?" Cohl asked.

"*Vengeance is mine saith the Lord*,"[22] Marian quoted. "I told her she should leave it to God. She said God uses people to do everything else—help the needy, carry the gospel to the unsaved. She argued that in Old Testament times, He also used people to fight battles and dispense justice, so she prayed that God would use her to bring justice to whoever was behind her father's murder."

"And you didn't approve," Cohl repeated.

"Her grandmother and I both warned her to be careful what she prayed for," Marian said.

"About the evil man—" Cohl started.

"I do not appreciate your pushing me to break a confidence, Mr. Cohl," Marian chided.

---

[22] Romans 12:19

He stood, paced the room, then asked, "Did she pick up some of Captain Box's Texas drawl, or does she maybe fake it now and then, like Buck does?"

"I would not say she fakes it, but it comes and goes with Jady," Marian laughed. "Perfect diction one minute, pure Texas the next. Mrs. Garcia has been teaching us Spanish—it is not hard, having studied Latin in school—but Jady understands it better than she speaks it. No matter how hard she tries, she just cannot roll her 'R's."

Cohl nodded, made another lap around the room and took a different tack with his questions. "Tell me about her last night here, and did you see her in the morning afore she rode out?"

"We sat up half the night talking while she packed," Marian said. "I almost missed seeing her off in the morning. I rushed out when she was mounting up. We traded lockets so we would not forget each other, as if we ever could."

Marian displayed a dainty bit of gold, engraved with the letter J.

Cohl eyed the piece. "That worth anything?"

"Daddy presented matching lockets to Jady and me to celebrate our friendship," Marian smiled. "Knowing Daddy, they were pretty expensive."

"Then there's something you might do," Cohl said, "write up a lost and found advertisement for your locket with the M on it. Run it in the papers around here and maybe some at a distance. Mrs. Box shouldn't get worked up over that."

"Should we do the same for her gun?" Blaine asked. "I had it custom made by a gunsmith over in Baker City."

"Is it like that flashy silver showpiece of yours, with gold inlays?" Cohl asked.

"That would not have pleased Jady," Blaine chuckled. "It's blued steel with walnut grips custom

179

carved to fit her hand. There is some scrollwork on the frame, but it's not real showy."

Cohl nodded approvingly. "The notice better make it real plain we don't just want the gun," he said, "Offer a reward for information. Maybe come right out and say we want the owner of it alive and well."

Another lap around the room and Cohl asked, "Buck, any chance you can get Jade's picture away from Mrs. Box?"

Marian laughed and pointed at a stack of albums filled with tintypes and sepia tone photographs. The top book yielded an extra copy of Jadene's graduation picture, as well as two copies of one of Jady on SoBig and Marian on a gray mare.

"That's Sweetpea, the horse Jadene trained for me. She kneels like a camel, so I can get on and off," the girl said.

"That what your dad gave her the locket for?" Cohl asked.

"Heavens, no," Marian laughed. "Daddy insisted on paying Jadene generously for training Sweetpea. That's another thing—in the inside pocket of her jacket she had five hundred dollars she earned training and selling horses. She wanted to give it to you, Blaine, to help hire a good attorney. The locket was just for being my friend."

"No offense, Miss Copeland," Cohl puzzled, "but I'm not seein' how you two would be such close friends."

"It was a miracle," Marian declared. "All through primary school, there were bullies who tormented me because I cannot walk properly. I prayed that it would be different at the academy, but they started in worse than ever the very first day. Jadene and I had barely met, and she had been so shy in class she could hardly speak. After school, six of them set upon me—it was a fearsome situation and I had no idea what to do to escape. Suddenly, there was Jadene—I don't know how she did it, but she sent them all running with just a word and a look.

"From that day on, Jadene was my guardian angel. She even switched classes to be with me all day the first week. That moved her from art to choir, which was pretty bad," Marian chucked at the memory, "but the next semester I signed up for art, too, and I cannot draw so much as a straight line."

"The bullies," Cohl asked, "they give you any more trouble?"

"None that Jadene did not settle in a hurry," Marian said. She recalled several small incidents, including the threat on the bridge.

"Where do I find Billy Ellis?" Cohl asked.

"New Jersey," Blaine said. "Sheriff Sage came by Mother Faye's last night. He talked to the Ellises after Billy threatened her and again when Jady went missing. Seems Billy had heard his father and some others expressing concerns over Jady's tomboy ways. They all swore it was not a threat—just the same sort of concern Mother Faye expressed herself on a regular basis."

"How does that put the bully boy in New Jersey?" Cohl asked.

"Kid wants to be an attorney like his father," Blaine said. "He will be attending Princeton University come September."

"Shouldn't take three months for him to get there," Cohl calculated. "More likely they wanted him out of here."

"Perhaps," Marian said, "but Billy is a city boy. He absolutely could not have trailed Jady across the desert."

"He might know who did," Cohl said. "I'll ask the boss to make inquiries. Now, Miss Copeland, could you write out a detailed list of everything you saw her pack, especially anything unusual or of some value."

"It will take a while," Marian said, disturbing the cat as she reached for writing materials.

"Buck, do you know the trail Miss Jade would've taken out of here down to where she probably tried to ford the river?"

"I sure do," Blaine said.

"Well, if you're not scared to venture out, let's ride it while Miss Copeland writes that list," Cohl proposed. "See what we find."

* * * * * * *

By mid-morning, Blaine and Cohl were trailing south through thick sagebrush, Blaine taking the lead as Cohl studied the picture Marian had provided.

"Her hair's not as dark as her ma's and her sister's," he observed.

"No," Blaine confirmed, "it is a light brown. Dar calls it mousy." As Cohl continued to study the sepia-tone, Blaine warned, "Sun will fade that clean away."

Cohl gazed at it another minute, as if fixing it in his mind, then eased it into his inner vest pocket. "She sure don't look like a kid," he said.

"Doesn't," Blaine chuckled. "Kid or not, she is too young for old men like us."

"I'm not near as old as you," Cohl allowed.

* * * * * * *

Fresh grass was pushing up through fire-blackened soil, and spring rains had coaxed charred sagebrush trunks to bud with new life.

Blaine reined Steel off the trail and worked his way up to a break in the rimrock that gave access to the mesa-top. When Cohl came alongside him, they were overlooking a narrow, steep-sided valley and the remains of a burned-out soddy.

"Had a good corral set-up," Blaine said. "We called it north horse camp. It did not get much use because it is so far from the ranch. Wildfire last summer wiped it out."

182

Catching the strained quality in Buck's voice, Cohl listened silently.

"The spring after the Captain died, Jady wrote asking me to meet her here when she had a few days off for Easter," Buck related. "Only I never got her letter, so I was not here."

Buck swallowed hard, "Someone else was. Said his name was Al. Said he was an old friend of the Captain's, here on account of the letter the Captain wrote to your Mr. Ethridge. He got her to tell him everything she knew. Said he would take care of it—she need not worry anymore."

"Ethridge don't have no Al workin' for him," Cohl growled. "What's he look like?"

"Like Marian said, it does not matter," Blaine gritted. "He let her get to sleep, then he came for her. That derringer Lincoln found in the river—Jady stuck it in his ear and pulled the trigger."

Cohl gave a low whistle. "A damn good girl!"

Blaine nodded. "I wandered in the next day, just happening by on my way to Boise, taking her revolver to her. Jady was digging a grave. I finished it out. I never told anyone and did not think she had, but it seems Marian knows."

"Not a girl to mess with," Cohl approved.

"As I told you before, any man who messes with Jadene can expect to wind up dead," Blaine agreed.

CHAPTER 7

They rested their horses at noon and ate some of the food Mrs. Garcia had packed. "Visited the police stationhouse last evening," Cohl drawled.

"I told you not everyone in Boise is a friend," Blaine replied.

"Really?" Cohl feigned surprise. "They admire you so much they've got your poster front and center— someone penciled in 'alias Blaine Box,' corrected the height, doubled the reward and X-ed out the 'or alive.' But that's not what I was after—didn't let on I even noticed it, just flashed my badge and asked to go through their dodger collection. Lot of smallish southerners, but no big knife-scarred Canadian. Then I dropped in on the Ada County Sheriff, but he was out— visitin' you and Mrs. Box, you said—so I talked to a deputy name of Reidel. Real close-mouthed."

"Rollie Reidel hates bounty hunters—likely read you as being one," Blaine nodded. "Lowell Sage is Jadene's godfather. If I had known where you were going, I would have told you where to mention my name and where not."

After they crossed the railroad tracks late that afternoon, the trail forked. "Both routes go down to the Snake," Buck said. "The west fork is the stage route and a much better road, but Jady surely took the east fork and swung by Lemuel Walker's Bar None, where I should have been waiting for her."

Cohl nodded and started Red down the eastern trail.

184

Another hour passed and Blaine took a hard left, saying, "Lem's ranch is just over this rise. He's her sweetheart."

As the ramshackle ranch came into view, Cohl grunted sourly, "She's really sweet on this guy?"

"Has been for years," Blaine deadpanned. "Jady and Lem make quite a team."

A black and white dog yelped a greeting. The cabin door creaked open, and a grizzled old man peered out. "Why, I'll be a sorry son of a jackrabbit," he cried, "Quiet, Tipper, you know Buck. Dang am I glad to see yuh, boy, first good thing's come muh way in a month o' Sundays. Been a turrible spring, what with losin' our li'l sweetheart an' havin' some nogood'n do in pore ol' Trapper, an' then make off wi' muh Brandy, too."

Blaine swung down and gripped the wiry old-timer's hand, saying, "I.C., meet Lemuel Walker, proud owner of the Bar None. Lem—I.C. Cohl, our friend and the man who is going to find Jady for us."

"Find 'er?" Lem's face lit up, "You mean the Basque's wrong when he tol' me my sweet li'l Jady drowned?"

"Jady will be very disappointed with you," Blaine teased, "if she ever learns you believed she was dead without seeing proof." Inside, he filled the oldster in on what they knew, while Lem watered down his stew, declared it to be soup, poured it into three bowls, and set the pot down for Tipper to wash.

"Lem's cooking never killed anyone," Blaine assured Cohl.

"Shorely not," their host agreed, "Tipper keeps ever'thin' spic 'n' span. When yer done, jus' put yer bowl down an' she'll tend to it."

Cohl nodded, and the dog got a full serving that night. "You said someone stole your liquor?" he asked after Walker slurped the last of his portion.

Perplexed, Lem said, "My licker? Whut?"

"Brandy is a horse," Blaine told Cohl, "prettiest little bay colt you could ask for, by Steel out of Lem's mare, born a year ago last September."

"He's a dandy," Lem agreed. "I been hopin' ol' Steel'd mebbe visit Rosy agin'. Thought I'd be ridin' Brandy by th' time she rounded out. I wuz workin' 'im some, even put shoes on 'im. Then Tipper an' me come back from he'pin' Basque John move sheep, an' ol' Trapper were dead, an' Brandy were gone, an' thet wuthless piebald were hangin' 'round. Three-four days later, the Basque tol' me 'bout Jady."

"When was this?" Cohl demanded.

"Oh, week 'r two ago," Lem guessed. "I kinda lose track."

"Miss Box disappeared twenty-two days ago, Mr. Walker," Cohl said. "Was your horse stolen afore or after that?"

"It don' seem like it been thet long," Lem puzzled. "Basque John could tell yuh fer shore—marks ever'thin' down in 'is book. As I recollect," he added, "it were the day after Jady come by—mebbe two days."

"You saw her?" Blaine cried.

"Nope, movin' them sheep took three-four days a runnin'," Walker recalled. "The one day, I come home an' saw her sign—felt real down havin' missed her. Next day or th' day after, Brandy were gone."

"She left a note?" Cohl asked.

"Now why'd she do thet?" Lem frowned, "Jady knows I cain't read. Just lef' me a sign, like always." He pointed to the wall which was papered with sketches. "That'un." He poked a gnarled finger at a colt's head, with a heart drawn around it.

"That's Brandy," Blaine said.

"Yup," Lem swallowed hard. "All I got lef' of 'im—"

"Notched right ear," Cohl observed. "About a thumb's width down from the point?"

"That cut is Lemuel's mark," Blaine nodded.

186

"You mentioned a piebald, Mr. Walker," Cohl said, "Can you describe it?"

"See fer yerself—I cain't git rid 'o th' critter," Lem groused, leading the way outside and pointing.

In the growing dark, the animal's white patches stood out as it grazed behind the small barn. It came readily when Blaine shook a little grain in a can. It was an exact match for the horse Sheriff Leinert had described.

Blaine winked at Lem as he put Steel in with Rosy for the night, leaving Red in a separate paddock. Before the younger men bedded down in the barn, Cohl prodded a few more details out of Walker.

Judging by the tracks, Brandy was taken by a man wearing boots bigger than Buck's. The man had come and gone from the east on a horse with hooves the size of dinner plates. He seemed to have stashed a pack just over the rise that sheltered the Bar None, loaded it on Brandy, and continued northeast toward a railroad stop called Cleft, moving at a lope, leading the colt on a short line.

They slept in the hay and Cohl was breakfasting on cold biscuits from Mrs. Garcia's provisions when Lem called them to bowls of grits inside. Accepting only the offer of hot coffee, he brought his own tin cup.

After Blaine and Cohl were saddled and mounted, Lem said, "Almos' fergot one thing—thet big feller what kilt Trapper an' took Brandy went through muh house, too. Took muh new army blanket, one I brung back from th' war."

Lemuel pointed out the direction he had trailed the dog-murdering thief, but no tracks remained for them to follow.

The railroad agent at the tiny hamlet of Cleft was certain Jadene had not been through, nor had he seen Brandy or a big stranger.

"Trail's gone cold again," Cohl muttered, as he wrote a message to be wired to Ethridge.

"Let's pay a call on John Bastida," Blaine suggested.

The Basque sheep rancher confirmed that Brandy's theft occurred the day after Jadene disappeared. Neither he nor his people had seen anything, but some of his men had reported that someone camped at the rock corral the night Jady disappeared. They would keep watching. Before heading back to Copeland's, Cohl gave him a Sacramento post office box number to write to if anything turned up.

* * * * * * * *

They were going over the list Marian had prepared when a door slammed open elsewhere in the house and hurrying footsteps pounded in the hallway. Both men sprang to their feet, Blaine taking a position behind the door where he would be out of sight if it opened, and Cohl standing, light on his feet, ready to draw, on the other side.

The door swung wide, revealing a solid-built, middle-aged man with a full head of iron-gray hair and a worried look. Peering over his shoulder was an older version of Marian, without the limp. "Daddy, Mama," Marian cried, "You gave us such a scare."

"We gave you a scare!" Delwin Copeland retorted, "We saw the horses out back, and Inez said two rough men were here yesterday and returned today. Are you all right?"

Marian laughed delightedly. "More than all right," she said. "The Lord is answering our prayers. You remember Jadene's brother, Blaine, and this is his friend, Mr. Cohl. They have found evidence that Jady is alive!"

"Praise God!" both Copelands cried, drowning out Cohl's qualifier:

"Might be."

Shaking hands with Blaine, Copeland said, "It has been a long time, but I believe we met at the swearing in ceremony when Gideon was first seated in the Legislature."

188

He extended his hand toward Cohl, but the gunman just stepped back.

Covering the awkwardness, Blaine said, "Yes, Senator, you remember right. I hope we were not out of line coming here."

"You are Gideon's son and Jadene's brother. You will always be welcome," Copeland said. "The Boxes have been good allies and better friends. I hope Mrs. Box told you that I am eager to assist in resolving your legal difficulties."

"Mother Faye does not hold with taking advantage of friendships," Blaine said, "I appreciate the offer, but finding Jadene comes first."

"Speaking of finding things," Maude Copeland said, perching on the arm of her daughter's chair, "the most peculiar thing happened in Denver.

"While Dad was at the bankers' meeting, I went for a little walk and found myself on a street that was not the sort of neighborhood I normally would go walking in, certainly not unescorted," she said. "When I turned back, I noticed a jewelry display in a store window—it was what they call a pawnshop. Well, you know how I am about jewelry, so I paused to look and—" from her pocket she withdrew a piece of tissue paper and handed it to Marian to unfold. "Now doesn't that look just like the lockets Dad bought for you and Jadene? It even has our initial on it."

In the stunned silence, she added, "The link that connected the chain to the clasp had pulled open so I took it to a jeweler and had it repaired. I hope you do not mind my having one, too."

"Mother," Marian said in an awed voice, "Jadene and I traded lockets. She was wearing mine when she disappeared."

"What's the chances it's the same locket?" Cohl asked.

"It looks just the same," Marian said, opening it. "We were going to put our pictures in them, but we never did."

189

"I cannot imagine how it got to Denver," Senator Copeland said, "but I had those lockets made to order. There should not be another exactly like it."

"If Miss Jade drowned in the Snake, her body could turn up downstream, and someone could take the locket off and pawn it," Cohl calculated aloud. "That would put it north or west of here, maybe even all the way to Portland—but not in just three weeks' time. Denver means she's not in the river."

"And that, praise God, means she is alive," Marian rejoiced.

"Might be," Cohl repeated. "Mrs. Copeland, tell me everything you can recall about that pawnshop."

"Why, I do not even know where it was for sure," Maude sighed. "It was a horrid place and the woman charged me an exorbitant price when she saw how much I wanted that locket. She was a strange person— quite tall with coarse features and tobacco-stained teeth. She wore a purple gown and was painted like, well, like a woman of ill repute. She had big hands with large, gaudy rings on every finger, several wide bracelets on each arm, a huge brooch, garish earrings, jeweled combs in her unnaturally red hair..."

"Did she say how she came by the locket?" Cohl asked.

"She said a poor woman brought it in, and that she, the pawnshop woman, that is, overpaid for it out of pity, so she could not give it to me for anything less than forty dollars," Maude Copeland harrumphed, "but I do not believe that woman ever did anything out of pity."

"Denver," Cohl said. "If I can get Buck on the train without the local law getting in the way."

"I will arrange for your tickets," Del Copeland offered. "The ten-ten will get you to the mainline at Nampa in time to catch the next train east. It is a local, I am afraid."

"That's good," Cohl said. "It'll give us a chance to ask questions all along the line—better haul our horses, just in case we hit upon a trace to follow."

The hours until the train departed gave ample time to review the lost and found notices Marian had prepared and replace the ad for the locket with one seeking Lemuel Walker's colt. Cohl also wrote out a message to be wired to Ethridge—and pumped Mrs. Copeland for more details about the pawnshop.

After supper, Inez served coffee and tea cakes in the library. While the others chatted, Cohl paced impatiently. Pausing to study the photo on the harpsichord, he idly dropped his hand on the keyboard and ran a scale.

All conversation stopped as Blaine and the Copelands stared in amazement.

"G's going flat," the gunman observed.

"You can play that?!" Blaine marveled.

"Been awhile," Cohl shrugged, "it's smaller'n Mother Ethridge's piano, but it works about the same—needs tuning though."

* * * * * * * *

Long before they reached Minidoka, Blaine and Cohl heard about a grisly robbery that occurred less than a week after Jadene disappeared.

Banker Warren Webster had been knifed to death by someone who took his satchel containing five-thousand dollars cash. When it happened, Minidoka Town Marshal Haley Pinkham, who was supposed to be watching out for Webster, had been busy talking to a man about a missing girl.

Blaine and Cohl laid over in Minidoka to talk to the still distressed lawman. Pinkham told them what the man he knew as Robert Glasgow had told him.

"Sounds like your missing girl, all right," the marshal said, "though I can't figure why she'd take a shot at Glasgow. He's as nice a gent as you could ask for. Sells mining supplies, I believe. A shade taller than

191

you, Mr. Box, weighs probably two-twenty or so, no fat, just big. Real friendly. I've met him more'n once takin' a turn in Ralph Paulson's barber chair."

"He may have been the last person to see Miss Box," Cohl said, "How do we get a hold of him?"

"He was over east in Pocatello to catch the Northern to Montana," Pinkham recalled. "Seems to move around, wherever there's mining—over to the Owyhees, up in the Sawtooths, Idaho City. He's down from Alberta, but I don't know as to whether he travels back up there regular."

"Canadian? Does he spend time at Denver?" Cohl asked.

"Not that he's mentioned to me," Pinkham said. "Next time he comes through, I could ask him to contact you. He was real anxious to help—minute he saw me, he come right over and started tellin' me about gettin' shot at. He's a peaceable sort, I've never even known him to pack a sidearm—think it rattled him, especially it being a girl. He's a handsome gent—expect he's not used to ladies bein' unfriendly."

"And while he had you distracted, a man died and the cash disappeared," Cohl concluded.

"It's a tragic thing," Pinkham mourned. "Bad enough losing five thousand dollars, but young Webster was a fine man. He had been runnin' his father's bank in Blackfoot, but he married a girl from here last summer. His bride's in a family way—wanted to be closer to her folks, so he bought the bank here."

"How'd it go down?" Cohl probed.

"We were about to board the train," Pinkham said, "Warren got on and I was about to step up, when Glasgow came up to talk. When the conductor called, 'all aboard,' I jumped on and waved goodbye, then went in. The car was empty except for Webster and he was dead. The trainman said there was two fellas that bought tickets and boarded, but they were nowhere to be found."

192

"A big Canadian with a knife-scarred face and a small southerner?" Cohl guessed.

"How'd you know that?" Pinkham asked. "We stopped the train and checked it over good, but didn't find anything more to go on."

"Glasgow?" Cohl queried.

"Lent a hand lookin' until it was time for his train to pull out," Pinkham said, "He was just as sick over it as me."

CHAPTER 8

Blaine stepped out of the outhouse that served the train station. A moment later, he felt the muzzle of a revolver prod him in the back.

"Blaine Box," an unfamiliar voice said, "you're wanted for a double murder."

Blaine slowly raised his hands before turning. The stranger was about his height, but not lanky, with flowing hair and mustaches, affecting the style of General Custer.

"You ain't gonna make it that easy for me, are you?" the man taunted, lowering his gun. "Wanna show me how fast you—hey!"

A steel vise had closed on his wrist, twisting it so he could not maintain his grip on his gun.

"Mr. Box is in my custody," Cohl said, placing his foot on the fallen pistol.

The bounty hunter sneered down at the smaller man. "Don't see how that can be, runt. He's still packin' iron."

"Protective custody," Cohl said. He flashed his badge, then ordered, "Sit."

The stranger squatted on a bench, ready to spring.

"Your name?" Cohl demanded.

"Francis Pitcairn and that bounty's mine."

"And why do you think there's a bounty on Mr. Box?"

"Hell, I seen the poster up to Gimlet—got his name on it and gives a real good description," Pitcairn

194

smirked, "Mayor offered me double the reward. Shoulda dropped the sucker soon as I seen him."

"In which case," Cohl gritted, "I'd've dropped you. The charges against Mr. Box are false. You want to collect anything, Pit, you might try telling me about this so-called mayor."

"So, you've heard of me," Pitcairn crowed. "Yeah, I answer to Pit, but I ain't in the business of sellin' stories."

"Well," Cohl withdrew a fat money clip from his left pocket, "that's what I'm buyin'. You want paper or lead?"

Pit swallowed hard. "Always glad to help out the law," he lied. "Mayor's name's Wilbur Frey. Told me him and his town marshal'd been tipped off this outlaw was headed their way, so they was set to arrest him. Then the marshal seen some shifty snake-oil peddler muckin' around, so he goes to run him off. Next thing anyone knows, this'n up and guns the marshal. The peddler caught a wild shot.

"Frey said they caught him, tried him, and got set to hang him, but his gang rode in and busted up the town and broke him outta jail. They made up a poster, not really knowin' who he was, then they found out he's the same outlaw they'd been told to expect, so they fixed the poster and upped the reward," Pit ended.

"You been told a pack of lies," Cohl said as the eastbound beside the platform built a head of steam.

"Who cares?" Pit sneered, "Now pay up or give me my man."

Cohl handed his clip to Blaine. "Peel off two hundred," he directed. When Blaine had done so, he said, "Give it to Francis, here, then take this piece of crap I got my foot on and drop it in the can." He tipped his head toward the outhouse.

Pitcairn gave an enraged howl but snatched the money. "Don't you throw my gun in there," he ordered, "don't you dare."

Blaine dared.

Pit was still trying to fish it out when the train disappeared down the track.

* * * * * * * *

"I owe you," Buck said, as they settled into the rear seats of the last passenger car.

"Easy come, easy go," Cohl shrugged.

"Ethridge keeps that money clip loaded?" Blaine asked.

A half-grin tugged at Cohl's mouth. "Found a game in Boise after my chat with Reidel."

"You are dangerous, my friend," Blaine chuckled.

"Ain't I, though," Cohl agreed amiably.

He fell silent, pondering, the humor draining from his face.

"What's the chances," he mused, "of two big Canadians being in the same area at the same time and not being a team?"

"Probably better than you think," Blaine replied. "Even if the other two are the same ones who tried to rob the Jordan Valley stage, Glasgow might not know anything more than that he saw Jady three weeks ago."

"Trying for the stage puts them on the wrong side of the river to run into Miss Jade," Cohl said.

"Maybe Glasgow is that 'honest puncher' you were speculating about," Blaine said, "Maybe she's hurt too bad to tell him where she belongs, so he is asking around trying to find out."

"Then why doesn't he just come right out and say he's got her?" Cohl countered. "Why go all the way to Minidoka afore talkin' to a lawman? He passed up more'n one doctor getting that far. Blast! We should've had notices in the papers."

"Maybe not," Blaine allowed. "A stranger who called himself Simon Taylor accosted Mother Faye right after Jady's graduation ceremony. He claimed to be an old friend of the Captain's and was over-eager to meet

196

Jady. Mother Faye said she expected Jady to be at her home the next evening, and he promptly invited himself to supper. When Taylor arrived and found Jady was not there, but Sheriff and Mrs. Sage were. He did not stick around—he really raised Sage's suspicions and it seems likely to me that the same people who sent Al after her sent this man Taylor, and also sent the person who shot at her at the river. If they think they killed her, I hesitate to publish notices that would get them back to hunting for her."

"They might already know exactly how that came out," Cohl speculated. "Might've grabbed her when her horse came out of the water. There was a struggle and she lost the derringer. Where Glasgow would fit with that, I don't know, but she's little and young, like you said—no match for a cabal killer. I don't want it to be so, Buck, but chances are we're too late— unless they kept her alive as bait to get you. We hear anything from them, it'll likely be a trap."

* * * * * * * *

A telegram was waiting for Cohl when they reached Pocatello, where the Oregon Shortline rails met the tracks of the Utah and Northern.

Cohl gave orders for the horses to be transferred to the southbound train and directed Blaine to get aboard while he fired off what Blaine supposed was a reply. The train had nearly cleared the station before Cohl swung onto the rear platform of the caboose and made his way forward.

Slacking into a seat across from Blaine, he announced, "Ethridge wants you in Sacramento."

"After we check out Denver," Blaine agreed.

"Considerin' that business with Pitcairn, the boss wants you stashed away," Cohl said. "I'll handle the fieldwork alone."

"Mr. Ethridge is not *my* boss," Blaine replied, "Jadene is my sister and I am going directly to Denver to look for her, with or without you."

"Sacramento," Cohl gritted. "Looks like Pit was right about one thing, you better hand over your gun."

To Blaine's dismay, he realized Cohl had the drop on him.

"That is not necessary," he said.

"The gun," Cohl commanded. When Blaine reluctantly handed it over, he emptied the cylinder and thoughtfully shifted the shells in his left hand.

After a long silence, he asked, "I really remind you of that cousin of yours?"

"Not at all," Blaine admitted. "The two of you have similar coloring, but when I said you reminded me of someone, I did not mean Drake."

Cohl nodded, still juggling the cartridges. "I been feelin' a bit insulted."

"Actually, I.C.," Blaine said gently, "watching you, I got to wondering if my father had been married sometime to a Mexican or Indian lady. He would never talk about some things that happened early on. I thought maybe his other wife died in childbirth and the Ethridges raised the baby."

Cohl turned that news over in his mind, as he turned the shells in his hand. Eventually, he asked, "I remind you of Gideon Box?"

"Quite a bit," Blaine admitted.

"That's as fine a compliment as I ever heard," Cohl nodded thoughtfully. "'Course, if Mrs. Ethridge had raised me from the get-go, I'd've turned out more respectable, despite the permanent sunburn. Reckon you're right relieved I'm not your half-brother."

"Actually, I.C.," Blaine said earnestly, "I am a bit disappointed."

Cohl reloaded Blaine's revolver. "I want to stay on Miss Jade's trail, too, Buck," he spoke as if thinking out loud, "but Ethridge wants you in Sacramento, so that's where I gotta take you—gotta get you there in one piece—Ethridge and Miss Jade'd both be down on me if I brought you in with a hole in you—truth to tell, Buck,

198

I'd be down on me, too. So there you have it—you gotta quit buckin' me and follow my lead, hear?"

"Sacramento, then," Blaine nodded, and Cohl handed his gun back.

* * * * * * * *

At the bustling Ogden terminal on the mainline, roustabouts rushed to transfer Red and Steel to a stock car they had hastily added to a westbound freight train.

"Harvey Munson's the engineer, Sir," the stationmaster said as he escorted them to the caboose. "He's honored to have you aboard and says he aims to set a record for delivering 'Ice' to Sacramento."

"Good man," Cohl said, voicing no objection to being called Ice.

"Sir? Honored? Invited to ride in the caboose?" Blaine wondered aloud. "What did you do for these railroaders?"

"Nothing much," Cohl answered. "A set of plates sorta got misplaced in shipment awhile back. Ethridge had me get them where they needed to go."

"That must have been quite a set of china," Blaine said.

"Not that sorta plates," Cohl allowed.

199

CHAPTER 9

After collecting Steel and Red from the stock car at Sacramento, Cohl guided Blaine along broad avenues, finally stopping at the first carriage house on an alley that was wider than most streets in Boise City.

The carriage house was empty.

"She must be out," Cohl said. He directed the horses to unused stalls and showed Blaine where to get grain, hay and water for Steel.

Carrying their saddlebags and bedrolls, they climbed the stairs to the back porch. Cohl opened the door without knocking. The aroma of yeast bread rolled out. A gray-haired woman, her black arms white with flour, looked up from her kneading. A broad smile filled her dark face. "Boss said you's acomin' so I's makin' cinnamon buns."

"Agnes," Cohl deadpanned, "you'll get me to propose yet."

"Do you no good," she bantered, "you much too old an' slow for me."

"Too blasted slow," Cohl agreed. "Reckon Mr. Ethridge is up to seeing us?"

The answer came from the dining room door. A beautifully modulated feminine voice said, "Actually, Mr. Cohl, he is gone."

"Mrs. Ethridge! You're here. The boss is gone?!"

She laughed at having alarmed him. A beautiful tinkling laugh. "I expect him momentarily," she said. Looking past Cohl, she stepped forward, smiling, holding out her hand, saying, "And you must be Mr. Box."

Staring, mouth agape, Blaine was slow to respond. "Oh," she frowned, "Mr. Cohl does not shake hands either."

Blaine recovered in time to capture her silken hand, but was unable to speak. Cohl had mentioned a Mrs. Ethridge, but this willowy blond looked to be less than thirty, with huge green eyes shaded by long dark lashes, and full lips that curled into a teasing smile as she said, "And now that you have decided it is safe to take my hand, do you intend to keep it?"

"Yes, ma'am," he said, "I mean, no, ma'am, I..."

"Come," she said, taking his arm, "We have coffee waiting in the parlor."

The parlor was roughly the same size as Mother Faye's entire house.

"You moved things around," Cohl said nodding toward a grand piano.

"Yes," she said, "We thought you might be more inclined to play if the bench were where you would have your back to the wall."

He walked over, raised the cover on the keys, and ran a scale. "Maybe," he said, closing it. "Where's the boss?"

Glancing out the window, she said, "Come and watch."

A handsome enclosed carriage pulled to a stop.

"Buck, let's go lend a hand," Cohl said.

"No," Mrs. Ethridge objected, "come and watch."

The driver opened the carriage door, set down a step stool, and raised his hand to assist his passenger. A sixtyish gentleman in a bowler hat and tailored suit, with a gold watch chain, accepted the hand. Using a silver cane, he carefully stepped down.

The driver handed the man a second cane and he walked haltingly up the sidewalk. Leaving the second cane in a stand at the base of the stairs, he gripped the handrail and worked his way up the steps.

"When did *this* happen?" Cohl sounded amazed.

"Not long after you left for Nevada," the woman replied. "We had a terrible row. He said, 'It has been four years, Jeanne, it is time you quit wearing widow's weeds.' I told him, 'You will sit in that chair the rest of your life, and I will wear black the rest of mine.' He would not speak to me for a week. Then he had Agnes call me to his suite, as if there were an emergency. I went rushing in, and he was standing there. He took three steps, sat down at the desk and said, 'Jeanne, you have an appointment with your dressmaker.'"

Cohl stepped into the vestibule and opened the door. "I.C.," Ethridge boomed, collecting the cane waiting there, "can a man not even walk into his own house without being accosted by some semi-reformed villain? Why there ought to be a law."

"If there was," Cohl drawled, "you'd know the citation."

Jonathan Ethridge settled into a wing-back chair, removed his bowler, and patted down his thinning hair. "Blaine Box, welcome," he said, "You sure do favor Ruth."

After Jeanne left the room, Cohl leaned toward Ethridge and suggested in a confidential tone, "Good to see you're gettin' out now, but with me being out in the field so much, we better get you a bodyguard or a pocket piece, or both."

Ethridge chuckled and extended, handle first, his silver cane. "It is a 10 gauge," he said. "I have to sit down or it knocks me over."

Cohl gave a low, approving whistle. "Does she know?"

"I sent her to her dressmaker," Ethridge chuckled. "She ordered this from the gunsmith next door."

"We want you up for dinner, Father," Jeanne interrupted, bringing in a wheeled invalid chair, "so let me get you to your room for a little rest."

"I.C., walk with me," Ethridge said, refusing the chair. "Jeanne, you can get our guest settled in."

202

"Mr. Cohl has a wicked sense of humor," Jeanne said when they were alone. "I take it he did not prepare you for us,"

"He mentioned a Mrs. Ethridge and her piano," Blaine recalled, "but—well, I pictured a motherly type."

"Daniel thinks I am motherly," she smiled, "but if Mr. Cohl said anything favorable about a Mrs. Ethridge, he meant Lillian. The piano was hers. We lost her to cancer four years ago, and Mr. Cohl will likely never forgive me."

"He blames you for her dying?" Blaine puzzled.

"Not for Lillian's death," Jeanne explained, "but I was adamant that there be no guns at her funeral. They were working a smuggling case and there had been death threats, but I insisted—I said it was inappropriate to bring guns into the chapel, especially for the pallbearers—I insisted and I was quite pleased that everyone complied."

"I.C. went unarmed?" Blaine asked in astonishment.

"He appeared to," Jeanne said. "When they carried the casket out of the chapel, they walked right into an ambush. My Johnny died instantly and his father went down with a bullet in his spine," she shuddered. "Somehow Mr. Cohl suddenly had his gun in his hand—he killed three of the assassins right there and hunted down everyone else he thought was involved. Not a one lived to stand trial—so I am the only one left to blame."

"I.C. should not blame you at all," Blaine said. "But now I see what he meant when he said you folks were 'otherwise occupied' four years ago."

"Yes, 1883 was a horrid year," Jeanne sighed, "Lillian died the first of March, Johnny was killed at her funeral, which was on the fifth, and it was November before the doctors quit expecting Jonathan not to make it through another night. If I had not had Danny to hold onto—"

Blaine was still trying to work up the courage to touch her shoulder comfortingly, when she recovered her composure enough to continue. "Mr. Cohl thought the world of Johnny—they would sit on the back porch and talk for hours—it was like he had lost his only friend."

"Back home there was a boy named Johnny who went missing and is likely dead," Blaine mused. "Only time I have seen I.C. get rattled. I thought it was because Mr. Mundy preaches whenever he talks, but maybe it was the name being the same."

"Perhaps," Jeanne said, "but I am afraid Mr. Cohl has had nothing but grief from us 'church people.' He left town rather than stand up for Johnny at our wedding, but the next year, when I had Daniel, he reacted as if I had done the most wondrous thing in the world. We were thrilled—he even agreed to be Danny's godfather. But at the christening some of my father's parishioners made him feel unwelcome. After that, there was no getting him into a church—until Lillian's service, that is—and it was a death trap."

"That cane's a good piece," Cohl said from the doorway.

"I am glad you approve," Jeanne replied. "Daniel is visiting his grandmother. I will go invite them to join us for dinner, if you will show Mr. Box to his room—the bed in the room across from yours should be long enough."

"Should've warned you," Cohl muttered as he led Blaine up the stairs to the third floor.

"If you had warned me about Jeanne Ethridge," Buck laughed, "You would have had far less difficulty convincing me to come to Sacramento."

"Should've figured she'd have the same effect on you as she did on Johnny," Cohl growled.

"Is that who I remind you of?" Blaine asked.

"Just a bit, but not in what's important," Cohl allowed. "I did my level best to teach Johnny to shoot, but he just didn't have the hand or the eye for it. You

204

do, Buck, so don't you go givin' up your guns for that gal. Like Johnny, you're too tall to dodge lead, and like he proved, Bible citations don't stop bullets."

The tinkle of a dinner bell echoed up the stairs, calling Blaine and I.C. to the dining room.

Mr. Ethridge was listening politely to a silver-haired lady at the opposite end of the table. Jeanne and a towheaded lad of about seven sat on one side, their backs to a mirrored buffet. Cohl pointed Buck to the seat facing Jeanne and took the chair across from the boy, who was grinning delightedly.

"Mother, Danny, this is Blaine Box," Jeanne said. "Mr. Box, my mother, Mrs. Richard Stanton, and my son, Jonathan Daniel Ethridge, the third."

"Hilda," Ethridge said, "can I trust you to say a *short* grace?"

Hilda Stanton had the same tinkling laugh as her daughter. And she did keep the prayer short. "It's Reverend Stanton who will have you eating cold soup, if I do not nudge him under the table," she confided, after the Amen. "The Reverend has been asked to fill a pulpit on the way home from convention, so I would like to keep Daniel for an extra day."

"But, Uncle I.C.'s here," the lad protested.

"And I am certain he will be here for some time," Hilda said, as she passed the dinner rolls.

"Actually," Ethridge said, "perhaps Jeanne could spend the night with you so the boys can have a little time together. I.C. will be leaving in the morning."

"No, Grandpa," Danny cried. "Uncle I.C. can't leave so soon. I have all kinds of things to tell him and we've gotta do stuff together and..."

"I ain't inclined to share my bunk with a man who back-talks the boss," Cohl warned.

Danny instantly quieted. "I can sleep with you?"

Cohl shrugged. "Depends," he said. "I was hopin' you'd look after Red while I'm away—think you're up to that, Dan'l, if I show you how afore we turn in?"

"Yessir!" Danny chirped. "Can we play the piano, too? Grandmother's been teaching me."

"Bet she ain't taught you Camptown races," Cohl deadpanned.

* * * * * * * *

By the time Cohl reached Truckee, Nevada, on the Central Pacific, a stack of telegrams awaited.

In Owyhee County, Johnny Lauchlin's body had been found, hung up on a snag less than half-a-mile downstream from Mundy's south ferry landing.

At the Box Ranch, Drake hadn't been able to raise a crew to comb the sandbar, so Sarge Hankins was working alone. So far, he had found only a few scraps of tattered paper that likely came from Jadene's pack, plus a waterlogged schoolbook.

Senator Copeland forwarded a string of advertisement responses. He had his own people following up on those close to Boise, but several had come in from points south, closer to the transcontinental rail line. Cohl made the first of many side-trips on rented horses. Checking replies was slow going. The investigator grew short-tempered with people who couldn't tell a .22 from a .32-20, or nickel plating from blued steel.

Looking for Lemuel Walker's colt, Brandy, went no better. The ad clearly described a young, thirteen-hand, blood bay with tall black stockings, a notched ear and no white except for a powdery snip that made the colt look as if it had snuffled a flour sack. A man near Elko, showing a white-stockinged liver chestnut declared, "He's a nice little horse. Thought you might want to buy him if you can't find the one you lost."

Cohl thought it proof of his self-restraint that he didn't shoot anyone. And proof of people's greed that they responded so wildly to Copeland's generous reward offers. Taking advantage of the train's frequent stops, Cohl showed Jadene's picture to every reputable lawman, newsman, stationmaster, merchant and horse trader he knew. Eager to assist the man who had recovered the hijacked printing plates and delivered them safely to the U.S. Mint in San Francisco two years earlier, they all promised to keep both eyes peeled and pass along anything that might be of interest.

July twenty-seventh at Kelton, Utah, at the northern tip of the Great Salt Lake, a telegram directed Cohl to a horse broker in Albion. He bought a sorrel horse—a so-so animal, but the best available—and headed north-northwest on the wagon road to Idaho, thinking, while he was up that way, he would check in with Pinkham again.

* * * * * * * *

"Got 'im in a pen out back," Russell Johnston said. "Goin' to be awhile 'fore he's in shape t' sell. Pore little feller's been used bad. Got a bowed tendon, but he's a youngster, so I'm hopeful it'll come around."

Rounding the stable, Cohl saw a thin bay pony standing hip-shot, head down. Size and markings were right and the set of the ears with the distinctive notch was straight out of Jadene's drawing. He called, "Brandy!" The colt's head bobbed up, ears perked, and a hopeful glint lit the soulful brown eyes. Cohl slid through the bars, took the willing head in his hands and rubbed around the ears with his long fingers. "You don't know me, boy," he said, "but we're going to get you home to ol' Lemuel."

Johnston had what seemed to be proof of honest ownership. Brandy had come to him from Les Perry, a trader at Pocatello who didn't want to be bothered with doctoring. Perry passed along a handwritten bill of sale showing that a man named Pete Jackson—who signed with an "X"—had owned the colt from birth, then sold him to a Bob Devlin, who signed him over to Perry as part of a trade. "Les don't do things the way I would," Russell allowed. "I don't often take stock from him, but I felt sorry for this little guy."

"Glad you did," Cohl said, taking out his money clip. "I'll cover your costs, time and trouble if you'll ship Brandy back to his rightful owner."

207

"Don't seem right for you to be out that much," Russell said, "but it looks like you can afford it easier'n me."

Cohl shrugged, then pulled out a sepia tone of a young lady. "Ever see her? Might be dressed as a boy and was likely the one who rode Brandy."

Russell studied the picture. "Don't look like no boy to me, nor a horse thief, neither," he said.

"She's not," Cohl said. "Whoever palmed Brandy off on Perry likely stole the horse to carry her. You hear anything, let me know the same way as you reported finding the colt. I want her back—real bad."

"I can see why," Russell said.

* * * * * * * *

Reaching Perry's spread at Pocatello, Cohl indicated the sorrel he was riding and said, "Like to trade this'n for a long-legged mover."

"Like 'em fast, do you?" Perry smirked.

"Fast and red," Cohl allowed. "As they say, if you're not on a red horse, you're afoot an' don't know it."

Perry waddled over to a corral, spat a stream of chewing tobacco and pointed, "Wal, if you're wantin' a red horse that moves, that'n there's got yer name on it."

Cohl gave a low whistle, causing the animal to turn to him. "Hullo, Red," he said. After checking the gelding over and trying him out, he said, "Shoulda pretended I didn't like him. Now you're gonna jack the price."

Perry's ample belly shook with laughter. "Hell, I always jack the price. Boys like you gotta expect it." In a serious tone he added, "It'll be two-hunnert, but I'll give you a bill-a-sale that'll keep you from gettin' hung."

"I get hung, it won't be for horse thievin'," Cohl rumbled. The asking price didn't make a visible dent in his money clip.

"Shoulda said five," Perry grumbled, starting to write out a bill of sale.

208

"There's something else I'd pay for," Cohl allowed.

"Name it," Perry responded eagerly.

"You had a bay colt in here." Cohl showed Perry the bill of sale Perry had written when he acquired the colt and waited until Perry recovered from choking on his wad.

"This Bob Devlin who brought Brandy to you has something else I want," Cohl said. "Where do I find him?"

"That'd be a right unhealthy thing for me to know," Perry said.

"I'm not lookin' to gun him," Cohl said. "I just want back what he's got—and I'll pay well." He thought better of showing Jadene's picture to the crooked trader, instead giving him a page out of a newspaper's classified ad section.

"Give this to Devlin, he'll know the right one when he reads it. When I get the whole package—in good condition—he gets paid and so do you. Is he back from Denver yet? Sooner I get my package, the better the pay."

"Denver? Hell, there's no tellin' if Dev'll be back at all," Perry claimed. "Just 'cause a jasper trades with me onct don't make him a reg'lar."

"But Devlin is," Cohl said with certainty. "You about done writing that sale bill?"

"Yeah ," Perry said, "Whut name'd you want on it?"

"Eichman'll do," Cohl said, giving an alias he was sure the cabal hadn't yet linked to him.

"I-C-E-M-A-N?"

"Not how th' ol' folks spelt it, but it'll work for me," Cohl said.

CHAPTER 10

In Denver, U.S. Marshal Henderson provided a list of pawnshops known or suspected of serving as fences. The name Devlin rang no bells, nor did Glasgow, but Pete Jackson was a name that had been used by Jack Peat, also known as Two-Gun Peat—a fast man said to be even faster with his left than his right. The dodger showed an average-size gent with a sour face and dark, thinning hair. Henderson thought he was still in jail in Wyoming, so it probably wasn't the same man.

Cohl started with pawnbrokers within walking distance of the Grand Hotel. The third place on his list was operated by the jewelry-bedecked person Maude Copeland had described. Cohl pegged the pawnbroker as a man, despite the gaudy orange gown.

"Looking for something special?" the proprietor asked in a contralto voice.

"I'll know it if I see it," Cohl replied, searching the merchandise for anything from Marian's list. After nearly an hour in the cluttered shop, he passed, for the fourth time, a cheap embossed saddle setting atop a vintage army blanket. Bruning's saddle. Lem's blanket. He raised an eyebrow.

"I can make you a good deal on that little beauty," the pawnbroker offered.

"I'll bet you can," Cohl scoffed. "It's a chunk of junk. Surprised you gave Devlin anything for it."

"Ahh," the fence purred, "you're acquainted with Devlin?"

"He has something I want," Cohl said. "Thought I might get a line on it here."

"Perhaps the item has already sold," the broker said, "if you could describe it—"

"A custom .32-20 revolver," Cohl said, "blued steel, walnut grips fitted for a small hand—"

"Ahh, a lovely piece," the fence purred. "It will likely be here later. Devlin decided to try it himself first but, of course, that gun's not going to work out for him. As you said, it was made for a small hand, not those big hams of his. I could take your name and hold it for you. Will you be wanting the holster and belt as well?"

"I want the whole package," Cohl emphasized. "If it's likely to come in in the next few days, I could check back."

"Few days? No, he said something about maybe having a use for it at his butte place," the fence recalled, "It could be months. You know, dearie, you have exquisite hands. If you'd like to come in the back I have quite a selection of guns that would suit you better than that .32-20."

"I'm always interested in guns," Cohl allowed. "I'll take a look, but I still want that .32-20 package—the whole package."

"Ahh, a gift perhaps?" the fence brushed through a curtain to the rear.

Cohl admired a number of guns and bought a mate to the Smith and Wesson Schofield he wore, saying, "Never hurts to have a spare." Paying, he laid out an extra twenty and wrote "I C C 13-13 Sacramento" on the margin. "That's to cover the telegraph when my package arrives. I'd just as soon not wait months," he added, "If there's a way to get word to Devlin, tell him I want the whole package, undamaged, and the price will be to his liking."

The twenty disappeared into the front of the orange gown. "Pleasure doing business with you," the pawnbroker smiled hungrily.

* * * * * * * *

"Butte," the fence had said. Cohl wrote and sent his report, hunted up a high-stakes card game to replenish his front money, and, come morning, loaded himself and his horse on a northbound train.

First stop, the Wyoming Territorial Prison at Laramie. Jack Peat had been released the first of June, having served five years after he, two Canadians, and a Georgian named Jefferson Davis Zeeb had been convicted of stealing a mine payroll.

As young, first-time offenders, the Canadians got off with one-year terms. Their names? Devlin and Madden Burke—brothers from Alberta.

Zeeb, a hard rock miner, also served a single year, having been found guilty only of abetting in that he waited with fresh horses for their unsuccessful getaway.

"Butte might be the place to look," Warden Snowcroft said. "When I gave those boys their stay outta trouble talk before cutting them loose, Devlin said he had a girl waiting there. Said he was going to collect his 'Sweet Candy,' and never cross the line again. I'm sorry to hear he may be back with Peat—we should have hung that one."

* * * * * * * *

August fifteenth—Jadene's eighteenth birthday—Marian Copeland paid a courtesy call to Mrs. Box and found her ignoring the date. It was a struggle for Faye to remain civil when Marian attempted to inform her of how the search was progressing.

"I can live with picturing her safe in heaven with her father," Faye said. "I cannot bear to think she is alive somewhere because every possibility is too horrible to contemplate. Besides," she added, "I met that man and I cannot see how anyone could believe him. Do you not see he is just after money?"

"All we have paid for is the advertisements," Marian protested, "and the reward for the horse. Mr. Cohl has not asked for a penny, not even for expenses."

"He will," Faye predicted. "Will he ever."

212

* * * * * * * *

Serena delivered a baby girl on August twenty-fifth. She named her Naomi Jadene, in honor of the child's dead grandmother and aunt.

Three days later, Sarge Hankins ventured in, hat in hand, to admire the newborn. "Where did you get that?" Serena shrieked, pointing at a cut-glass butterfly stuck in his hatband. A treasured possession of Grandmother Box, the trinket had been claimed by Jadene after grandmother's passing.

Sarge had combed the sandbar for two months, finding nothing but scraps of paper and the remains of a lady's fancy stickpin. Nothing Miss Jady would use, he had concluded, tucking it in his hatband.

* * * * * * * *

Informed of the find, Cohl scratched the hatpin off Marian's list. Jadene's hat hadn't fit right over her graduation hairdo, so she had resorted to using the pin, Miss Copeland had explained.

Jadene Box had come out on that sandbar, all right, but that was three months back. Cohl was in Butte, exploring what he hoped was a fresher lead.

As Cohl unloaded Red, a burly roustabout backed another horse over Cohl's bedroll. It seemed accidental but the man made a show of apologizing and insisted on buying drinks.

"Never pass up a free round," Cohl claimed, agreeing to meet at the White Buffalo that evening.

"Got a game goin' back here," the man beckoned from a back room when Cohl walked in.

Cohl entered the back room, but the man led him right past the poker table, through a passageway and upstairs to a windowless office stacked with papers.

"We playin' stud or draw?" Cohl drawled.

The roustabout grinned and shook his head. "I been advised not to even play Old Maid with you. Name's Harry Bechtold. What do you need in Butte?"

213

"Man named Devlin Burke has a place 'round here, maybe with a gal he calls 'Sweet Candy.' Big man. Canadian. Also answers to Bob Devlin or Dev, and maybe to Robert Glasgow. Might be workin' with Two-Gun Jack Peat," Cohl replied.

"Peat got run out of Montana before I signed on here," Bechtold frowned. "Not likely he'll return. Never heard of Devlin Burke, but I'll ask around. As for Candy, there's a gal by that name working here, been pining for some old lover long as I've known her. I'll have the barman send her to tend the little bar in that back room we came through, you can see if she's your mark."

He led Cohl back downstairs to the poker table. "Ace here's gonna play my hand for a round or two while I check on something," he told the players.

When the dealer turned the cards face up on the third round, Cohl knew they were playing seven-card stud. Hell of a way to get acquainted with four strangers, he thought. It was a low-stakes game, so he deliberately lost that hand and the one he dealt, but easily took the next two small pots. Half-way through the betting on the third hand, a buxom barmaid drifted in, took drink orders, and then stationed herself behind the little bar.

"Harry slip a ringer in on us?" asked the next man up to deal. Cohl shrugged. "Well," the dealer said, "just in case, I'm callin' threes, sixes, and nines wild."

The foursome found that very amusing. Cohl received a three and a nine down and an ace up. He anted, folded, and left the table.

The barmaid, painted to disguise years of hard use, leaned forward on the bar, displaying her assets as Cohl ambled over.

"Back here's where we keep the good stuff," she cooed.

"So I see," he drawled.

She giggled. "Scotch? Rye? Candy?"

214

"Candy?"

"Yeah," she breathed, "I'm Candy."

"Thought you looked real sweet," he fibbed. "Let's start with a shot of rye, water alongside. And one for yourself." He laid a twenty dollar gold piece on the counter, sipped the drink, nodded, and gave her an appraising look. "Been in Butte long?"

"Awhile," she said wistfully, "all my life in Montana."

"You wouldn't happen to be Devlin Burke's Sweet Candy, would you?" he ventured.

The blood drained from her face and she turned, as if to flee. Reaching across the bar, Cohl took hold of her upper arm with his left hand. "You got a room close by where we can talk?" he asked.

"Yes," Candy nodded, trying to pull free, "but I'm workin' now."

"Pay's better in your room," he said, picking up the gold piece and dropping it in her cleavage.

"I'll get in trouble if I leave now," she whispered.

"I'll handle it," Cohl rumbled, leading her around the end of the bar. The men at the table pretended not to notice.

She indicated the corridor, and they went through, past Bechtold's office, up a second flight of stairs, to an attic room. "You're hurtin' my arm," she whimpered.

He released his grip, closed the door and noted the fear in her eyes as she lit the lamp, turning it low.

"What do you want?" she asked, unlacing her bodice.

"No offense," he replied, "but I'm just after information." Her hands stopped, but the fear rose in her eyes. "What do you know about Devlin Burke?" he asked.

"I—I don't know nothin'," she started. "It's been so long. I gave up ever even hearin' his name again.

215

Why are you huntin' him? Can't people ever leave him alone?"

"I'm not exactly hunting him," Cohl said. "He found something I need to get back. Fact is I'll pay well to get it back. Pay you and pay Devlin, too. Pay enough for you to go wherever you want. Someone in Denver said he had a place at Butte."

"If Devlin was here," Candy said, "I'd know it, but he ain't—never came to Butte far as I know. And I'd know." Taking a deep breath, she added, "It's been so long, what I know won't help you."

"Let me judge that," Cohl rumbled. "I'll pay for your time."

"You're sure you're not lookin' to—" she eyed his gun.

"I just want to buy back what he's got," Cohl assured her. "I reckon he's eager to sell—just hasn't found a buyer yet. You help me connect with him, he'll appreciate it."

"I don't see how knowin' what happened ten years ago'll help, but," Candy sank down on the bed, "Devlin's family had a place on the Milk River. There was a terrible fire, and his folks got killed in it, and the law was lookin' for someone to blame, so they locked up Madden—that's his brother—but Devlin broke him out, and they come across the border.

"My folks had a little saloon and café up at Sweetgrass. Minute Devlin walked in, I fell for him. He's the most gorgeous man I ever saw and he's got this wonderful smile, and his laugh, and he can do about anything. Ma and Pa liked him, too. And he liked us. He liked me—a whole lot," she sniffed.

"But then there was Madden. I think he'd probably be almost as handsome as Devlin, but he has these terrible scars on his face, and he was always gettin' in some kind of trouble, and Devlin would bail him out, and that's what ruined everything for Devlin and me," Candy sighed.

216

Prodded by Cohl, she continued, "There was a fight, and Devlin went to pull Madden out and got pulled into it, and he fights like no one you ever saw. He's got the biggest hands I ever seen, and he's got the reach on everyone, and he kicks French-Canadian style, too. When—when it was—when it was over..."

Cohl patted her shoulder. "Someone was dead?" he asked softly.

"Two," she sobbed, "and three others likely were never right again. But it wasn't his fault. It wasn't."

"Was there a trial?" Cohl asked.

Candy nodded. "They were gonna hang him. I couldn't let that happen. I got horses ready, and when I took dinner over from the café I hid a key in it. He said to meet him in Butte. I took my folks' cash box and came here, and I've been waitin' ever since."

"When I find him," Cohl said, "I'll let him know, if you'd like."

She nodded, her face buried in her hands.

Lying on a scarf-draped crate that served as a bureau was a pale rectangle with a heart penciled around the words "Devlin + Candy." Cohl turned it over and saw a fading picture of a fresh pretty girl and a large handsome young man. Taking the picture, he left five twenties, knowing it was too much, and not enough.

When he got to Bechtold's office, he went in and sat in the dark until he heard Candy pass by half-an-hour later, then he lit the lamp and started going through a file drawer marked A-D. It didn't take long to find the yellowing file. The dodgers were old and the drawings didn't do Devlin justice, judging by Candy's picture. Devlin Burke was six-foot-four, Madden, a shade shorter. According to a yellowed news report, Madden had carved up a girl who refused his advances. As the town marshal and the girl's menfolk wrestled Madden into jail, Devlin lit into them. The Burkes wound up locked in the cell, but not before Devlin inflicted mortal injuries on two of them, and left several others permanently incapacitated. A jury sentenced them to hang, but they escaped, leaving the Sweetgrass jailer dead of a crushed neck.

"Why's Ethridge got you on such an old track?" asked Bechtold, when he returned with no additional information.

"A young lady went missing in Idaho in early June," Cohl replied. "We've got reason to think Burke found her."

Scanning the news clippings from his predecessor's file, Bechtold said, "If Madden got her, you gotta reckon she's dead."

"He was wrong side of the river," Cohl said, "It's likely Devlin."

"If there's a girl with Devlin Burke," Bechtold opined, tapping the picture, "she wants to be. Man like that don't have to handle them like you do, Cohl. Hell, he'd make a model for an artist."

* * * * * * * *

Candy came to Cohl's hotel room as he was packing to leave the next morning. Bechtold had let slip that the item Burke had that Cohl wanted was a woman.

Making sure he saw the bruise on her arm, Candy said about what Harry had said, "If your girl's with him, it's 'cause she wants to be. Devlin doesn't have to force girls."

Cohl picked up two telegrams before boarding the southbound Northern. Ethridge warned that the fence Cohl had identified was known to have connections to the cabal. Any message from Denver would likely be a trap. Del Copeland confirmed that the ads had been pulled and Russell Johnston had been paid for finding and shipping Brandy.

* * * * * * * *

The train inched its way up the Rockies, stopping at Melrose, Dillon, Red Rock, and Molinda before the track topped out and dropped into Idaho.

218

At Beaver Canyon, town marshal "Smitty" Smithton had just received a new packet of dodgers from Bingham County Sheriff Ray Wilde, offering rewards for the Burke brothers, Jack Peat and Wolf Zeeb.

Four men matching their descriptions had robbed an army paymaster on the Fort Hall Reservation the previous week. Wilde advised every lawman in Bingham County to be on the alert.

Continuing south to Blackfoot, Cohl called on Sheriff Wilde.

"Jack Peat rode with the Reed gang, back when my pa was the only lawman hereabouts," Wilde recalled. "Last time I seen him was six or so years ago— had him in my jail. It was just one cell in the corner of my old town marshal office back then. Had a nice old man, Linus Gormley, as my helper at the time. My sister came in, needing help talking to someone—she's deaf so some folks have trouble understanding her. When I got back to my office, Peat was gone and Mr. Gormley was dead—someone'd wrung his neck like you would a chicken."

"Same as Devlin Burke did to the Sweetgrass jailer," Cohl said.

"Sounds like it," Wilde agreed. "Next I heard, Wyoming had Peat and the three others in the lock-up. Last two summers and into the fall, it seemed like every big payload that moved around here got hit by two big Canadians and a scruffy little southerner. Sure enough, Wyoming'd turned the Burkes and Zeeb loose. Only arrest we made was Merle Oswald—a horse from one of the holdups turned up over to his place outside American Falls. We got him for receiving stolen property."

"Where do I find him?" Cohl asked.

"Downstairs," Wilde pointed, "Ozzie's in the cell on the left. Swears he bought the horse legal from a Canadian named Bob. Claims he didn't have any sale papers because he can't read. You try talking to him—

he doesn't give me anything—been a guest of ours before. I'll finish up here and we can go talk somewhere private."

* * * * * * * *

Neither the offer of a cigar nor twenty dollars coaxed more than a grunt out of Oswald.

"You don't know a damn thing," Cohl taunted.

"That's what I been tellin' the law," Ozzie whined. "My ranch is goin' to pot, me sittin' here. Tell that damn Wilde to lemme out."

"If I get you out," Cohl offered, "will you show me Bob Devlin's hideout?"

"I cain't show you what I don't know," Oswald grumbled. "I'm a inner-cent man, jus' traded hosses with a stranger, not knowin' nuttin 'bout nuttin."

"What did this stranger look like?" Cohl probed.

"I don't remember—jus' big, that's all I know an' I ain't sayin' no more less'n you get me out," the prisoner declared.

"You'll have more to tell me if I get you out?" Cohl asked.

"Told you I don't know nuttin'," Ozzie sulked.

"Then I've no reason to get you out, have I?" Cohl ambled toward the stairway, hoping that Oswald would call out to stop him with an offer of information, but the man remained silent.

* * * * * * * *

The sheriff was saddling his horse when Cohl went to collect Red.

"Last fall," Wilde confided, "we set up a trap for them—leaked word about a big payroll coming through—but they'd left the country."

"Sounds like you had another kind of leak," Cohl observed.

"Sometimes I think the walls have ears," Wilde agreed, "but we can talk freely at my ranch out on Lincoln Creek. The rangeland's leased to my neighbor

220

so I don't keep a crew. Only soul around is my sister, and she can't hear a blessed thing."

As they rode, Cohl told about the disappearance of Jadene Box. Wilde had neither seen nor heard anything that might be relevant, but promised to keep silent and watchful.

When they turned off the main road, Wilde tugged on a light rope that ran along the lane. "Have to give Mattie fair warning," he explained, "this raises a flag at the house so I don't startle her."

Miss Wilde shyly slipped into her room as the men entered. Cohl heard a bolt turn after she closed the door behind herself. In Ray's den every lamp was burning brightly and a pot of fresh coffee and a plate of warm scones awaited the lawmen.

"Mattie's a little odd, but she takes wonderful care of me," Wilde said.

"What's the layout?" Cohl asked as he accepted coffee and a scone.

Pointing to a map on the wall, Wilde explained, "Dang county runs clean from the Montana line almost to Utah. To get enough people to qualify to be a separate county a couple years ago, the powers that be had to take a big chunk from Oneida as well as Alturas. It's hell for a lawman to cover." He eyed the slim gunman speculatively. "You ever wear a badge, Cohl?"

"Time to time," Cohl allowed, "I need to keep on this track just now."

"Then you need that badge," Wilde said. "Expect you heard about the Webster murder—that was the Burkes and Zeeb. Then nothing from them all summer until this paymaster heist—them again plus Peat. We've got a mine payroll coming through next week. I'll be surprised if they don't try for it."

"Any idea where they hole up?" Cohl asked.

"Thought we had them a couple times hereabouts," Wilde indicated an area called Three

Buttes. "But they vanished into thin air, then popped back up for another hit."

"Hmmm. Could be Burke's hideout is in a butte, not at Butte. I'll have a look around," the gunman declared.

"Not without this," Wilde replied, fishing a deputy's badge out of a cubbyhole in a roll-top desk below a large mirror.

Cohl allowed Wilde to swear him in, and pinned the badge to the lining of his jacket without showing Wilde the badge he already wore inside his black leather vest. "Not a word to anyone," he warned.

"You've got my word on that, Cohl," the sheriff said.

CHAPTER 11

"They shall mount up with wings as eagles,"[23] the girl whispered, although the birds circling below her definitely were not eagles.

From atop Pillar Butte, she scanned the wasteland of sand and broken lava that seemed to stretch endlessly in every direction. Just as the vultures searched for death, she searched for some sign of life, but with less success.

She eased a slim leather case from her shirt pocket and sat down, drew her knees up to her chin and wrapped her thin arms around her equally thin legs.

The case held two sepia-tone photographs. One picture showed a soft-featured girl with dark curls. "What did I pray for, Marian? What did I pray for that you warned me against?" she asked, neither expecting nor receiving an answer.

The second picture was of a tall man with light hair—her brother, she thought. His flashy outfit, tooled gunbelt and engraved Colt revolver suggested a performer in a Wild West show, not an outlaw, yet she remembered rescuing him from a gallows.

She sat in the sunlight atop the butte, going over the shards of memories that had kept her company since she first awoke, crumpled in the crevice between the bed and the stone wall of the tiny cabin at the bottom of the hollow core of the butte.

Fearing she had been buried alive, she had cried out, "Deliver me, Oh my God."[24]

---

[23] Isaiah 40:31

Instantly, she had heard her father's voice singing, *"Fear not, I am with thee, O be not dismayed,"*[25] but when she inched her way out of the crevice, she was alone.

She had crawled to the door, looked out and found herself surrounded by soaring sandstone cliffs that formed a hidden hole within the butte. *"Stone walls do not a prison make..."* she had groped for more of the poem, but found only a fragment, *"...a hermitage."*[26] She adopted the word as a name for the place in which she found herself.

When she had first spied the corral, she had instinctively nickered like a mare calling its foal—calling the buckskin colt she remembered in every detail—but Dustdevil had not come to hug her with his neck.

And then she remembered the outlaw, Devlin Burke, laughing and saying she rode a buckskin horse only in her dreams. Why, she wondered, could she recall Burke's name, but not her own or her father's? She recalled Pa calling her Baby, and Burke calling her Em, but neither man answered when she cried out.

"He leadeth me beside the still water,"[27] she had murmured when she found the cool spring beside the corral. She had lowered herself to drink, then used the remains of a bucket as a wash basin, to clean herself of vomit and excrement, taking care not to foul the spring.

She had recognized the putrid bandages she peeled from her arm and shaven head as the remains of an embroidered petticoat.

"Pray for me, Marian," she sighed. "Morning and night and in between."

Those early days she slept more than she was awake, often dozing off beside the spring and waking only long enough to drink.

---

[24] Psalm 59:1
[25] Isaiah 41:40 also the hymn *How Firm a Foundation*
[26] *To Althea, from Prison* poem by Richard Lovelace, 1642
[27] Psalm 23:2b

In the following days, she gritted her teeth against the agony that punished every movement, yet she drove herself to explore her tiny world and the small bundle that seemed to hold all her worldly possessions. She set aside an odd brown garment with legs as wide as skirts, a matching bolero jacket and a high-necked lace-trimmed white bodice, but rejoiced upon finding an embroidered, polished cotton reticule.

"Why, Marian made this for me!" she had exclaimed. Unknotting the lavender ribbon that held the reticule closed, she found a small sewing kit and various toiletry items, including a tiny jar of acrid-smelling black salve. Massaging the soothing salve into the wound behind her left ear, she had worked loose what appeared to be the remnants of thread, as if someone had sewn her scalp together.

Her first meal had been a handful of cornmeal mixed with water and set in the sunlight that briefly reached the floor of the hermitage. When the sun moved on, she bowed her head and whispered, "*Thou preparest a table before me,*"[28] and gratefully slurped down the barely warm under-cooked porridge.

When she had looked up, a stray sunbeam glinted off a pile of rusty cans and shattered bottles at the base of the canyon wall opposite the cabin door. The next day, she had focused the brief sunlight through the convex bottom of a broken whiskey bottle onto a pile of dry leaves and soon had a cook fire going.

Among her few possessions was a poor-quality folding knife with a small cutting blade and an odd hook. "For opening cans," she had murmured. "Not much of a knife, but Pa carried it 'cause it was a gift from me." She had searched for, but never found the two better-quality knives her father had also carried.

She had tried to open one of the few tin cans of food she found in the cabin, but ten days passed before she was able to exert enough force to punch even a small hole. She had sucked out the liquid and

---

[28] Psalm 23:5

eventually enlarged the hole enough to shake out the beans, one by one. She had eagerly gobbled them up.

She had carefully removed enough of the decorative embroidery thread from her reticule to fashion a snare which she set in a rabbit trail leading to the spring. When the snare yielded a young jackrabbit, she had cried, "A gift from God!" When neither her arm nor the knife proved up to gutting and skinning her "gift," she burned off the fur, roasted the hare whole, and consumed it hungrily.

As the weeks turned to months, she had ventured outside the hermitage from time to time, to explore the dangerous territory beyond. Scaling the butte the first time had nearly turned her into buzzard bait, twice over. First, because she had slipped and nearly fallen. Second, because, the lake-like shimmer she had seen to the west had lured her into the scorching Snake River Desert.

Pursuing the lake that was a mirage, she had been struck down by what she came to call a "blind headache." It started with blank spots in her vision, exploded like dynamite within her skull and drove her to her knees in pain. She had pounded her head in the sand as great ugly birds brushed her with their wings, lifted off and circled, eager for her to stop moving.

She had choked out words: *"My God, my God, why have you forsaken me?"*[29]

The fury of a dustdevil had answered. Whether it was real or a memory from when she and Pa rescued a newborn foal—the Dustdevil of her clearest memories—she did not know. The whirling sand swept the buzzards away and she plunged into blackness.

She had revived, shivering in the cold of the desert night. The migraine had passed, leaving her physically drained but with clear vision. Stumbling and crawling, she had turned back to the butte that towered black against the starry sky. At dawn she had found

---

[29] Matthew 27:46

the hidden entrance and collapsed beside the spring, safe within her hermitage.

Scaling the butte came easy now, thanks in part to hand and footholds she had scraped out. Piecing her memory together was still tortuous.

What was true? What imagined? She did not know. Burke had claimed to have rescued her and doctored her injuries, yet she also had a horrid memory of him attacking her. Her memories of Pa—"Call him the Captain!"—were equally jumbled. Mentally she grasped at a comforting shard of memory—they were singing as they rode stirrup-to-stirrup—*"It is well"*—only to be stabbed by the memory of finding him lying dead. Worse yet were the nightmares in which he attacked her as Burke had. She squeezed a trigger and felt again the spatter of brains on her face. Had she killed them both? Was that why she was alone? Why no one came seeking her?

She had scratched a line in the sandstone wall beside the cabin door that first day—low on the wall because her shoulder screamed when she tried to raise her arm. As the days passed, the lines formed an arc, not unlike a horse's arched neck, as she forced herself to reach higher and higher. The arc now stretched above her head, but she was still alone with her broken brain. Nothing *was* well.

She put away the fading sepia-tones, stood, stretched, and began working her way back down the butte. An hour later she reached the hidden entry to the hermitage.

The tracks of two shod horses were clear in the sand. Fear mixed with hope as she peered through the concealing brush. Two brown horses stood beside the cabin door. The larger one wore Burke's saddle, with a rifle in its scabbard. The other carried an empty pack saddle.

She eyed the saddled horse covetously, wondering whether she could leap atop it and gallop away, and where she should go if she did.

When she stepped clear of the brush, the man spoke from within the cabin. "Figured you was aboot." Burke flashed a disarming smile as he stepped out, but her last memory of him clicked in hard and clear. "Expect you're right pleased to see me, eh," he grinned.

"Not hardly," she gritted. "Last I remember, you were trying to force yourself on me."

"Eh? Your head's broke for sure," he declared. "I never have to force no gal, but big as I am and little as you are, if I tried I'd sure as hell get the job done, eh."

"I-I jabbed you in the ear," she said uncertainly.

He laughed. "Only way that'd stop a man is if you jabbed with a gun and tripped the trigger, eh. Mebbe you're recollectin' somethin' from afore I pulled you outta the Snake, eh, and puttin' it to me 'cause you don't remember no one else. I swear, Emma, I left you sleepin' like a baby right there on the bed, eh."

"I woke up on the floor behind the bed—head feelin' like it was split open—thought I'd been buried alive," she said.

"Must a rolled off, eh," he suggested, shoving the bed tight against the wall. "Looks like you're gettin' around right fine, eh, 'cept your memory's sure enough broke all to hell."

"Have you found out who I am?" she asked.

Burke had learned nothing, but that did not keep him from answering at length. "Your pappy was a kill-for-pay gunman, eh, got hisself shot all to hell by a posse. Them tin stars was dumb enough to turn their backs on you," the outlaw lied.

"Law don't know enough to put out a dodger anybody'd know you by," he added. "Reckon you'd best keep on answerin' to Em, eh."

Em. Emma. Well, she certainly was not going to ask him to call her Baby.

Once the horses were in the corral, Burke looked at Em appraisingly. "You got to where you're good for anything?"

"Lot's of things," she allowed. "I'm good at figurin' out how to do whatever needs doin'. I've been livin' mostly on jackrabbits I catch in a snare. I cook them over a fire I start with the bottom of a broken bottle when the sun comes down."

"Must not be much good with that snare," he sneered. "You're down to skin over bone, eh."

"Can't catch what's not there to catch," she shrugged. "Can't fix what's not there to fix, but I sorta recollect Grandmother teachin' me to cook—just need some fixin's."

"Oughta be somethin' there you can cook up, eh," he indicated a pile of supplies beside the bed.

Em sorted through the stack, which ranged from a set of sheets to a fifty-pound bag of dried pinto beans. "I'll put some beans to soak, but they won't be ready to eat until suppertime tomorrow," she said.

"What else you got?" he demanded.

"Don't you know what you bought?" she asked.

"Hell, I didn't buy nothin' but this, eh," he said, hefting a bottle of whiskey.

Em set aside a bag of apples, a few cans of peaches, a rope of sausages and some cast iron cookware, then picked out flour, lard, salt and baking powder.

"Wonder how biscuits will turn out, made with water instead of buttermilk," she mused. She put the Dutch oven on the fire to heat.

Once the biscuits were baking, she slit open several sausages, broke the meat apart in the skillet as it fried, and added water and flour.

Burke ate the biscuits and gravy enthusiastically. "Grandmother taught you good," he admitted. "But, I got no use for a cook, eh."

"Point me toward the nearest ranch or café where I might find work. I'll walk away and won't be a bother to you ever again," she offered.

229

His laugh sent a chill up her spine. "Hell, Em, when you an' me part ways, you won't be walkin' or talkin' any which-a-way."

She turned his words over in her mind, trying to make them mean something other than what they clearly meant. "You mean you will kill me?"

"Depends," he shrugged. "Got a feelin' you might be worth somethin'—been a helluva disappointment up to now, eh."

He considered a moment, then rummaged in his saddlebag and pulled out a tightly coiled gunbelt. Em's heart leapt when she recognized her revolver.

"See if you can make yerself useful with this," he said. "Last time I give you a chance, you couldn't hit a post at ten feet, eh. Set up a target across the way and show me what you can do now, eh."

Once she had the target set, he pulled a big .44-40 Smith and Wesson Single Action Frontier from his saddlebag and aimed it at her before handing her the holstered .32-20. The belt, unoiled since its bath in the river, was stiff and ill-fitting, but the gun itself had been cleaned, and the cylinder spun smoothly. As Em loaded it, she pictured the speed and smoothness of her draw and the sureness of her aim.

She made several draws without firing, testing the action of her arm under the weight of the small pistol. The contrast between her memory and how she actually moved was as sharp as the contrast between the music she heard in her head and what came out of her mouth when she attempted to sing.

The gun hung up in the holster, making for an awkward draw. Her first shot barely jiggled the can, and a twinge in her shoulder said she wasn't as healed up as she'd hoped. She drew and fired twice more—slowly, clumsily, with worsening results.

"Reckon it'll take time," she said, settling the gun back in the holster. "The belt needs oil. Think my shoulder does, too."

When she started to turn to face Burke, his huge hand clamped down on her shoulder painfully and he pawed her gun from its holster. "Hell," he said, "you ain't even as good as me, eh."

But he didn't object when she found some saddle soap and Neatsfoot oil among the supplies. While she cleaned and oiled the leather, he removed the shells from the little gun, tossed the spent casings into an old can and pocketed the live rounds.

Em oiled the rig twice, then buckled it on and stepped outside. Burke handed her the gun and six shells. He filled the doorway, the whiskey bottle in his left hand, his right poised to snap her neck.

The .32-20 no longer hung up in the holster and her arm moved more smoothly each time she drew. She fired all six shots, but only the last two creased the can.

"The pack's gonna eat you alive, eh," he sneered.

"The pack?" she puzzled.

"Jack Peat—he's my partner—boss, he'd say, but he ain't. Then there's Madden, my damn fool kid brother, and that bastard, Wolf Zeeb, eh," Burke replied.

"They won't like me?" she asked.

"Like you? Peat's real p'tic'lar aboot dames—sure as hell won't have one along on the trail, eh. Madden'll want to cut you up, ain't but one gal he fancies and she ain't real partial to him, eh. Wolf, now, he never met any gal he didn't fancy. Even ugly as you are, you'll give him a ride or he'll shove a stick of dynamite up your ass, eh."

"You won't let them—" Em cried.

"'Cause you cook good?" he laughed. "What else you gonna do for me?"

"My shooting arm is coming back," she said. "I just need a little time."

"The pack won't give you no time, eh," Burke sneered. "Jack's shootin' like he never been away, eh. You bein' a girl, he'll be on the prod to dump you."

231

"Stand up to him! Show everyone you're as much the boss as he is," she urged. "You're the only boss as far as I'm concerned."

"Hell, I own you, eh," he challenged. "You want me to keep you around, you gotta make yourself useful."

"I will!" she cried. "Tell me what needs doin' and I'll do it."

"You'd drop a lawman for me, eh?"

For a moment, a broken shard of memory came clear and she saw again, as if from a distance, a rage-filled man who wore a badge—the lawman drew his gun and eared back the hammer—she was running but she could not get there in time—a kindly white-haired man fell—she could not recall who he had been, but the man who fired back was the tall blond bronc rider of her photograph—her brother.

"Well?" Devlin Burke demanded again. "Will you drop a lawman, I say so?"

"Yeah," she gritted, with a slow nod. "Anytime you say it needs doin'."

"Suppose I say to drop your drawers, eh?"

She mixed a nod and a shrug. "Big and handsome as you are, Boss, you don't really want ugly little me to, uh, drop my, uh, my drawers, do you?"

He laughed. "Not likely, but if I tell you to take care of Wolf, you do it, eh."

Again, she nodded slowly. "You want him taken care of, Boss," her hand caressed the butt of her gun, "you just say so—I'll drop him real quick."

He laughed again. "That ain't what I meant."

She shrugged. "Well, that's how I do it."

"And if I tell you to drop them drawers for me, eh?"

"You're the boss, Boss, reckon if you're that hard up..." her voice trailed off.

CHAPTER 12

As Jack Peat, Wolf Zeeb, and Madden Burke came through the slit three days later, they heard carefully spaced gunfire.

"Why's Dev practicin' when he's got us, eh?" Madden jeered.

"It's not Devlin." Wolf was in the lead and the first to see the tiny shooter in rumpled canvas jeans and a chambray shirt. The boy was bare-headed, showing a short mop of light brown hair.

A look of loathing settled over Madden's face at first sight of the scrawny youth.

"This here's Emmett," Devlin announced, "Wants to lend us a hand, don't you, Em?"

Em shrugged.

The one wearing a double-gun rig indicated the .32-20 and asked, "You any good with that, son?"

"I'm not your son, Mr. Peat," Em glowered. "Been laid up awhile, but it's comin' back. Just need a little practice."

"Where'd you get this piece a crap?" Madden sneered.

"Fished Emmett outta the Snake," Devlin laughed. "Got kicked in the head and don't remember much, eh. Been healin' up while we was busy."

Peat's eyes narrowed as he studied the small shootist. A quick draw holster rode on Emmett's hip and the kid's waist belt sported a slotted metal plate. "Where the hell'd you get a Bridgeport rig?"

"Emmett came with it, eh," Burke grinned. "Got it from his pappy."

233

"You know how to use that, son?"

Em nodded. "Ah handle th' Bridgeport jus' fine," she gritted in a pure Texas drawl. "Keep callin' me 'son,' ah'll show yuh how fine."

"Mouthy pup," Peat growled, "Who's your old man that he give you a rig like that?"

"Was," Em corrected. "Rig got to be mine after Pa got killed."

"Your pa had a name?"

"Expect he did," Em said, "but ah can't recollect it—can't even recollect muh own. Got kicked in the head, like the boss said. Would've drowned if the boss hadn't come along."

"Devlin ain't the boss," Peat objected.

"My boss," Em said.

Peat thought on that, then asked, "If you don't recollect your own name, how'd Devlin come to call you Emmett?"

"Got it off somethin' he had on him, eh," Devlin answered.

"What'd your pa call you?" Peat asked.

"Nothin' ah want yuh callin' me," Em gritted.

"Son," Peat smirked. "Yuh don't recollect what folks called him?"

Em shrugged, "Cap, I think. Cap'n."

"Cap'n!" Zeeb whooped, nearly dropping his cigar. "Bet he was a unreconstructed rebel, same as my old man."

Em wasn't sure what that meant.

"That damn Lee give up, but the South will rise again—" Zeeb paused to send a series of smoke rings skyward. "Rise like thet bluecoat paymaster with a stick o' dye-no-mite up his rear."

"Ridin' through Hell," Em muttered.

* * * * * * * *

234

Madden howled when Zeeb snagged the last biscuit and used it to wipe out the bean pot.

"Next time, make more, son," Peat ordered, "I still got a hole in my belly."

"You keep callin' me 'son,' there won't be no next time," Em warned.

"Mouthy pup," Peat repeated, as the kid retreated into the cabin.

"Be fun to cut his tongue out, eh," Madden offered, pulling a knife.

Em returned with a peach cobbler. Peat grabbed it and scooped a quarter of the dessert onto his plate. Madden used his knife to claim an equally generous share.

"Hey," Devlin yelled. "Quit hoggin', eh." He grabbed the pan and sat down, eating directly from it. Wolf edged over and managed to scoop a small portion onto his plate.

Em shrugged and ate an apple, then scrubbed the cast iron pots with sand and scalded her plate and eating utensils in boiling water.

"Ranch trained, eh," Devlin shrugged.

He leaned back, rolled a smoke and passed the makings around.

"I was by Perry's earlier," Peat said as he built a cigarette, "You know someone calls hisself Iceman?"

"Should I?" Devlin asked.

"He bought a hoss from Les. Asked after Bob Devlin and knew the name Pete Jackson so it must be from a ways back since I ain't used that handle in five-six years," the gunman replied. "Dark face but light eyes. A sliver of a man with a Schofield planted on his hip. A shootist, Les figured. Don't ring no bells with me."

"Me neither," Devlin rumbled. He instantly recalled naming Pete Jackson on Little Bay's sale papers, but wasn't about to mention that slip-up to

Jack Peat for the same reason Perry hadn't. "Perry give him anything, eh?"

"Said not. Seemed kinda eager to talk to you. Iceman asked if you was back from Denver and said he'd pay extry the sooner Perry aimed him at you," Peat replied.

"Iceman," Em echoed softly.

"What'd you say, Piece-a-crap?" Madden demanded.

"Nothin' to you, Madman," Em growled. "But hot as it is, ah'd welcome an iceman."

When Devlin headed for the corral, Em followed.

"May I go with you, Boss?" she asked, as he started saddling up.

"Hell, no," he grinned.

"Then may I have some shells so I can practice?"

Burke laughed and counted out six. "Don't kill no one 'fore I get back, eh."

She nodded, but said nothing.

As Devlin rode away, Em silently calculated: Three men—six shells.

In the preceding days she had found that she could shoot fast and straight using the Bridgeport belt, just tipping the gun up with the belt supporting the revolver's weight, but her accuracy plunged when she switched to her holster.

Her speed had impressed Burke, but her hand seemed disappointingly slow to her and the voice in her head coached, "Speed doesn't count for anything, if you cannot hit your target."

Ignoring the pack, she practiced drawing the .32-20 from the holster, just drawing and pointing, retraining her body to the movement, but not firing—not wasting her few precious shells. The kink in her right shoulder slowly unkinked until, at last, her gun rose smoothly and her grip held firm.

Shooting light would soon be gone. Could she down the likes of Jack Peat, Madden Burke and Wolf Zeeb with just six shots? Not likely, even if they just sat there and let her—which they wouldn't.

Devlin Burke would be suspicious if she didn't burn any of the shells she had begged for.

Em picked a target, drew and fired. The shot took the seed cluster off the top of a dried sourdock stalk beside the trash heap.

A snort of derision sounded behind her. Peat, supposing she was aiming at a can several feet to the right of the weed, swiftly drew his left gun and drilled the can, chasing it with lead as the shots sent it skittering through the weeds. Without pause, he shifted to his right gun, continuing the display.

"Damn, Two-Gun," Wolf drawled, "Doin' time shore didn't hurt yer aim none."

Peat scooped up the ragged remains of the can and sailed it toward Em. "That's how it's done, son," he taunted.

"Told yuh, ah'm not yer son, Mr. Peat," Em brought her .32-20 around in a steady two-handed grip, to center on the sour-faced outlaw. "Thet was right purdy shootin', but yuh'd be dead now, 'cause yore double empty an' ah've got five ready to burn."

The blood drained from Jack Peat's face as he hurriedly reloaded. "You got me there, Emmett," he admitted. "I know better. Guess I thought I was among friends."

"Yore lucky, Mr. Peat," Em gritted, "Boss said not to kill no one 'fore he gets back."

"I told you, Devlin's not the boss," Peat objected.

"My boss," Em declared, her gun still leveled at him. "Said yore his partner. Ah suggest yuh play it thet-a-way."

"You play poker, Emmett?" Wolf asked.

"Not thet ah recollect," she growled.

Em continued working with the gun until the last vestige of light was gone. She fired two more shots. Both hit where she aimed.

The men were still playing cards by lantern light and passing around a bottle when she retired to the bed in the cabin. She slept fully clothed, her back to the wall, her gun in her hand.

* * * * * * * *

When Devlin returned late the next morning, Madden whined, "Piece-a-crap hogged the bed. Cabin here's too tight for all a us, Dev. Let's go back up to Three Buttes, eh, it's bigger 'n' better."

"Time we was workin' our way south," Devlin replied. "Maybe winter in Mexico, eh." Giving Peat a hard look, he jibed, "Your friend from Perry's pocketed a badge yesterday. Sheriff called him Cole."

"Your friend," Peat replied. "Hell, south is good. Reckon we about cleaned out this end of Idaho, anyhow."

"Except for a mine payroll they figure to trap us with," Devlin agreed.

* * * * * * * *

Em didn't complain when Devlin pointed to the pack horse and ordered, "Git on," nor did she ask for help mounting. With the leadline looped to form makeshift reins, she led the beast to the rail and climbed the corral fence. "Settin' all catawampus," she murmured, as she eased herself atop the load.

Although straddling the pack was not comfortable, she figured no one was interested in assuring her comfort. "Do what needs doin'," she murmured. The horse was inclined to follow the others, so she didn't really miss having the control provided by a bit and stirrups—at least not until they reached the Snake River.

The men knew of a safe ford and rode in without hesitation and the pack animal followed. Panic-stricken, Em clung to the ropes that held the pack in place.

"Oh, Lord," she murmured, and the same words she had sung when last she had crossed the Snake flowed through her consciousness and washed away her fear:

"*When through the deep waters I call you to go, the rivers of sorrow shall not overflow, for I will be with thee, thy troubles to bless, and sanctify to thee, thy deepest distress.*"[30]

* * * * * * * *

From a small rise, late that afternoon, they viewed a ragtag homestead.

"Damn country's fillin' up," Peat growled. "People and fences and lawdogs."

"We'll be long gone b'fore them lawdogs figger out we didn't fall for their trap, eh," Devlin grinned.

"Be gone a lot farther, eh, if we didn't have Piece-a-crap slowin' us down," Madden groused.

Em watched the sodbuster below. The man was plowing with a mismatched pair of draft horses. Closer to the house, a rough corral held a band of mustangs.

"If wishes were horses," she sighed, eyeing them longingly.

"Emmett, let's get you a horse and saddle," Peat offered.

Em looked hopefully at Devlin. "Gimme your rig," he ordered. "A kid packin' a sidearm'll get folks talkin', b'sides, Jack shoots good enough for two, comes to that. Don't do nothin' that'll catch that manhunter's eye, eh."

"Yes, sir, Boss," Em nodded. She handed over her holstered revolver.

Peat kneed his mount close to the pack horse and Em shifted onto his gelding's rump, taking care not

---

[30] How Firm a Foundation, verse 3

to touch the man. "I'll do the talkin'—say I'm your uncle," Peat said, as the Burkes and Zeeb rode on.

Galen Wicker left his team when a man and boy rode in double. He and Peat drifted away behind the low barn as they talked. Em eyed the covey of broom-tails in the pole corral.

Two ragged little girls left off cleaning a water trough and moseyed over.

"I'm Carrie," the older one said. She was about eleven, with a hungry-for-company look. "This is my sister, Mary."

Em nodded and continued to study the ponies.

"What's your name?" Carrie pressed.

"Emmett," Em replied. She slipped through the corral bars.

"Them's awful wild," Mary warned.

"Come outta there, Emmett," Carrie pleaded.

Em ignored the girls. Moving confidently among the mustangs, she calmly appraised their conformation and temperaments. Several had potential, she thought. One in particular reminded her of the buckskin that pranced in her head, though this animal was an unusual dappled brown. He was small but stocky, well-muscled and the only one in the covey that had been gelded.

She rubbed his withers, felt him relax into her hands, and continued working over his body, hand-grooming him. He lifted each hoof readily, letting her tuck it between her knees and keep it until she was done cleaning with her jackknife.

Peat and Mr. Wicker returned leading a long-backed, hammer-headed sorrel packing a shabby slickfork saddle that likely outweighed Em.

"Git over here, boy," Peat ordered. "This is all he's got that's broke."

Em eyed the beast distastefully. "One of these ponies'll suit me better," she said.

"Mustangs off the range," the owner sneered. "Sell 'em for dog meat."

"How much?" Em demanded.

"We don't have time to break a horse," Peat growled.

Both girls were biting their lips. "This your horse and saddle?" Em asked.

The girls nodded sorrowfully, but their father cut them off. "Them brats don't need no horse. Get back to work, slackers."

"Mount up," Peat ordered.

"I'll take the McClellan," Em said, pointing at the remains of a cavalry saddle hanging on the side of the barn, "and that pony." She pointed at the gelding with the curious ears.

"Baddest of the lot," the owner jeered. "Fella I got him off called him Trouble. He'll throw you clean to hell, bet me."

Em nodded, turning to hide the grin that tugged at the corner of her mouth. It was as she thought. The gelding wasn't raw from the range. He had been handled before and there was a look in his eye she recognized.

"Critter'll fool yuh on the ground," Wicker was telling Peat, "but when yuh get aboard he explodes. Took top horse money at more'n one buckin' contest b'fore he turned killer. No one 'round here'll get on him no more."

Leading Trouble by a handful of mane, Em put him in a broken-down corral and was pleased when he stayed although one section had only its bottom rail remaining. She helped herself to the best bridle and blanket in Wicker's small collection of tack, and settled the worn McClellan on the dappled back. The stirrup leathers were bad, but they were so long she had to double them to get the stirrups high enough for her short legs. That also doubled the chances that they would hold up to use, at least for a time.

241

Trouble stood calmly as she cinched, and he readily took the bit. Free-lounging the gelding, Em turned him right and left, whoaed him, and tested her weight in one stirrup and then the other.

"Okay, here's the bet," she announced. "I ride him, he's mine. I don't, uncle pays for the sorrel but doesn't take it, 'cause it won't be needed."

"Kid's gonna get hisself killed," Wicker warned. Peat shrugged.

Em swung fluidly into the saddle and immediately began working the mustang in tight circles and figure-eights. She asked for a trot with a soft nudge of her knees and instantly got it, slowed him back to a walk, signaled for a canter and jumped the gelding over the single rail. She rode a circle around the barnyard, brought Trouble back to a walk, turned and made a wider circle at a smooth lope.

Stopping in front of the astonished owner, she drawled, "Trouble tells me he don' like spurs or quirts or cursin'. We'll get on jus' fine, an' ah thank yuh for him."

"That's a hundred-dollar horse," Wicker blurted.

"He didn't throw me anywheres near Hell," Em drawled, "but ah reckon uncle has a fiver for th' tack, an' mebbe an extry dollar or so if yuh put shoes on 'im."

* * * * * * * *

Trouble easily kept pace when Peat jigged his significantly longer-legged mount into a lope. Em kept her pony's nose even with the outlaw's stirrup until they were out of sight of the Wickers, then she quit holding Trouble back. A mile or so later, she pulled up in the shade of a locust tree to wait. She wondered if she had made a mistake. Jack Peat was clearly not a good man to anger. But when he rode up on his lathered beast, Em was surprised to see what passed for a smile on the gunman's face.

"Let's not mention this, Emmett," he said.

"Ah don' keep secrets from muh boss," she said.

"Tell Dev if you like, on the quiet," Peat said, "but Mad likes bettin', and I like takin' that damn fool's money. Deal?"

Em considered that. "Deal, Mr. Peat," she nodded. "Jus' among friends."

True to her word, she kept her mouth shut, although the other three outlaws made disparaging remarks about the little horse when she and Peat rode into camp that evening.

"Piece-a-crap on a piece a crap," Madden jeered as they saddled the next morning. "Gonna hold us back. Thought you was smarter'n that, Two-Gun."

"Emmett's real light," Peat shrugged, "I bet he keeps up better'n you do."

"Bet?" Madden's eyes narrowed. "Fifty bucks says I leave him behind before we cross the Utah line, eh."

"Fifty's kind of steep," Jack sounded regretful, "and you're talkin' a good three-mile run. What kind of odds you offerin'?"

"Five to one," Madden crowed.

"So it only costs me ten if Emmett loses, but I collect fifty if you're behind?" Jack mused, "Guess I can spare that."

Em was just swinging into her saddle when Madden spurred his mount. He was six lengths ahead before Trouble stretched out. The others hit their saddles and joined the race. The dappled mustang pulled even with Madden's horse within a quarter mile. Once Trouble took the lead, the others saw nothing but his tail.

Not knowing where the border was, Em leaned forward and let Trouble fly until she heard two gunshots. Looking back, she saw the men had stopped. Peat had fired in the air to signal her, but Devlin was off his horse, rifle in hand, drawing a bead on her.

She instantly whirled Trouble and shouted, "Victory!" As she loped back, the word sparked a broken

243

memory of another song, "*vict'ry unto vict'ry—*" She struggled to conjure up more of the words with dangerous success.

Peat had been laughing aloud as Mad angrily paid off the bet, but his face darkened when Emmett rode up singing, "*From vict'ry unto vict'ry His army shall He lead, til ev'ry foe is vanquished and Christ is Lord indeed—*"[31]

"What the hell!" Peat roared. His left gun came up incredibly fast and Em saw it lining up on her. She bumped Trouble sharply and the mustang jumped sideways. Em heard the click of the shell tumbling in the air as it passed her ear.

Devlin grabbed Peat's arm but Madden attempted to wrestle his brother away, shouting, "Let 'im go, Dev! Let 'im shoot Piece-a-crap."

Devlin downed his brother with a sideways kick and wrapped Peat in a bear hug.

"Why's he tryin' to shoot me?" Em puzzled.

Devlin laughed, while still holding onto Peat. "Hell, Emmett, Two-Gun ain't gonna stand for that singin', eh."

"I sing bad enough to make Mr. Peat want to kill me?"

"Aboot," Devlin laughed.

"I don't give a damn how you sound," Peat raged, "but you sing out with that crap again, Dev won't move fast enough to save you, y'hear?"

"It-it's a victory song, Mr. Peat," Em stammered. "I won so you won—vict'ry unto vict'ry—I'm havin' trouble recollectin' all the words."

"Hell, Two-Gun," Devlin said, "Emmett got stuck in one of them church orphan homes while his pa was doin' time, eh. His brain bein' broke, half the time he don't know what he's sayin'."

---

[31] *Stand Up, Stand Up for Jesus*, hymn by Reverend Dudley A. Tyng, 1858

Devlin cautiously released his hold on his reluctant partner.

Peat shook himself. "Damn places, them orphan homes," he muttered. "But I ain't gonna put up with no damned preachin', Emmett. I shore as hell ain't."

Em nodded soberly. Keeping the strange words that rattled in her head from tumbling out her mouth would be an added challenge on top of the life-or-death game of keeping the pack thinking she was a he.

Fortunately, Devlin—who spun lies quicker than most folks could spit out the truth—was her ally in the deception and was obviously enjoying fooling the others.

When the men paused to relieve themselves, he said, "Ride off a piece, if you gotta, Emmett." To Peat he added, "Kid can't pee if anyone's watching."

"Piece a crap, like I said, eh," Madden sneered.

"You ain't the first to have that problem, son," Peat said. "You'll outgrow it in time. We ain't gonna wait, but you'll catch up easy enough."

As Em disappeared into a thicket, Devlin called, "Don't you dawdle, eh."

"*Dawdle*"—the word rang familiarly in her ears.

Actually, she continually gave thought to doing more than dawdle. She imagined Trouble could outrun and outlast the men's larger mounts, but she had no answer for the question that echoed in her head: *Whither shall I flee?*[32]

* * * * * * * *

Trouble delighted Em. The little horse was responsive to her slightest cue, faster at a walk than the men's mounts, gentle at a jog and smooth at a canter. Being astride him brought a smile to her face, but listening to the talk of her travelling companions wiped away all mirth.

---

[32] Psalm 139:7

The men competed with boasts of past misdeeds and eager hopes for future—what was the word? Devilment.

Em wanted no part of it, but she could not shake Devlin Burke's declaration that she would live only so long as he found her useful—and she wondered whether death might be a better choice than life.

As she lay awake that night, her revolver in her hand, she looked up at the stars in the vast sky above and a long-ago conversation played in her mind.

"Your bein' real handy with a sixgun can be a blessin' or a curse," a baritone voice drawled. *"Your choice."*

The statement had not been directed to her, but she had listened, like a mouse in the corner.

"Don't worry, Pa, it's just a game—I'll never gun anyone down," a laughing tenor had replied.

"Now ah am worried," the baritone had said seriously. *"There's times it quits bein' a game—yuh ever run onto such a time, don' throw your life away—do whut needs doin'—evil prevails when good men do nothin'—stay alive and do what needs doin'."*

Not the words of a kill-for-pay gunman, like Devlin Burke claimed her father had been, Em thought. Might be he got the Cap'n wrong—or might be it was someone else she'd listened in on.

She holstered her gun and counted the stars until sleep closed her eyes.

CHAPTER 13

Cohl spent his first week as a Bingham County deputy scouring the Three Buttes area, where Wilde's posses had twice lost the Burke gang. He crossed a game trail that seemed to lead nowhere, poked through the brush and found a disguised gateway to a small box canyon that sheltered an over-grazed pasture with a natural spring. The freshest horse droppings had dried for a week or more.

A roomy four-bunk cabin was built into the bluff, but no perishable provisions or personal effects were in evidence.

"A dream hideout," Cohl mused. "They'll be back, but likely not real soon."

Rendezvousing at Wilde's ranch, Cohl described the hideaway and marked it on a map that Wilde kept in the safe in his den, along with other confidential papers.

"Empty a week or more, you say?' the sheriff mused. "I bet they're getting set to try for that payroll tomorrow."

He lost that bet. The next day, the shipment passed through Bingham County without incident, frustrating Wilde and his waiting posse.

* * * * * * * *

"The minute I hired on, the Burkes disappeared," Cohl wrote to Ethridge. "The sheriff swears he told no one about our arrangement, but I smell a rat and it may be Wilde himself."

The day after he posted the report, a large packet, mailed a week earlier, was waiting for him when he returned to Jorgensons' rooming house. Retiring to

247

his room, Cohl took a photograph from his inner vest pocket, where he carried it every day, over his heart. He carefully propped it up on the bureau and said, as if to the girl in the sepia-tone, "Looks like the boss has lots to tell us."

Topping the stack of papers in the packet was a child's drawing of a long-legged yellow-haired man leading a boy on a red horse and a lady on a gray. "Not bad for a kid," he tilted the drawing as if showing it to the girl who was only a photograph. "But it looks like Dan'l doesn't much need me anymore.

"Letter from Buck," he continued conversationally, "He spent the summer clerking and reading law for the boss. He's in San Francisco now studying at Hastings College of the Law—it's connected to the University of California."

Cohl started to read the letter aloud, but didn't get far before his voice failed.

"*I find you have a well-deserved reputation for seldom being wrong, my friend,*" Blaine wrote. "*Sadly, we now have proof that you were right when you told me on the train that we were probably too late. Mr. Ethridge's contacts have confirmed that cabal killers were offered a $1,000 bounty for Jadene. A man tried to collect it in Boise—possibly Simon Taylor who called on Mother Faye. Jadene got past him, but there was someone else waiting down south, close to the ranch. The second man collected. I have written to Miss Copeland. Thank you for trying.*"

Ethridge's letter detailed the confirming information. Cohl knew the sources. They were reliable. Word had it that the man who collected deliberately left evidence suggesting that Jadene might be alive, to distract Blaine from the killer's trail.

"Shift your attention to the Gimlet matter," the prosecutor directed. "Take the enclosed letter of introduction to my old friend, Asa Samuelson, who is now the sheriff in Alturas County. It should not take long. Daniel and I want you home for the winter."

I.C. Cohl sank down on the bed and stared at the photograph on the bureau.

Alternately, his long fingers crumpled and then smoothed the pages of the letters. When it got too dark to see the picture, he went out.

A shot of whiskey did not help.

He slacked into a chair and was dealt a hand of cards. He anted without looking at them. "How many?" the dealer asked. Cohl left the cards and wandered out.

Back at Jorgensons' he gathered his gear.

"Leaving?" the old man asked. "You're paid up through the end of the month."

"Keep it," Cohl said wearily.

He stopped at the sheriff's ranch just long enough to hand his badge to Miss Wilde, who smiled oddly at him.

Four months had passed without a single report of a possible sighting—except that first one from Glasgow who was really Devlin Burke. Cohl had shown Candy's picture to Pinkham and confirmed that. Was it Burke, himself, who had collected on her? The outlaw did not fit the pattern for that, but Burke had seen something that had made him curious enough to ask a few questions. Seen what? Cohl hoped Burke didn't get himself killed before they had a chat.

He crossed the line into Logan County, passed Pillar Butte, and rode northwest through the night-shrouded Snake River Desert, his route arcing toward the mountains where the Alturas County seat of Hailey was situated.

Yes, he would clear up the Gimlet matter for Blaine Box, but he would also complete Jadene Box's failed quest to identify and bring to justice whoever had ordered the death of her father.

Cohl very much regretted having never met Gideon Box. Even more, he regretted having never met Jadene Box. The regret was a physical pain, like fire and ice, deep in his breast.

249

"The boss may want me home," I.C. Cohl gritted aloud, "but I swear I will follow the trail of the Snake until I have personally settled up with every last man who was involved in killing Miss Jade."

* * * * * * * *

Several days down the trail, Devlin announced what he called a "scouting trip."

"I ain't gettin' stuck here with Piece-a-crap," Madden objected.

"Git along," Peat ordered. "You, too, Wolf. Dev, gimme all the .32-20 shells yuh got and bring back more. I gotta get Emmett shootin' good as he handles wild hosses."

Em grinned and happily set up a makeshift target range.

Instinctively, she held to her old pattern, using her revolver as if it were a single shot pistol. Firing once per draw, she took pride in placing her shots where one did the job. Peat was not impressed and refused to give her cartridges to top off the cylinder.

"Light gun like that ain't gonna put a man down with one shot," he coached, "You gotta throw some lead out there, Emmett—three-four shots at a time. Never've shot a man, have you?"

"Four—over 'n' over, in my head," Em corrected. "Blew the last devil's brains out with a single shot—the others..." her voice trailed off

"Like Dev says, yer recollerter's broke," Peat said.

Em shrugged, "Think I used my carbine—Boss says I lost it in the river."

"Prob'ly somethin' heavier—mebbe a .44-40— light pistol like you're packin' now's different," Peat said. "Try slippin' the hammer."

When Em gave him a blank look, Peat demonstrated the technique. "Lock your finger on the trigger and slip the hammer with your thumb."

Em tried and found, after practicing a bit, she could empty her gun in four seconds flat while maintaining a tight pattern.

"You got it there, boy," Peat approved, "Time we found you some action."

Em didn't argue but she didn't like empting her gun. Better to fire three or four rounds, then top off, she silently decided.

"Git saddled, Emmett, you an' me're goin' huntin'," Peat ordered.

Em saddled Trouble and followed Two-Gun. Nearing the rimrock overlooking the stage road to Preston, Peat dismounted and left Em holding their horses while he looked over the rim. Four times he shook his head and moved on before signaling her to join him, bellied down on a rocky outcropping.

A light buggy was stopped beside the wagon track along the White River, apparently with a cracked axle. The horse was gone, likely carrying the driver to town for help. A young mother sat on a blanket reading, a babe in her lap. A small girl cuddled beside her, scribbling on a tablet.

"Not what I hoped for," Peat told Em, "but you gotta prove yourself."

"What do you want me to do?" she asked warily.

"Go down there and take whatever that dame has that's worth takin'," he ordered.

Em looked at him slanchwise. "I could do that," she agreed, "but shootin' them'd draw that manhunter. Boss wouldn't like it."

"Don't shoot her unless she comes up with a Greener. I'll be watchin'." Peat patted his rifle significantly.

* * * * * * * *

Claudia Nichols smiled when Em rode up. "Hello," she said, "did you meet my husband on the road?"

"No," Em said. "Got any money?"

251

"Any money? Why, of course he has money," Mrs. Nichols said.

"Not what I asked." Em brought her revolver to rest on the saddle horn with the muzzle angling down at the woman. "You got any money?"

Mrs. Nichols's mouth sagged. "You're a bandit? But you're just a child!"

"I'm not wantin' you to get hurt," Em warned, "so you gotta give me whatever you've got that's worth anything."

"All I have here is diapers," the woman cried.

"Dump out your bag," Em ordered. In addition to baby things, it held a napkinful of molasses cookies, and— "What's in that envelope?"

"Just my egg money," Mrs. Nichols said.

"Bring it to me," Em demanded, "I'll take those cookies, too, and," she swiveled the gun to the little girl.

"No!" the mother gasped, "not my child."

Em shook her head, "I don't want the kid, just what she's got."

The mother took a deep breath. "Give me the tablet, Molly," she said.

"An' the drawin' stick," Em demanded.

Clutching her baby, Claudia held up the small treasures and saw the little bandit waver. The brown eyes that had seemed so threatening flooded with torment, the hand that reached for the loot first softly brushed the infant's cheek. The bandit sighed.

"Robbing little children," Mrs. Nichols scolded, "you ought to be ashamed."

"I'm just doin' what needs doin', Serena," Em gritted. She took the meager loot and wheeled Trouble away.

"Wait," Mrs. Nichols called. "Can you read?" Em mixed a shrug with a nod. The woman scooped up her book. "Then take this!"

252

Em backed Trouble and reached down to accept the black leather volume. "It worth anything?"

"Oh, yes," Mrs. Nichols said, "it is priceless. Please read it, it will help you ever so much."

* * * * * * * *

"You make a big haul, Emmett?" Peat jeered when Em rejoined him.

"Cookies an' egg money." Em handed him the envelope. It contained three dollars and forty-five cents in change.

"More'n you'd make punchin' cows all day," Peat said. "Reckon you can keep it. What was it she give you when you went to leave?"

"A book," Em said. "I-I wanna see how good I can read."

"Gimmie," the outlaw ordered. Glancing at it, he said, "Crap, Emmett, I warned you—I ain't gonna put up with this bullshit," but he tucked it inside his shirt.

Disappointed, Em bit her lip and didn't risk showing him the pad and pencil.

When they returned to camp, the Burkes and Wolf were back.

Although Em had told Devlin before he left that they were short on provisions, all he had brought back was whiskey.

Peat pulled a cork with his teeth and chugged nearly half the contents. Sitting down by the fire, he pulled out the book he had taken from Em, tore the cover off and fed it to the fire. As he related the tale of Emmett robbing a lady with a broken down buggy, he continued to pull on the bottle and steadily tore page after page from the book until it was entirely burned.

"'Course holdin' up some unarmed dame ain't the same as pullin' a real job," Peat said. "I ain't sure Emmett really pulled off them killin's he recollects—but he's handlin' a gun good enough."

"How aboot it, Emmett?" Devlin smirked, "You ready to show Jack you're man enough to drop a man, eh?"

"If it needs doin', Boss," Em shrugged, "but killin' thet don' need doin' jus' buys trouble."

"Says who?" Peat demanded.

"Ah don't rightly recollect," Em puzzled. She looked at Devlin. "You, mebbe, Boss—not wantin' to draw that manhunter?"

"Prob'ly thet damned orphan home," Peat said, draining the last of his bottle.

"Might could be," Em shrugged. "Important thing's stayin' alive—don' worry, Mr. Peat, when it comes down to it, ah don' play games—ah do whut needs doin'."

"Killin' most always needs doin, to my way of thinkin'," Peat nodded. "Hell, if yuh really done all thet killin' yuh recollect, yuh gotta know droppin' a man's the best feelin' there is."

"Second best, I'd say," Wolf smirked. "Yuh ever been with a woman, Emmett?"

"Reckon not," Em growled.

"We shoulda took yuh to our wild woman, 'fore we headed south," Wolf grinned.

"Piece-a-crap gets anywheres near the wild woman, I'll whack off his pecker," Madden threatened, knife at the ready.

Devlin nearly choked on a burst of laughter, then pulled the cork on another bottle, Peat having finished the first on his own.

Em ate her stolen cookies while the men passed the bottle around.

"You like whiskey, Emmett?" Wolf asked, offering her a pull.

"Not thet ah recollect," she replied.

"Give it a try, eh," Devlin ordered.

She sniffed the bottle and wrinkled her nose, took a half-swallow, gagged and spit it out. The Burkes and Wolf guffawed, but Peat howled, "Don't waste it!" He lunged tipsily to his feet, grabbed for the bottle, stumbled, lost his balance and tottered on the edge of falling into the fire.

Em jumped up to steady him just as Madden gave him a hard shove. Peat slammed into Em, knocking her to the ground and landing atop her.

With a stunned look on his face, Peat pushed himself up with one hand. Unmindful of the bottle gurgling out its contents into the thirsty ground, he grabbed her shirt with his other hand and looked down her front.

"What the hell," he roared, scrambling to his feet. "Damn you, Dev, yuh don' wanna draw thet gunner's eye, but yuh brung along a damn dame."

"Figures," Wolf leered, "Devlin pulls someone outta th' Snake, it's bound to be a gal—not much of a gal, mind yuh, but—hey, she as good in bed as she is with a gun?"

"Hell no, she ain't even worth the trouble," Devlin laughed.

"I knowed it was a piece-a-crap!" Madden cried, pulling a knife. "Lemme git rid of it, eh."

"Not just yet," Devlin smirked, "but if Em don't take proper care of me—say she lets me get shot up— then you got my okay to carve her up, Madden—just see that Wolf gets his ride first, eh."

"What the hell do we do with her now?" Peat demanded.

"Same as when you all thought she was a he, eh," Devlin shrugged. "We go right ahead with our plans."

"With a dame?!?" Peat objected.

"No one'll notice, eh," Devlin predicted. "I took 'er for a boy, first time I seen 'er. You all took 'er for a boy. Hell, Jack, you been teachin' 'er to shoot even better'n she could when she downed the whole damn posse that killed her pa, eh. You're ready for action now, ain't you, Em?"

The girl drew her revolver as she silently recalled the baritone advice, *"Don't throw your life away—stay alive—do what needs doing."*

Thoughtfully, she turned the cylinder—six small cartridges—four murderous men—

Devlin's hand came down hard on her shoulder, his fingers closing on her throat. "Well, ain't you?"

In a voice hard as flint, she replied, "Ah do whut needs doin', Boss."

It Is Well with My Soul

1. When peace, like a riv - er, at - tend-eth my way, When sor-rows like
2. Though Sa-tan should buf-fet, tho' tri - als should come, Let this blest as-
3. My   sin— oh, the bliss of this glo - ri - ous tho't— My sin— not in
4. And, Lord, haste the day when my faith shall be sight, The clouds be rolled

sea - bil-lows roll— What-ev - er my lot, Thou hast taught me to say,
sur - ance con-trol, That Christ has re - gard - ed my help-less es - tate,
part, but the whole— Is nailed to the cross and I   bear it no more,
back as a scroll: The trump shall re-sound and the Lord shall de-scend,

Chorus

It   is well, it   is well with my soul.
And hath shed His own blood for my soul.   It is well . . . . with my
Praise the Lord, praise the Lord, O my soul!
"E - ven so"— it   is well with my soul.   It is well

soul, ... It   is well, it   is well with my soul.
with my soul,

Continued in

Martha McKeeth Ireland's

THE TRAIL

OF THE SNAKE

VOLUME II:

PART 3

...hath regarded my helpless estate...

PART 4

Even so—it is well...